Children of the Red Dot . Falling

Katharine Ann Angel

First Edition published 2018 by
2QT Limited (Publishing)
Settle, North Yorkshire BD24 9RH United Kingdom

Cover design: Tom Cockeram (Tang Mu)
www.tang-mu.co.uk

Cover art: from Brightfield by Meg Wroe
www.megwroe.net

Printed by IngramSparks Inc

@katharine59
katharineannangel@gmail.com

A CIP catalogue record for this book is available
from the British Library
ISBN 978-1-912014-34-7

*For Christopher, Elizabeth and Simon
with love*

Contents

"We cannot become another. But the challenge of getting close or at least closer, of glimpsing, hearing, touching other realities, is thoroughly compelling to us."
Steven Feld: The Sound World of Bosavi

"When people don't have an outside navigation system they walk around in circles."
Bear Grylls

1

A Distant Scream

The lanky girl with the sapphire-black hair hauled herself up a twisted vine, one of millions of woody ropes that hung in curtains from the forest ceiling. She pulled it gently to test her weight then yanked it several times until she trusted it to carry her across the narrow stretch of sage swamp. Because of the ants she zipped her navy sweatshirt up to her neck then in one fluid movement jumped, coiling her arms and legs tightly around the vine the way she'd been taught in PE. She let go, landing with a thud on the other side. Birds of paradise fluttered in all directions, their extraordinarily long feathers flicking out behind them, silver, orange, red, black.

''Scuse me,' said a small voice, 'can't you just stop a minute?'

The lanky girl sighed with exaggerated exasperation. There was quite enough to think about without being interrupted. Even so, she stopped and turned to see a squat, sturdy girl squelching after her through the swamp, ankle-deep in wobbling lichen.

The child stepped up onto firmer ground, an area of impacted earth carpeted with huge leaves, holey and brown as overcooked pancakes. She stamped her sodden trainers, forcing the water out over the tops, then bent down and lifted the leg of her tracksuit. 'Sumpfinks wiggling,' she said, matter-of-fact. Sure enough, a leech had attached itself to her ankle. Without hesitation, the child squeezed the free end of the creature between two fingers and pulled its shiny, black body, stretching it out and away. She scrunched her face, tongue between her teeth in concentration, 'Stuck.'

The lanky girl's sharp jaw lifted. Her eyes darted high and low, scanning the impossible foliage, 'Did you see any grown-ups?'

'I came out the side. It was all cloudy. I seed nobuddy. This slug's got all stuck on me, see?' She gave it another pull and muttered, 'Sticky.'

'What about the pilots? The guardian?'

The small one shook her head. She let go of the leech so it pinged back and shrank into itself. She stared at the throbbing black blob, fascinated by the sway of it as it fattened itself on her blood.

The lanky girl shrugged, turned her back on the child and pushed on through the undergrowth, dividing the liana and slender brown reeds with the awkward pull of a lopsided breaststroke swimmer. The little one (with the leech attached) trotted behind like some orphaned chick that instantly bonds with the first living parent it sees.

The pair soon came to a clearing, a flat expanse punctuated with ebony rocks, some the size of a man's skull, some bigger than a bus, and one resembling a huge hedgehog, glassy-smooth on one side, but sharp as shrapnel studded with jagged holes on the other. Overhead, a leafy canopy framed a vast yawn of clear blue sky. The girls stared up at the place from which the helicopter had fallen, smashing into the tree tops before descending, thump-by-terrifying-thump, crashing through the branches, skinning the gigantic windmill blades with gunshot-snapping, glass-cracking, liquidised screams.

Silence.

*

'I was asleep,' declared the sturdy child, 'an' the front sunk in the big swamp.'

'Where the grown-ups were. I know.' A statement. Matter of fact. Like these things happened all the time back home in England.

The child nodded, remembering how the adults had sat laughing and yelling above the engine, doing grown-up talk. She chuntered some more, expecting the bigger girl to pay full attention, 'I sleeped next to Elle-Marie and Freya. Freya was that one what was scared of flying, what bited her own arm.' The child gnawed the back of her hand to demonstrate the feel and the truth of it.

The tall girl looked about wildly, her eyes flashing

high and low for an escape route. No buildings. No cars. No people. They should have been allowed to keep their mobiles, then at least they'd have had hope, something to hold on to. 'It was cloudy. Dust. Smoke. I didn't see anyone else get out. Oh, yes, maybe the extensions girl - her with the eyebrows . . .'

'You mean Claire? Yeah, I saw her. She's the one what drawed them thick triangles on. And the fake nails. She crawled away before I got out. Our seatbelt, mine and Elle-Marie's, was hard to undo. We was hanging funny by our tummies.' The child grimaced and clutched her stomach, 'What's your name?'

'Mizuki.'

The small girl waited to be asked her name, but Mizuki was distracted so she said it anyway, 'I'm Katey with a yer at the end. Do you think them's apples?'

Pale green, knobbly fruits weighed thin branches almost down to the ground. Puzzled, Katey tugged at a fruit until it came away in her hand, so the branch bounced away and, despite its strangeness, she bit into the fruit, surprised by its tender flesh and sweet smell, not at all apple-like. Sticky juice ran down her chin onto her tee shirt. Katey grinned and bit again, 'Mmm, s'nice.' She held the fruit out to her new friend, but her gift was ignored.

'Wait here. Back in a mo.' Mizuki flicked her hand, signalling to be left alone to explore without having to talk. She ducked beneath some creepers and found herself in a tangle of trees, their trunks exploding with ferns and funnel-shaped sticky leaves lined with fierce curves of spiky brown teeth. Mottled shadows mingled with web-slung holes and rotting vegetation. Small creatures leapt through the canopy above. The silhouette of some kind of winged guinea-pig glided overhead then crashed onto a branch that shook, scattering leaves and miniature lime-green bananas onto the forest floor. Mizuki ducked then quickly recovered. She picked up a banana and squealed as a humungous spider with hairy, fat legs emerged lazily over the top. Mizuki dropped the fruit and watched with thudding heart as the tarantula crawled away. She calmed herself, slowing her breathing, telling herself not to be such a stupid coward, but to lift the banana again. This time, she held it well away from her body, between her thumb and finger, turning it over and back to check. Only when she was positive there were no bugs, she peeled back the skin and placed the tip of her tongue against its flesh. The texture was vaguely familiar, so she nibbled the tip of it. When nothing terrible happened, she bit a larger piece, chewed it and swallowed it, thrilled by its burst of fabulous sweetness. Delighted, Mizuki gathered more bananas, inspecting each one before tucking them into her hoodie pockets as a gift for the little girl she'd just met. Already she'd forgotten the child's surname, but that it ended in a 'yer.' And then she was hit by a twinge of guilt for leaving such a small child alone in the wild. *That girl – I left her and she's only little - got to find her again.*

Mizuki glanced back the way she thought she had come. It dawned on her she had no idea which way 'back' was.

'Hello?' Mizuki called into the hopeless, vacant

space. A multi-coloured bird with a huge hooked beak squawked and flapped through the overflowing foliage. Mizuki turned on the spot. She called again, louder this time, her voice trembling, 'Hello girl? Can you hear me? Are you there somewhere?' She pulled back some giant leaves then pushed between a vast mesh of web littered with dead and dying flies and broken-winged moths. 'Little girl?' she shouted, her voice weak with nervous panic so that her cry fell flat and went nowhere. After a couple of steps Mizuki came to a clearing that must surely be the right one, but if it was where she'd come from then the child who'd been told to stay put had disobeyed her command and vanished. No child. And no, this was not the same place at all.

Here, bright sunlight splashed swathes of lilac, lilies and orchids, enormous star-patterned beauties overshadowing millions of delicate fern fronds, uncurling welcoming smiles. Yet such beauty lent no comfort. Mizuki's heart beat faster. She spun around several times. It was impossible to decide on the best direction.

Behind her the foliage rustled. 'Are you there?' Mizuki whirled round to see something approaching - not the little girl, but some kind of hideous, strange beast. Not a beast, but a bird with an outsized black beak on a triangular-shaped head atop an unnaturally long, electric-blue neck. Mizuki stepped back for fear of attack, but the monster meandered nonchalantly into the clearing to peck at a mound of fungus. Mizuki exhaled. She gawped at the daft bird's shiny plumage, pointed casque and flap of red skin flip-flopping beneath its blue neck and when it did not attack her, she laughed with relief.

'You got blood on your head,' Katey said as she popped out from a tumbling mass of greenery. Ignoring the bird she added, 'Come on, Mizuki, you better come with me. Come through this bit here, 'n we go down there to them black rocks where there's more girls.'

A surge of relief washed over Mizuki, so much so that she felt light-headed and unable to speak. She wiped her forehead with the back of a ripped sleeve. When she lowered her arm she realised there was blood on it. She bit her lip, fighting self-pity. Never cry. Never cry. Never cry.

'Stop being such a misery-guts! You don't get to hold your own pity party,' spat a voice from Before. Her mother, screaming, most likely drunk. Mizuki blinked away the memory. Never cry. Never. Never. Never.

The sturdy child noticed the way Mizuki's bottom lip was quivering, but she said nothing. She watched Mizuki feel her forehead again, more gently this time with only her fingertips, pressing a flap of skin that hung loose above her right eye and, when Mizuki inspected her fingers, tiny pieces of grit turned out to be tiny flies invading and drowning in the damp, fleshy mess.

Mizuki shrugged. Blood and flies, so what? Nothing's as bad as the loathsome residential care home where boys and girls of all ages arrived and departed like waves on a shingle beach. Any shred of security Mizuki had ever mustered shifted the instant any of the others moved on. And after they'd left it was as if those kids had never existed. Nothing was worth hanging onto, not the colour of their hair or pattern of their scar nor the expression on their face. Twice, Mizuki had dared to confide in a newcomer, hoping to form a special friendship. Twice the chosen confidante had been fostered or adopted. Gone. No one ever stuck beside her. There had never been a 'bestie' yet in less than ten breaths that child with a 'yer at the end' of her name had come to find her because . . . because she cared. A single tear fell without permission. Never cry. Never cry. Never. Mizuki's top lip whitened where her bottom teeth bit into it.

'When d'ya think they'll come 'n get us?' Katey said, tugging at the bobble on her pony-tail, pulling it loose. She shook some ash or dust out of her hair, then replaced the bobble so it hung in a lank flop between her shoulder blades.

'They?'

'The 999 people.'

'We're not in England you know.'

'But it's a 'mergency.' Katey's bottom lip quivered. 'My mum said . . .'

'You haven't got a mum . . .'

'My mum said to ring 999 if she O-D'ed. But I was asleep. I didn't know to ring no one, and she . . .'

'She died?'

'No, she never. But someone told them and they took her away. Social got me out of bed and put me in a resi. After, I got a foster mum, but she said I was a "proper little madam" so I got put back. My real mum's goin' to come and get me when she's better from doing rehab. Is your mum getting you any time?'

Mizuki jumped up, 'Come on you! Show me the way to the next room.'

Katey led the slender girl through an archway of saplings leaning into each other, on a path trodden by creatures yet unseen. In the clearing, Mizuki recognised the hedgehog-shaped rock. Around it sat eight diminutive girls in identical, custard-yellow tracksuits, all grubby and torn. Seeing Mizuki they leapt up, squeaking and mewing, butting against her legs as they giggled, 'We're being kittens!'

Mizuki feigned a brief smile. Those mini-brats. They'd been introduced at Heathrow, the whole irritating gang of them, and she'd ignored them ever since.

'I'm sweaty hot,' said one, removing her sweatshirt to reveal a white aertex, especially donated by the British government for the children of the Transfer Hope Project, embroidered above the pocket: THP. The other girls followed suit, scattering their tops here and there, floppy and bright as water-lilies.

'There's prob'ly spiders,' Katey warned, wishing Mizuki would be the one to speak - 'what crawl inside your stuff.' The little ones listened to Katey and, scooping up their tops, they chucked them onto a rock. Forgetting spiders, they tumbled and squealed until as one entity, and for no obvious reason, they stopped perfectly still as if an adult had entered the room and shouted, 'Shut up!' All were instantly super-aware and super-afraid of the jungle as it exploded overhead, whooping and whistling, jabbering and jittering, chattering and clacking, as if every sound ever created had been flung hilariously into one single space and time.

Taking advantage of the moment, Katey pointed to her new friend, 'Right, ev'rybuddy, look here. Her name's Mizuki. She's got blood, see there - on her head. Can someone be a nurse?' Several girls pointed to a round-faced child with a neat bob and thick fringe shielding her eyebrows, the impressive result of her first ever visit to a real salon. The chosen one proudly tossed her hair to assert her authority. Swish.

'She wants to be a nurse when she's growed up,' said one whose aertex hung almost to her knees.

Katey glanced at Mizuki for approval, but when no response was forthcoming she continued, 'Okay, so we'll just have to pretend she is growed up. Anyone sore or bumped has to go to her. What's her name?'

Most, but not all, of the girls chorused, 'Donna's-a-Goner-Moore.'

Donna jumped up grinning, 'I got plasters!' In the excitement of being chosen, she flapped her hands and the others saw a livid bruise across her arm that fanned out like the smudged wings of a moth. Sensing the girls' stares, Donna rubbed the bruise self-consciously. She disappeared behind the rock and returned lugging a tangle of colourful handbags and school rucksacks from which she extricated a blue plastic shoulder-bag studded with diamante on which a laminated label had been stuck. The label read: 'THP Donna Moore

Blaze House'.

The chief medic rummaged through the messy depths of her bag. She withdrew a clear packet, unzipped it, and shook out a dozen interlinked safety pins, some sterile packs, antiseptic ointment and, as if to validate her new appointment, a shower of sticking-plasters in various sizes.

'That stuff's stealed frum her 'dopting parents' bathroom,' said a girl with two bald patches showing through her dark, straggly hair, 'She's a bad stealer, she is.' The girl folded her arms. She pursed her full lips to show that no one was supposed to argue with her.

'Don't say stealed, Pearl, 'cos it wasn't me!' insisted Donna, 'It was their boy what took them. That Bradley. He was always doing bad stuff to blame on me. He stood on the bog and took the key off the top of the metal cupboard what they thought I couldn't reach. He poured Calpol pink yuk all over the floor and shook powder all in it and stuck his finger in like this - and he wrote Donna on the mirror. He washed his hands and shouted, "DAD!" and Bradley's dad came stomping upstairs like this – and shouted in my face, "Come here, young lady, it's your last straw."' Donna drew breath. Encouraged by all the attention she swished her neat bob so it rocked around the base of her neck, then hastily continued, 'So obviously I did my invisible chant what makes me invisible from Bradley's dad.' She closed her eyes and opened them again. The others were all staring at her aghast. Donna leant forward into them. 'This is me in his face, "Invisible, invisible, I didn't do nothing,"' Donna flapped her hands in Pearl's face. 'Watch what's next. This is me being Bradley's dad,' Donna pushed her nose right up against Pearl's nose and snarled; '"Right, you've had it. Tomorrow Blaze House staff will pick you up. We're sick to bleedin' death of you. Utterly sick, do you hear? You listenin' to me, you utter bleedin' nutter?"' Donna's shoulders broadened, her hands formed fists, she glared hard at Pearl the way Bradley's dad had glared at her, like he wanted to belt the living daylights out her, but she knew he'd never dare hit her because she'd tell social and he'd get done.

Donna shrunk back into being herself, 'So anyway I got the key off of the top of Bradley's dad's secret cupboard because I had to fetch this bag, see. It's for me for when I'm growed up, because no one's ever gonna give me the proper stuff what I need to be a real live nurse. . .' Donna's voice dropped to a whisper, 'so I went and gived it to myself.' Story over. Donna stepped back. *Them girls won't tell, will they? What if they get rescued and tell Transfer Hope I nicked stuff?*

'Bradley's dad's gonna be ma. . . ad!' Pearl chanted, leaping up and tugging her own hair, pulling chunks of dark curls from her head.

Three of the Blaze House girls, Vix, Joy and Melissa echoed, 'Donna's-a-Goner! She's-a-Stealer! And Bradley's dad's gonna be mad at Donna's-a-Goner-Moore!' Donna laughed because Bradley's dad was miles away on the other side of the world, so he couldn't hear them telling on her. She wiggled her hips and waved the first aid bag in triumph.

Katey cut in, 'You all from Blaze House then? I'm

from Castle Care. It's by the seaside but the sand isn't yellow like in Finding Nemo. It's brown and sinky and you need a guide to go on it or it sucks you under and you die. The rest at Castle Care was all boys except Naomi Wilson but she's thirteen so she was too old to get picked for Transfer Hope, so I got chosed all by myself.' Katey looked around, 'Hey, anyone seen Bronwyn Bowen? She talked to me on the England plane. She's from Wales but they moved her to England. She runned away on a train without even a ticket, back to her Wales house where she lived before. A lady came and said, "Your mum and dad's got put in prison and don't live at that house no more," so Bronwyn put fire in the letter box and burnt the house to pieces, then social brung her back to England, because in Wales they said she's impossible, what's why she got s'lected to come here.' Katey took a huge breath with the effort of relating Bronwyn's life. She ended with a whimper, 'All us Transfer Hopes are *impossible* blinkin' nuisances.'

'We're six and seven and eight and nine years old, and that's all,' announced a pixie-faced child, her golden hair shaped into a sharp crew cut. 'My name's Melissa and I'm nine. Donna Moore's eight. Vix and Joy are six. Joy's that one with white hair. She's got a 'dentical twin who's not a THP girl. Pearl's ten, but she's a big baby, aren't you, Pearl?'

Pearl pouted. She stuck her thumb into her mouth and pretended to suck.

White-haired Joy said, 'Julie's my real-life twin sister. She's six, same as me. She didn't get to be

Transfer Hope like me. She got adopted 'cos she's the good one. I'm difficult. I've got a new sister called Vix, she's my bestie now. We're besties for ever, aren't we?' Joy high-fived Vix then wandered across the clearing to retrieve her backpack, a glossy lilac bag printed all over with princesses and fairies.

'You missed telling us about them three.' Katey pointed to two tiddlers who were rifling through their bags for sweets, and a large girl, the only child still wearing her oversized sweatshirt, who was curled at the foot of the black stone, seemingly asleep.

Pixie-faced Melissa explained, 'Them two is Nadia, she's the India girl what bites, and Evie who's growed up with her. They speak YaYa to each other.'

'YaYa, what's that - is it like French or sumpfink?' asked Katey. Mizuki smiled.

Nadia lifted her drooping eyelids. She flicked her eyes at Evie and they shook their heads in unison. *No, not French. What's French anyway?*

'Yabilly paskini yaya,' said Nadia, to prove her point.

'Billy yaya tic,' was Evie's reply.

'They 'vented it when they was babies, sharing a cot,' said Melissa, 'I heard staff say their two mums left them alone all the time. They're not real sisters but they think they are. They understand everything what you say but no one told them how to talk proper like us. They only do YaYa. Oh, and that other girl over there, that fat one sleeping . . . her name . . . I forget. She started at Blaze House just before we left. She never speaks to no one.' Melissa completed her

14

speech with a half a dozen star jumps, imitating Nadia by yelling, 'Yabilly paskini yaya! Yabilly paskini yaya!' and everybody giggled.

'Won't her name will be on her bag label?' asked Katey.

'Nope, 'cos she aint got no bag. She left it in the taxi. Staff's going to post it here,' said Joy, and the other girls nodded, recalling this thing that had happened long ago in a crowded, faraway land.

Katey squatted to pick through the medical equipment, 'Pick up them plasters, Donna Moore, and put this cream on Mizuki's head to stop the flies. They hate the taste of stinky cream.'

'How do you know what flies hate?' asked Joy, but Katey wasn't listening. Katey unscrewed the cap from the ointment. She reached out to take Donna's hand in her own, then squeezed some of the antiseptic onto Donna's finger. The onlookers held their breath, in awe of this child-nurse who dared soothe such a terrible wound. Mizuki closed her eyes. She bowed her head and waited for Donna to heal her pain.

Donna's arm shot back, 'Ugh! That's mega disgusting! You can't make me touch that 'gusting gunk.'

'Well, you got to do it 'cos you're the actual nurse,' commanded Katey, secretly relieved that she hadn't volunteered to stick her own finger into the wound.

'But it's too yucky!' Donna blew a raspberry and pulled her 'disgusted' face, an expression usually reserved for congealed baked beans and lumpy semolina. She flicked the precious cream off her finger. It flew through the air and landed on a leaf. Everyone watched the cream ooze downwards like a ghastly living thing, a white slug, a slick of snot, a just-hatched alien.

*

They all heard it. A loud shout, 'Hey!' followed by screams that pierced the jungle, and a fluttering of wings as many birds ascended, wheeling up, up, up, until they were dark flecks against the sky. Mizuki opened her eyes. She craned her neck, not to see, but to discern the direction of the screams.

The girls shuffled together, clinging to one another, alert to the towering forest, the screeches of unseen creatures, the stifling heat and the black rocks looming. Donna, who'd been rubbing the remains of ointment from her finger onto some itchy bites on her own arms and face opened her eyes wide at the distant screaming. There followed a new sound - not like the other - more like a person coughing close by, a man clearing his throat, then coughing again as if trying to get their attention; 'Ahem, ahem, hurm, hurm, hurm.'

With a finger to her lips, Mizuki beckoned the girls to cower behind the largest black rock, the one smothered in blindingly yellow shirts, and the girls obeyed, grateful for orders to follow and a shadow in which to hide. The sound of the coughing man returned. 'Hurm, hurm, hurm, o:sulu tepela,' was what they thought they heard.

'It's the bogey man,' they whispered, 'the one our mums said about, what comes to get the naughty children.'

*

Back in the UK, staff had assured the children, 'Aussies speak English, so you'll be fine. It'll be just like home, except you'll be living in Papua New Guinea,' but weird foreign languages were the least of their worries. Foreignness as a thing had never occurred to them. The girls had been shown You-Tube clips and photos of a man called Ethan Cook, a smiling Australian with his wife, Lilian, who'd selected each girl to join their government-approved Behavioural Intervention Centre where for two decades they'd run a successful programme for Aussie youngsters with challenging backgrounds. The Cooks helped young people restart their lives after a total break from their past. Their Transfer Hope Project created new opportunities for the future of each child as each was replanted into what they called "good soil" to be nurtured with values of respect and honesty, a healthy diet, an outdoor lifestyle, a balanced work/play ethic, and recreational activities designed to meet the needs of each individual. The THP children had every opportunity to become valuable citizens of the next generation. Ethan Cook believed that nurture could win over nature, through consistent teaching, loving discipline and a daily dose of positive feedback. If properly implemented, his three platforms - or "stabilisers" - teaching, discipline, and encouragement, could replace the children's negligent, shifting sand of their past. So far, Ethan Cook's results had proved outstanding.

The British government were on their knees with underfunded, erratic care provision, social services at breaking point, and a failing youth-justice system, so it was agreed by the powers-that-be to handpick nineteen girls to trial the famous Transfer Hope Project. Those without family attachments and unlikely to be fostered or adopted because of their age or behaviour, yet young enough to be taught a new morality and attitude to education. Ethan Cook would not only save their future but, in the long run, the project would save the British government millions of pounds.

'O:sulu tepela! Ahem! Hurm!' A black bird with an extraordinarily long, white tail flew out of the forest, its great, curved beak opening and closing; 'Ahem. Ahem!'

'A magical bird what talks like a man!' gasped Katey. All but Mizuki giggled with relief as they imitated the winged beast, chirping, 'O:sulu tepela, cough, cough! Silly old us believing in a bogey man. Them grown-ups jus' wanted to scare us!' How the children laughed, punching each other, gurning and rolling their eyes to the heavens. Scared of a stupid talking bird – whatever next?

But Mizuki was thinking of the screams.

2

A Grey Ghost

Some of the little ones were whining for food. Mizuki handed Katey her collection of miniature bananas to give to whoever would accept them, then Katey doled out the wrapped biscuits, salted crisps and previously rejected apples from their personal bags. All the fruit pastilles and Haribos had been scoffed during the interminable wait to board the helicopter at Daru Airport.

The Silent One woke. Her dull eyes wandered from child to child. At some point she'd removed one of her trainers, pulled out a lace and woven it through her mousy tangles to form a plait. Sighing heavily, she tugged at the lace and dragged it down and out, not bothered that it ripped her hair. Then, with serious intensity, she unplaited her hair, poking her fingers through the overlaps, pulling each strand apart as if it were the most important work in the universe. Once loose, she combed it all through with her fingers, divided a section into three parts and began a new plait.

Katey nervously held out a biscuit on the flat of her hand, the way a person offers an apple to a horse. The Silent One took it slowly and without thanks. She dangled in front of her eyes, rubbing it between her finger and thumb, then dropped it deliberately and glanced up at Katey. Their eyes met. A wordless conversation flashed between them: a flick of the eyelashes, a twitch of a cheekbone, a tightening of a lip.

What d'ya do that for? (Katey's eyes narrowed)

None of your beeswax.

If you don't want it, pick it up and give it me back. Don't you even breathe on it. It's mine.

The Silent One poked the biscuit with her big toe.

Mine.

Katey backed away. It wasn't about the biscuit, but she minded her effort at kindness being rejected. She looked in vain to Mizuki for moral support, so she said loudly, 'I saw on TV that if you're lost at sea you should stay with the boat. That's why we got to stay here and not move 'til the grown-ups come 'n get us.'

'What if they never come? We'll be here for blinking ever,' said Melissa, one of the Blaze House crew who top-trumped Castle Care's Katey in age and height. Melissa couldn't work out why the Blaze House girls were so quick to follow Katey's lead over hers. Also, she eyed Mizuki with suspicion. People like that unnerved her. She was far too quiet. You never quite knew what they'd do next.

'Don't they have search thingies on planes for

when they fall in the sea? Beepy sort of things that beep? I bet they're finding us by the beep,' said Donna, scratching her arms before smearing another liberal slick of ointment over her bites.

'In case you hadn't noticed, this isn't the sea,' Melissa said, moving to stand beside Katey. She spread her arms wide over Katey's head and turned full circle. 'When we was up there flying, I was looking all around. I saw mega-high mountains, sharp, sticking-uppy ones in the massivest circle ever, and millions of trees and . . .' Melissa drew breath. When no one interrupted she continued, 'You know, just . . . just millions of trees with white steaming stuff coming up off them in swishes. Like clouds but not clouds, and . . . and that's all.' Satisfied that the others had seen her standing taller than Katey, and that they'd heard her point of view, Melissa dropped her arms to her sides. *Even so,* she hoped, *maybe there is a beepy thing like Donna said.*

'Right. Who's got a secret phone what's not got smashed,' Donna asked, 'because didn't they say we could have new phones when we get to Transfer Hope?'

'But we're not in Transfer Hope, are we?' Melissa scoffed, 'In case you hadn't noticed, we crashed. Fact. No phones. No signal. We're stuffed.'

'Stop saying "in case you hadn't noticed,"' snorted Donna, 'like you know more than us. Hey, where're you sneaking off to Joy?'

'The bog.'

'Well, don't get bit on the bum then,' Donna giggled as six-year-old Joy vanished like Tom Thumb beneath a fountain of gargantuan leaves.

One minute the sky was bright, the next it was a stuffy, oversized quilt of semi-darkness. The children hastily reclaimed their yellow tops, shook them for spiders, and huddled in their 'safe place' at the base of the hedgehog-shaped rock, with Katey and Mizuki and Melissa instinctively guarding the outside. No one cried. No one moaned about hunger or fear. No one expected a worried parent to rush to their aid, to read them a story or give them a glass of water. And so they slept as they had so often done in the Before, with no choice but to trust to the care of strangers.

After many uncomfortable minutes Katey whispered loudly, 'What about tigers and lions?' She'd been imagining fierce cats hiding in the dark, orange and black and ready to pounce, baring their sharp, silver fangs and flashing their golden claws.

'What about them?' Mizuki felt faint. Her head ached, and her throat burned.

'Beasties in the jungle. Smelling us. Eating us.'

'I don't think those sorts of creatures live here.'

'Snakes then?'

'Maybe - I dunno.'

'What's that loud 'lectricity sound?'

'Beetles in the trees. They've got a funny name – chick . . . sick . . . sick adders or something. Our guardian told me about them, but I can't remember. They sometimes stop that buzz, but they don't bite.'

'Well I wish they'd shut up buzzing all the time,

'cos it gets under my skin.' Katey rubbed the back of her neck. Silhouettes of bats, large and small, disturbed the navy sky. The girls could not yet see the moon, but there were billions of burning stars huddled together in families, big, middle-sized, and insignificant ones.

'Let's sit back to back,' Katey said. She slid closer to Mizuki, drawing her knees to herself. Mizuki shuffled closer, grateful for the warm, dry ground and the comforting pressure of the smaller child's back against her own.

After some minutes Mizuki spoke; 'What shall we do about tomorrow?'

'I've been thinking . . .'

'About tomorrow?'

'Yes,' Katey dug her fingernails into the back of her hand because Mizuki was almost a grown-up and grown-ups were unpredictable, but Mizuki had ask for her opinion so Katey tried very hard to sound clever without being bossy. 'We could go back to the helicopter to see if anyone's there. If Donna's right and there is a beeper thing beeping, telling the grown-ups where we are, and if they come and get us and we're not at the heli, they might go away forever because they'll say we've been eaten by lions. Tomorrow we should go to the heli.'

'Sounds like an okay plan, but did you hear what Melissa said about big mountains and all them trees? The guardian told me we were flying over an extinct volcano. She said not to worry, it won't blow up because it's thousands of years old. She said the volcano's as big as a whole country but no one's ever lived inside

23

it because everyone's scared of spooky gods. We're all alone in a giant pit. Even if we go to the helicopter and something does beep, there's no signal. No one will ever hear it. No one will find us. If I don't find us a way out of here, we're doomed.'

'But the heli – can't we please go there tomorrow, just to see?'

'I suppose we can try. It was sinking, remember? Smoke everywhere. Our sandwiches are in the cool box inside.'

'I'm going to want them sandwiches.'

One of the little girls shouted in her sleep, 'No! Go away!' Nightmares always made the children cry out, so no one reacted. Katey shifted her back, pressing into Mizuki, who pressed back, wriggling until both were comfy. They rocked against each other, forwards and backwards, forwards and backwards, drifting through the shadows of half-sleep.

*

A mottled moon and countless stars cartwheeled through the night, finally succumbing to the uncluttered dawn of a cerulean sky. The little ones woke, rubbing the sleep from their eyes, complaining of thirst and stiffness. Some wandered off behind the scattered rocks to empty their bladders.

Mizuki scaled the tallest rock. She stood aloft, arching her back like Peter Pan with her hands on her hips. She beckoned Katey; *Come up here with me, come on!* Katey responded, her stubby legs struggling with the short climb, but she was determined to succeed, to impress the wonderful, beautiful, elegant Mizuki. Katey pursed her lips and gripped the jagged holes, scraping her stomach over the top ledge. She stood facing Mizuki as she rubbed away the pain.

'Speak to them kids,' whispered Mizuki.

'Me? Why me?'

"Cos I don't want to.' Mizuki's pale face dripped with sweat.

'Speak what?'

'That we gotta go back to the helicopter. Tell them there might be food. That we got to stick together walking in a line. You can be at the front. Me at the back. Or Melissa at the back if she wants.'

'But you're bigger than me. *You* be the boss of us. You speak.'

'I *am* the boss,' Mizuki said as she turned and scaled effortlessly down the backside of the rock to where two girls were bickering. She called up to Katey, 'You're just my talker.'

*

'Ow, get off of me, Vix, you're mashing my arms in!' Pearl, the stocky girl with patchy, dark curls was fighting with all her might against the wiry, ashen-faced Vix, the girl with crazy hair, messy as brambles. Despite her larger size, Pearl was already flat on her back with her arms trapped beneath Vix's bony knees, trying desperately to force her head up and forward, gnashing at the air, kicking her ankles wildly and ineffectively against the ground.

'You been in my bag, you nicked my food!' Vix screamed, slamming her fist down hard into Pearl's face. Pearl growled, gnashing her teeth like a dog. Vix leapt up, snarling. She kicked Pearl with her trainers, harder than any six-year-old should be able to kick, right foot, right foot, right again, then to give the right foot a break she kicked left, left, left the way her older brothers had kicked their enemies or each other without mercy.

Donna, the prime spectator, stood over the fighters. With every kick she flinched, her body tense, elbows out, fists tight, urging on the aggressor. She could hardly help herself from shouting, 'Stab her, Vix. Stick her with a knife!' Joy and Melissa added their voices to Donna's as they jumped up and down, chanting, 'Stab her! Stab her! Stab her!' Close by, the YaYa girls Nadia and Evie exchanged glances, grinning conspiratorially at the fun of the fight.

Pearl summoned all her pitiful strength. Hearing 'knife' and fearing a blade, she screamed with all her might, and at that exact moment, as her muscles clenched tight in the pit of her stomach, the floor of the mighty jungle rumbled. Vix froze, eyes wide, body alert, hardly daring to breathe. Every child froze, hearing the growl of the earth shuddering like an underground train beneath them. They were on the platform and a train was coming, but instead of slowing to a stop, it sped up, flying by with a deafening roar. Where to run? Nowhere to hide. The tall trees shivered violently from their roots up and their leaves broke away, fluttering down like confetti and then, all around, thud, thud, thud, as coconuts crashed to the ground.

The sky filled with so many squawking birds. A massive hairy rat, the like of which had never been seen back home, ambled through the clearing, politely avoiding Pearl's feet before melting out of sight between the bamboo stalks. No sooner had it gone, there followed an almighty crash. Somewhere unseen, a mighty tree had plunged to the forest floor. The skyful of birds beat their wings, crescendoing their complaints and, throughout the distant canopies, creatures great and small spread the news of yet another quake.

And then it was over.

The land returned an eerie silence.

The cicadas shut down. The bullfrogs stopped their throats. Even Vix submitted to the planet's fury and calmed down. She backed away from Pearl who had slowly, painfully dissolved into a foetal position, pressing her ear against the dangerous earth that had defended her against Vix.

Upon the high rock Katey sat petrified, digging her fingernails into her hands the way she always did in time of crisis. Her stubby legs extended from her calves over the edge of the rock. The sight of her own legs distracted her. She was strangely satisfied to see her own two feet sticking out over the edge, two meters above the heads of the others, yet not dropping off. 'My feet are attached to me,' Katey mused, 'and I am here. I am on a rock. I am me.' Her feet kicked in agreement; We are yours. We belong to you.

Although Katey could not see Mizuki, with all her heart she longed to obey her, to become Mizuki's mouthpiece, to speak to the group with Mizuki's authority. In the shocked silence that followed the quake, Katey took a deep breath and went for it, 'You lot, you all gotta do what I say because Mizuki says so. Mizuki says we're going to the helicopter 'cos there's sandwiches in a blue box - if it hasn't sunked in a swamp or got all burnt in the fire.'

Nadia and Evie reached for one another's hands. They looked down at the unpredictable earth, up to the voice of Katey and down again. It was Katey and not the earth, that made the next sound. In a small, uncertain voice she said, 'Does anyone actually know the actual way to the heli?'

No one answered because the shaken earth had turned the morning a funny colour and re-awoken in the children the shock of the crash. The night had been too dark for remembering the way to anywhere. Some of the girls huddled together the way fledgling wrens protect themselves from a hungry magpie, but the Silent One sat apart with her back against a different rock.

*

Donna Moore clutched her bag of bandages while scratching her bites, still quivering with exhilaration from witnessing Vix attack Pearl. Vix's eyes had scared her, the way they'd accused, glaring daggers deep into the soul of the larger girl. And Donna thought about another time, back home, when her older brother Dan had argued with their Uncle Lenny. If she hadn't gone downstairs to ask Dan for a glass of squash she wouldn't have witnessed the stabbing. She'd hesitated barefoot in the doorway, her dressing gown hung open over her snowman nightie. The two men were oblivious to her. They circled each other, eyeball to eyeball, in the tiny kitchen. Dan bawled at Uncle Lenny, something about money. Uncle Lenny swore back. He swore like a weapon, calling Dan every name, shouting 'I never stole no money!' Donna could tell Lenny was lying by the wobble in his voice. The bottle of bright orange squash was right at the back of the counter by the sink with its lid off. Donna wasn't sure if she'd be able to reach it and to pour herself a drink. Maybe the kitchen chair? Just as she stepped into the room Dan smashed a bottle of vodka on the work-surface. He cut his hand. Blood and vodka mingled, pouring towards Donna like serpents, rushing along the cracks in the tiles, tickling the soles of her feet. Dan stumbled, eyes skunk-crazy, arms akimbo. Forgetting her juice, Donna began to urge on her brother as if she was watching a film. Dan waved the broken bottle towards Uncle Lenny. Uncle Lenny's eyes locked onto Dan as his hand patted the work-surface feeling for a shard of glass. He found it. Picked it up. Stabbed Dan in the neck.

Donna touched Dan's arm. She punched the air. *Get him Dan!* Dan dropped to his knees in slow-motion. *Get him!* Actors rise again, but Dan slid down the cupboard door to the floor, then slowly down until he lay flat with his feet flopping sideways and those red serpents licking his shirt. Uncle Lenny dialled 999. He knelt in the blood and vodka crying, 'No, Danny, no!' Next thing the police arrived. A social worker came for Donna and her little sister Dee-Dee and . . . Donna forgot the rest.

Weeks passed.

Donna and Dee-Dee found themselves in a blue room with sky-high ceilings and a rain-dropping-chandelier and leaf-patterned brocade curtains that fell to the floor onto the deep-pile carpet. Above them, grown-ups acted politely, deciding where to sit around a shiny table, until they settled, shifting their bottoms, shuffling papers, busy, busy, opening iPads, glancing at Donna's mum, expecting her to make a scene.

'Love is not enough,' one was saying. 'Feeding your children should be your priority. School attendance has fallen to an unacceptable level. Visitors to the family home are unsuitable. And Lenny Briant is not their uncle.'

And so it went on, gabble, gabble over the heads of the children. Stuff Donna knew already. No one asked her opinion. She wished the grown-ups wouldn't talk so loudly about all the bad stuff their mum did because they made it sound real instead of pretend. And Donna's mum didn't know how to discuss. She always yelled and screamed, so when the pressure got too much she slammed her fist hard onto the table and all the mugs jumped, spilling hot coffee. Everyone jumped except Donna and Dee-Dee.

Donna watched the note-taker fight back tears as her mum yelled, 'You snotty bitches think you know it all. Right, I'll do you a deal. You can take the big one. She's a sodding nuisance.' Donna and Dee held hands under the table. Someone cleared their throat and said, 'Remember we are in the presence of minors.'

Both girls were moved on to a new family. Three months later the foster parents said, 'We're trying to love them both, but sadly, Donna's not good for Dee-Dee. She's destroying Dee-Dee's chance to bond with us.' And they were right.

Donna moved in with a new family. They gave her the box-room across the corridor from 'bloody Bradley,' (as his dad called him). Bradley landed Donna in a fat-load of trouble. That's how she ended up at Blaze House residential care home. There she was told, "You've been specially selected for the Transfer Hope Project."

The first photo Donna saw of Ethan Cook, he was outside Project House on a white veranda, his grey hair, twinkly eyes and Hollywood smile making him the most beautiful man she'd ever laid eyes on. Donna knew instantly Ethan Cook would choose her over all the children in the whole wide world. He'd adopt her and be her dad, and she'd be very, very good and stay with him forever.

A multi-coloured bird with a many-feathered tail crossed the clearing. Donna blinked. Katey and the others were rabbiting on about stuff. Mizuki was lying motionless, face-up on the ground, her eyes unblinking.

Donna pointed, 'Hey, you lot, what about that girl? She's had it. Look, everybody, that girl's proper dead.'

Sweat shone on Mizuki's cheeks. Her clothes were stuck to her body like she'd been swimming in them. Katey jumped down from the rock landing heavily on her feet. She rushed over and knelt beside Mizuki as the curious crowd gathered round to see what "proper dead" looked like.

Melissa scoffed, 'That's not being dead, Donna. It's a 'fection. Her head's all gammy. See that disgusting white stuff . . .'

'She is dead,' whispered Katey. Tears welled but did not fall. 'I never even talked to her before yesterday. She was going to take us back the heli . . . to keep us safe, to get us saved.'

'What's a 'fection?' interrupted Joy, picking her nose.

''Fection's when bad blood gets inside you and can't get out except for in hospital,' Melissa said, slapping her palms against her temples. She sighed an exaggerated, exasperated sigh, the way resi staff sighed when they couldn't be fussed answering endless daft questions. She yanked Donna's arm, 'You're the nurse, Donna. You're s'posed to do something.'

Donna examined her finger, still greasy from the ointment she'd used on her own bites. She rummaged in her bag for the first aid kit. 'Stuff you, Melissa! Nurses make sick people better. They don't do dead people and they don't do 'fections. I don't want to be a nurse no more. I'm going to be a hair 'n beauty person instead. Since you think you're so clever – catch!'

Melissa caught the kit in her left hand. She unzipped the transparent wallet and sifted through the contents, selecting two sealed metallic packets marked "antiseptic". She bit through one by picking a hole with her teeth. She extracted a square of antiseptic-soaked gauze which she unfolded and stretched across Mizuki's gaping wound. She flattened the gauze over Mizuki's forehead. Everyone stared as sage-green pus oozed through it. Melissa wiped her fingers down her tracksuit bottoms. She tore open the second foil pack and, using her teeth, she tugged fresh gauze out so it hung over her chin. She peeled back the repulsive gauze from Mizuki's forehead then, gentle as a mother, Melissa applied the clean dressing.

Joy offered a bottle of water from her bag. Melissa took it and tipped it carefully over Mizuki's lips. The water spilled down her chin. To their amazement, the tiniest tip of Mizuki's tongue appeared, licking at it.

Snot dripped from Katey's nose as a tear finally fell. She wiped both with the back of her arm. *Dead people don't lick water.*

'She's not dead no more,' announced Donna, irritated by the huge amount of attention Mizuki was being given. She took a huge breath, 'Do you know what? I've seen an actual dead person in real life.' To illustrate this, she raised her eyebrows, closed her eyes, opened her mouth and flopped her head to one side, then she grabbed her stomach and fell to her knees, slamming herself face down onto the forest floor. She lay perfectly still, holding her breath. When no one reacted she opened her eyes a tiny bit and peeked through. A striped beetle was walking straight towards her. Donna scrambled to her feet and stuck out her tongue, 'Don't care if you don't want to. Anyway, I didn't really see my brother dead, because he died in an ambulance and we weren't allowed to go in with him.'

'We can't go to the helicopter until she's proper well,' Katey said, taking the bottle so she could drip more water over Mizuki's face, 'so we'll have to make a camp here.' Although the idea sounded fun, no one moved because they didn't know where to begin and still the sun beat into the clearing where Mizuki lay drifting in and out of consciousness.

Katey said, 'She needs shade. Can you lot get some sticks to make a roof?'

Someone shouted, 'Yes, get sticks! Let's call this place Black Rocks.' This triggered a torrent of ideas, 'Holey Rock 'cos its full of holes,' 'Shiny Rock,' 'Hedgehog Rock,' 'Rock House.'

'Home Rock.' Vix sealed her own suggestion by stuffing a wodge of bamboo leaves into one of the jagged holes in the hedgehog-shaped rock.

'Okay,' Katey smiled, pleased with the kerfuffle she'd accidentally caused. 'This rock can be called Hog Rock, being as hedgehogs are spiky, and this whole place . . .' she swept her arm round full circle, spinning so fast she almost fell over, 'is Home Rock, like Vix said. Hog Rock is in Home Rock.' Everyone clapped, so Katey spun again then deliberately collapsed onto the ground, happy to be happy if only for a moment.

'Are we playing houses or mummies?' asked Joy,

distracted by a butterfly that was shimmering over the group, but Nadia and Evie were already at work, tugging at some skinny branches at the edge of the Home Rock clearing.

'Houses. And check for spiders. Don't get bit.'

The Blaze House girls played 'collecting'. Soon a motley mound of broken bamboo stems, liana and other slender branches had been gathered from the forest floor. Only the Silent One stayed alone, curled against the foot of her chosen rock.

Katey shook out the branches, leaves and twigs, unfazed by the sprinkling of beetles and spiders and a miniature, translucent frog that hopped quickly away. She selected a straight stick to poke into the ground, but it refused to go in. The ground was too hard. She hadn't yet worked out that in some places rocks lay just below the surface of the moss.

Melissa rushed out of the jungle, throwing her twigs in the air, shrieking, 'A ghost, I saw a ghost! You can't make me go back in that forest. On my gran's grave I swear it's true. There's ghosts here - real live ones!' Melissa was flapping her arms, her face powder-white.

Donna Moore had been standing lopsided, with one shoulder higher than the other, gnawing at her fingernails, watching the woodpile grow and thinking how Melissa had coped better than her at being a nurse. She sneered, 'You're a big, fat liar about ghosts, Melissa. Melissa, Melissa, stupid bed-pisser! Anyway, ghosts don't go out in the day.'

'I promise on my baby's grave, it's true,' Melissa

pleaded, then shot an evil eye at Donna Moore.

Donna retorted, 'You haven't got no baby's grave, so there in't no ghost and that's a fact.' Donna's ruling was final. She ambled away to assess Mizuki who lay so still and pale among them. After a long hard stare close into Mizuki's face Donna pronounced, 'She's proper dead now. I told you before. That's essackly what dead looks like.'

Katey rushed over to kneel beside Mizuki. She dripped more water over her cracked lips and peeled back the pus-soaked gauze that had begun to crawl with specks of tiny, drowning flies, 'Stop saying Mizuki's dead, Donna Moore, because she's not. I don't care about ghosts or graves so Melissa you better shut up and do me another bandage.'

Melissa protested with a stamp of her foot, 'But I did see. It had big eyes and a grey body floating towards me. I promise on any grave you want, I saw a ghost of a girl what must of got killed in the heli . . .'

'I'm not a ghost. I'm Freya.'

The girl drifted out from the jungle, her cropped hair matted with ash and her bruised face streaked smoky-grey. She wore pale-grey tracksuit bottoms stuffed into filthy, white socks and a pair of smoke-streaked Converses laced over her ankles. Her voice was hoarse and her eyes red-rimmed from crying. 'The guardian is dead. The pilots too. Bronwyn Bowen made a gang. She made us drag the bodies . . .'

'There's a gang?' Katey glanced up at the bigger girl. Melissa had been right after all. Here was a real-life ghost, a grey ghost in sunshine. Katey tried another question, 'Are you dead?' Freya blinked so slowly that Katey asked, 'Did you die the same time as them grown-ups?'

Freya shook her head. 'Water,' she managed to say.

Ghost or no ghost, Katey lifted her chin and raised her voice, 'My name is Katey and I'm from Castle Care. I met a girl called Bronwyn Bowen on the plane from England. Them girls there are from Blaze House, 'cept Mizuki. She's got a 'fection, so we're building a camp.'

The ghost girl wandered listlessly over to the woodpile. 'Water,' she begged, barely audible.

Katey offered her the dregs of the water bottle. 'We got more in our bags. It's yucky stuff. Kind of warm. Them dinky ones hate it.' Freya put the bottle to her lips, closed her eyes and gulped. Katey watched Freya's throat moving and the grey dust sticking to the sweat on her neck. She noticed on Freya's wrists a hatch of jagged scars, not caused by the crash.

Freya tossed the plastic bottle on the ground and wiped her mouth with the back of her hand. On tiptoes, she squatted down on her haunches beside the woodpile and selected a branch. Then another. With a twist of her waist, she moved each branch to its own space behind her, then added another and another until they lay in a ragged row.

'What you doing? That's our c'lection,' said Katey. Donna and Melissa stood beside Katey, a show of force, uncertain yet united against the gentle intruder.

Donna snorted, 'She's stealing our stuff, filthy beggar.'

Freya arched her eyebrows at Donna but continued to move sticks, this time laying them across the others until she'd formed a rough mat.

Donna spoke again, 'That's no good. We don't wanna do it like that 'cos that's not our Home Rock plan.' As she looked to Katey for back-up she noticed Melissa catch Freya's eye. As the nine-year-olds smiled at each other with shy understanding, a stab of jealousy shot through Donna, a familiar stab beneath her ribcage as if her heart had somehow twisted then pinged back into place. Donna's eyes narrowed as she tried to fathom what was happening. How come no one ever listens to me?

Melissa stepped quietly over to Freya's mat and squatted down beside her. She picked up some sticks and imitated Freya's weaving, all the time flattening the leaves and snapping off wayward twigs.

Nadia, Evie, Joy and Vix appeared, dragging more sticks and complaining of hunger. Pearl followed at a distance, not carrying sticks, but cradling several huge, yellow nuts that had fallen in the earthquake. Some had cracked and were spilling a creamy liquid down her tracksuit. Pearl dropped her bounty and grinned, 'There's loads more back there.' She licked her fingers, 'Mmm, sweet.'

Ignoring Freya, the girls fell on the nuts, some with hard skins, some softer and easier to break into. Before long they were digging into the split ones with their fingernails, or with pencils and combs from their bags, scooping the white flesh into their mouths, fruit that would have been rejected by fussy eaters in the Before.

'And I got bananas,' added Pearl as if she'd only just remembered, because she hadn't been planning to share. She lowered her lumpy tracksuit bottoms and shook out a dozen tiny green bananas. 'Hey, that's mine!' she cried, as Katey took a banana over to the Silent One and dropped it into her lap.

'What's your name?'

No answer. Eyes raised in distrust, anger. Hatred even. Go away.

'Eat. You want milk or water?'

The mouth of the Silent One pursed tight. Like, why should I speak to you?

Katey took a water bottle from the nearest shoulder bag and tossed it into the lap of the larger girl where it lay unacknowledged beside the banana. Katey crossed back to Mizuki, thinking to shade her dying body from the roasting sun with her own. Katey reached for Mizuki's hand and was shocked by how limp and hot it felt. She looked up, 'Someone help me drag her to some shade. Her skin's going all red.'

Donna folded her arms in refusal, 'She's meant to be red. That's how she was born and that's how she's gonna die.'

Melissa abandoned the stick-weaving to help Katey lift Mizuki's head. Supporting Mizuki under her shoulders they dragged her to the shade of the big rock. They checked the area for spiders before folding a sweatshirt to make a pillow.

Melissa peeled back the gauze on Mizuki's forehead and grimaced, 'Yeugh! Look at her skin. We'd best stick it back up.'

'Wash it first,' called Freya as she pushed another stick into the weave, over and under, over and under.

'I already did it with antiseptic,' said Melissa, though the wound was still grubby with flies.

'We should do it again. I'll get water,' said Katey. She returned to the Silent One to retrieve her water bottle, but while they'd been distracted the Silent One had downed the lot. The banana peel lay flopped open at her feet like a stranded starfish baking on the beach.

Katey found another bottle of water in another bag. She splashed its contents extravagantly over Mizuki's wound, swooshing the septic goo down Mizuki's temples and into her hair.

Melissa bit open a third packet from the first aid kit - not the same stuff as the gauze, but still, it smelt like hospital corridors. She pressed the pure white material against the unflinching patient, dabbing it here and there then, holding her breath, she lifted the flap of skin and did her best to lay it in its proper place, tapping and squashing the raw edges together. She then opened a pack containing a narrow bandage that unfurled like a ribbon. Melissa carefully lifted Mizuki's head off the ground and rested it on her knees. She wound the bandage under and over, covering Mizuki's forehead, until it was all used up, then safety-pinned it in place.

'Looks good,' said Katey, 'like in hospital.'

'I did first aid in after-school club. They did fake blood,' said Melissa, 'and we learnt what to do for choking, or if blood is spurting, or your mum has a fit.'

'I wish I did fake blood like you,' sighed Pearl, 'We never had any fun in my school.'

*

The girls worked and dozed, ate and drank, played and squabbled. The littlest children, the YaYa girls Nadia, Evie, along with best mates, Joy and Vix, explored the forest as far as their legs and imaginations would take them. Day after day they returned to Home Rock buzzing with excitement about the strange bugs and beasts to be discovered beneath every leaf or upon every breeze.

By the second and third nightfall most of the girls had woven mat-rectangles bigger than themselves. Freya requested fatter bamboo but it was too strong to cut, so they had to make do with weak, broken bits and they suffered a few frights fetching rotten wood. A bejewelled ribbon-snake had showed its fangs to Nadia who'd dropped the end of her branch and backed off, jabbering, 'Siu, coman misi,' to Evie who understood and rushed over just as the snake slithered speedily into the undergrowth. Giant woodlice scuttled, amphibians of every hue, (including an intriguing frog with tiny horns), hopped or crawled, but nothing bit, nothing attacked.

Freya stripped leaves from bamboo poles, then threaded these poles through the sides of each mat. She showed Nadia and Evie how to feel for the softer earth by jumping or pressing their feet on areas between the rocks, then how to dig using whatever tools they could find from their bag or the forest, because the soft earth would be where they'd sink the uprights on which to fix the mat walls. Their favourite "pick-axes" turned out to be the hard casings of nuts with which they chipped the ground, laughing as they flicked earth up into each other's faces. Laborious, but they were rewarded with a pile of roughly rectangular mats which they propped up to create "tents" open at each end. Katey, Freya and Melissa dragged Mizuki inside. That evening, Joy and Vix squeezed in beside the semi-conscious Mizuki, feeling safe because Donna Moore and Pearl were lying across the doorway. Katey slept in the open beside Melissa and Freya.

Only the Silent One refused to move, as she lay alone at the foot of her rock.

*

Shortly after dark they heard a shout followed by piercing screams. Some of the little ones cried out, 'What's that?' then 'I'm scared!'

'Shush, you lot, it's nothing - go to sleep,' Katey called above the general noise of the jungle, though the hairs prickled the back of her neck. She raised her ear off the ground to listen more intently. Beside her, Melissa gripped Katey's arm.

But Freya did not flinch. 'You should know what that is by now. Haven't you heard it before? I told you, Bronwyn Bowen's got a gang and they've got the helicopter. Bronwyn said there's demons in the jungle so everyone's got to shout and scream her made-up poem to scare them away. I said, "No, I won't scream your horrid poem!" so they kicked me out in the dark jungle all by myself. My feet got wet in the sinky stuff. Worms stuck on my legs. They sucked my blood and I couldn't get them off, so I went back and said, "I changed my mind, I will scream at them demons for you," but Bronwyn Bowen said - like this - "Beg all you like, darrrling. Your useless words can't save you. Gobble-gobble-gobble-gobble, I must do my work. Underlings obey without question. You challenged me. No obey, no stay." Bronwyn knows all the words from the Incredibles and other films and lots of songs and she says them loud, right in our faces. Bronwyn stuck her finger at me, like this . . .' Freya pointed her finger at Katey and narrowed her eyes. When she spoke again she changed her voice so deep and hoarse she could hardly force out Bronwyn's words, '"We must sacrifice the one to save the masses. Freya, Freya, Disobeyer, you are to be thrown to outer darkness."' Freya became herself again. 'Bronwyn made them girls grab me, an' they pushed my head into the ashes what made me cough, and they shoved me into jaggy leaves what scratched my face. Jody swinged my bag round and round her head. I yelled at her, "Give it me back," but they said, "Finders, keepers!" and the strap broke and my bag flied off by itself into the bushes.'

In the darkness each child lay, eyes wide open, listening to Freya's story.

Freya's voice broke, 'My tin were inside . . .'

Katey puffed out her cheeks. She blew into the night, 'You kept your memory tin? You brought your tin on the plane? That's not fair, 'cos we weren't allowed.'

Freya kept her tin. Unbelievable. Incredible.

'Yes. My tin with the photo of my birth mum, and mum's silver necklace with two dolphins. Staff said I could smuggle it to Transfer Hope because they didn't agree with Ethan Cook's rules that we mustn't bring our bad past with us.' Freya's eyes filled with tears but she didn't let them fall.

3

Vanishing Point

Long days collapsed into short nights as the jungle adopted the children born to concrete and corner-shops, nurturing them with wood and leaf and seed. The girls worked or played, chatted or slept - whatever, whenever. The Blaze House girls depended on Freya to suggest activities: mat-weaving, fruit-collecting, smashing nuts for the sweet milk. Inside the nuts, not only milk but an edible, fibrous substance, bland but filling and, as a bonus, those that chewed it benefitted from an accidental teeth-clean. Dust and grime coated their bodies as inadvertent sun protection. Hitherto white aertexes were streaked olive from brushing against foliage, so hide-and-seek became an impossible game - a girl could make herself invisible simply by standing stock still within an arm's length of the seeker. Fingernails were either bitten to the quick or grew into talons, effective weapons in the daily bickering. Pearl sported three vertical scars down one cheek after yet another spat with Vix.

*

Mizuki moved house once more. Freya, Melissa and Katey had hauled her into a new hut that was smaller than the first, no bigger than a one-man tent and still with both ends open. Joy and Vix had long since stopped sleeping beside Mizuki because she muttered constantly and stank unbearably and her matted hair stuck to the sweat around her face and neck. The triangular roof of the new hut was patched with leaves and grasses, with a hole in one side through which Katey and Melissa dripped water over Mizuki's lips. When the bottled water ran out, they used rainwater from leaf 'cups' or scooped from shallow mossy pools. Mizuki's cheekbones jutted ever more severely from beneath her skin. The lumpy crag on her forehead formed a clean scab.

And the Silent One remained aloof, sullen-faced, dull-eyed. Either she slumped by her rock, or she'd shuffle through Home Rock helping herself to random food, polishing off the last nut or banana, sometimes smuggling her loot under her sweatshirt to eat later. She guessed Katey would soon get fed up with looking out for her. Katey might be a Castle Care girl, acting all kind and concerned, but most likely she'd turn out to be no different from the Blaze House lot who'd snubbed her from her very first day at the resi. The dour girl lowered her head and dragged her fingers through her hair to separate the strands. She twisted these into a dozen skinny plaits. Finally, she threw back her head so the plaits fell backwards, stiff with dirt, and stuck out in all directions.

Of all the girls, Nadia and Evie were most fearless in the face of the bewildering forest with its peculiar creatures. They compared each newly discovered beast to those they were familiar with, using hand-signals as they gabbled YaYa; 'Bidan dog' ('bigger than dog,') 'Fat namper,' ('fatter than hamster,') or signing 'Flappy like budgie,' 'Noisy like cat,' 'Goofy guinea-pig thing.' Also fearless were the jungle creatures in the presence of humans. Humans were unknown. Humans had never hunted or killed here, never been a threat. Nadia and Evie would leave Home Rock via the same arch of saplings, venturing further and further from the camp, instinctively returning just before nightfall.

Six-year-old "pretend sisters" Vix and Joy, discovered a particularly glorious zone. A fairyland of flowers, butterflies and bugs, where reality blended with fantasy, where they could be inseparable and no one ever called them in for tea. 'We're princesses and this is our Flower Palace!' they cried as they danced freely, singing half-remembered pop or Disney songs at the top of their voices. Here, voluptuous flowers thrived for good reason - the daily downpour. When a heavy rainfall caught Vix and Joy, they ran dripping and squealing from the Flower Palace, further and further into unexplored territory. Breathless and giggling, they stopped beneath a dome of gigantic leaves shining like plastic macs as the water poured off. Together they squatted, holding hands, until the rain subsided.

A miniature rust-coloured deer wandered in to join them. It paused, raising its sharp nose to sniff the interesting human scent. Vix stood up to face it, knocking her head on the leaf above so the remains of the water showered over both of them. The deer froze, meeting Vix eye to eye, each with the same sharp face, delicate features and alert, inquisitive nature. Neither blinked as Vix approached the deer, reaching out to caress its stumpy antlers. The deer nuzzled her arm. Vix stroked its back, expecting soft fur, surprised by its coarse hair. The deer ambled on, picking delicately at the tips of shrubs, while Vix day-dreamed that it was leading her towards a paradise where happy children played and yucky adults were turned to stone. Joy limped behind, because of a splinter in her foot.

The deer wandered into yet another clearing, a vast, treeless expanse of flat rock, jet-smooth, but punctuated with soil-filled holes overflowing with drifts of purple orchids. The flattish surface enveloped a huge, pellucid pool that stretched as far as the eye could see, motionless but for the skim of water-boatmen and dive of faraway birds. Here and there the lake seeped through silvery reed-beds and over the flat rock into meandering broad channels through the undergrowth, creating areas of marshland, punctuated by millions of minute, white flowerheads.

Abandoning the deer, the girls rushed to the water's edge. They kicked off their trainers and stamped in the shallows, then lay on their stomachs enjoying the way the ripples tickled through their aertexes. Laughing, they arched their backs and slapped their hands together, barking like the seals they'd seen long ago in some distant zoo in a long-forgotten land.

*

Something small fell from the sky into the water. They heard it and blinked and missed it. By the time they'd worked out the direction of the sound, they saw only ripples, expanding hoops across the water. It happened again. This time they thought they saw a pebble flying towards them and heard it plop into the water some distance away. The splash disturbed an elegant grey-white heron that had been quietly fishing in the shallows. It folded its neck and stretched its wings wide, flapping dreamily low over the lake.

Joy watched the heron fly, fixing her eyes on it until it settled some distance away. By the time it was fishing again the splash had been forgotten. Joy's next fascination was a rotten log upon which a couple of flat-backed mottled-green terrapins[1] basked, extending their ancient necks to the sun. Joy touched one and it scuttled into the water. She shoved the remaining terrapins off their log and into the shallows and sat herself down in their place. Then, with intense concentration, she began to pick at the splinter in her foot. Her overgrown fingernails poked and tweezed until, at last, the end of the splinter emerged, then she doubled over, twisting her foot up into her mouth, and licked the rough end of the splinter with her tongue until she was able to grip it between her teeth to draw it out.

'Done it. I done it, Vix! I got it out all by myself!' Joy stood up. She twirled in triumph, scanning the dragonfly-laced reeds for her surrogate twin, 'Vix!' The intimidating lake stretched away, punctuated only by rocks and reeds and the occasional fish leaping. On the horizon, the bruised mountain tops threatened the innocent sky with their jagged dragon's teeth. This immense sky, despite being flecked with birds and butterflies, appeared vast and empty.

'V . . Vix?' Joy stammered. The displaced terrapins had her surrounded, breaking the surface of the shallows with their ancient snouts. For a moment, Joy lost concentration. She stopped worrying just long enough to admire the irregular diamond patterns on the terrapin backs. Then she remembered . . .

'I know who to call!' she yelled. And she cried out the name of the kindest person in the whole wide world, who right this minute was probably snoring soundly in a warm bed in Lancashire, 'Mr Blake!' Mr Blake, a staff member at Blaze House always had the answer. He'd tell the children in his care, 'When you're afraid, invent your own happy ending.'

'A happy ending, got to think of a happy ending,' Joy repeated out loud as she retraced her steps to the Flower Palace. She imagined Vix pouncing on her, jumping out from her hiding place with a 'Boo!' and a 'Got ya!' Joy laughed at her own imagination. She yelled, 'Ready or not, here comes Spot!' – a much-loved line from a once-favourite storybook – but Vix did not pounce or shout, 'Here I am!' Joy searched the shrubs, peering behind tufts of coarse heather and around grey boulders. Monster footprints beat their *thump, thump, thump* inside her chest. Scary, scary, scary. 'I give up! You win, Vix, come out. Come out, come out wherever you are.'

A rustle of leaves to her right. Joy spun around to see, but it was only one of those huge, hairy rats again, bumbling along without a care in the world. It didn't scurry or zoom like the scrawny kitchen rats in her Nan's flat, and it wasn't concerned by the presence of the tiny human, now shivering tearfully in the sunlight.

Joy wandered back towards the Flower Palace and as she walked she did what she'd always done *Before*. Grasping sadness in one hand and loneliness in the other she squished them together between her palms, then she stuffed the whole lot into her mouth, gulping it, sending it down her throat all the way to the dungeon inside her tummy button. Then, twisting her tummy button between her fingers, she locked it tight with the magic key so the horridness could never escape.

That done, she stopped to gape at what she thought was a skinny snake wrapped over and under and over a twig, its little black bridges decorated with alarming sulphur-yellow patches. She walked on, side-stepping an iridescent emerald beetle and ducking beneath a fly-infested web. Joy found her way back to the Flower Palace with its lush carpet and garish flowers that bowed to the silver-crowned girl because she was a princess.

'Oh no!' she clutched her stomach, but too late! Fear had unlocked her tummy button. It burst out.

'Vix! Vix!' she cried, panicky as a mother whose child is lost in a crowd, her voice smothered by a cacophony of cicadas, parrots and kookaburras. Joy rushed out of the clearing, along the path to Home Rock. A winged insect landed on her arm and stung her. She slapped it and killed it and kept walking. She heard voices.

'Im bin ver gud.'

'Can fly lick mm.'

Nadia and Evie, the dark-haired, unrelated sisters, were chuntering, discussing their 'cleckshun' of bugs that they'd unceremoniously plonked into their battered lunch-boxes. As Joy approached, the girls turned and grinned.

'Joy!' Evie grinned, 'See thi fly lick mm.' Evie held out a giant, black millipede, thrashing between her finger and thumb.

'That's not a fly,' said Joy, focusing on the only word she'd understood, 'No wings, see.' Nadia and Evie exchanged knowing glances. They giggled. Without warning, Evie threw the millipede onto Joy's head. It landed heavily, twisting and turning, struggling out of Joy's tangled hair, scurrying down her face and onto her shoulder. Evie jumped forward and snatched it back. She dropped it into the lunch box and snapped the lid shut. Joy did not flinch but glared at Evie, raising her shoulders, fists forming, squaring for a fight, boxing the air like a praying-mantis.

'Na, na!' Nadia reassured her, stroking Joy's shoulder and batting her eyes submissively. No, don't fight. *Just joking*.

Joy blinked and relaxed. She sighed, 'I lost Vix.

She was hiding and now she's gone,' but Nadia wasn't listening. She was distracted by a red tube-shaped beetle with black-and-white antennae trekking up a leaf.

Joy shrugged. She set off alone back to Home Rock.

*

Hog Rock was higher than an English shed, but the side with holes made for an easy climb. Every evening Katey scaled it simply to enjoy the calm of being alone yet not alone, and tonight was no different. She surveyed Freya below, pale and gaunt, running her tongue over her cracked lips as she wandered listlessly among the others. Freya had been working on a new hut design using bamboo of varying lengths poked vertically in rows where the earth was soft. Between the bamboo she wove long papery leaves. All around the base, she'd heaped soil and moss to deter crawling bugs. Four girls could lie side by side between the walls, but as yet it had no roof.

Katey smiled because Nadia and Evie were sketching again, creating naïve cavemen-style outlines of bugs or butterflies, and mammals with round eyes and zig-zag teeth. They liked to sit quietly, shoulder-to-shoulder as a single entity, reminding Katey of a weird sea creature from children's TV.

And there was Donna Moore, lost in her own little world as usual, gurning for the fun of stretching her face in all directions, or moaning to no one in particular about not having a mobile phone. Further away, Pearl, her chestnut hair flopping over her eyes like some neglected poodle, and arms hanging listlessly by her sides, flopped down, legs askew to pick seed heads off the long grass. Pearl avoided Donna ever since Donna goaded Vix to stab her. That was unforgivable. Forever.

The Silent One had removed her aertex in favour of her over-sized Blaze House sweatshirt, however sweaty and uncomfortable. Melissa was talking to her, trying to be kind, 'Sit with us. I'll show you weaving if you like.' And then there was Joy pacing Home Rock, crossing the clearing back and forth, circling the circumference, looking up to the sky and behind every rock as if expecting something, or someone, to turn up.

'Where's Vix?' Katey asked suddenly, for the first time noticing her absence. Nadia and Evie looked about, then at each other, shook their heads and chattered an incomprehensible mishmash of syllables.

'Dunno,' shrugged Joy, but she turned just in case Vix had crept up behind her. 'Gone, I think.'

Katey stood up. She checked the fringes of the forest. Most likely Vix'd be doing her business in the trees. 'Vix?'

Joy said firmly, 'She's proper gone.'

'What do you mean, gone?'

'We was playing and something fell out the sky and then I had a splinter and then I couldn't see her nowhere, so I come back here all by myself.'

'You should of telled us straight away,' Katey scolded, but it was no use stressing. To search for the totally, utterly lost was futile, especially if they chose to stay hidden. Hide-and-seek was an impossible game and Vix loved to hide. Stupid kid. Katey sat down and rested her chin on her knees.

Melissa stormed up to Joy and pushed her face into Joy's until their noses were almost touching. 'What do you mean, something fell out of the sky? Where? How do you know Vix is lost? You left her? When did she go? Why didn't you say so before?'

Joy stared her hardest right into Melissa's eyes. As with the millipede on her head, she knew how to hide her fear of angry, bigger people. To show fear is to invite pain. Fear made worse things happen. As Melissa yelled, Joy bit the inside of her lip; *Mr Blake said think of a happy ending. Don't answer back. Melissa's hating you. Can't tell the truth. She'll slap you.* Saying nothing, Joy stuck out her chest, broadened her shoulders and locked her knuckles under her ribcage tight as a wrestler's belt.

Melissa's breath blew over Joy's pursed mouth, 'You're going to tell us when you last saw Vix. Speak now!'

Joy found her voice, matter-of-fact, 'At the lake.'

'The lake? What lake? We haven't seen no lake, have we Katey?' Melissa sharpened her face and her eyes narrowed severely on the younger child.

'There . . . there's a very big lake.' Joy's arm twitched and pointed roughly to *somewhere out there*. Melissa stepped back, glancing up at Katey for moral support.

Katey stuck out her bottom lip. 'What am I supposed to do? Vix'll come back when she wants.'

Maybe because she was on Hog Rock and everyone seemed to be glaring at her, that Katey felt perhaps she should say more but she had no idea what. Her heart beat faster and faster. She wished Mizuki would wake up. She wanted to cry for a guardian to help. She opened her mouth but no sound came out.

Then, with a whoosh, so many words tumbled from her, scattering like a puzzle pieces out of the box and over the rug, 'The 'mergency people forgot us. Mizuki never talks. We're making this place all stinky. Vix is gone. There's no shops. No sandwiches. No milk. No phones. No TV. No more birthday parties.' Katey looked down at the bewildered faces, 'I think there's nothing.' Katey's lower lip wobbled. Below her the Blaze House kids looked as helpless as toddlers yet none of them cried for their mummies or begged to be saved or expected a grown-up to turn up to drive them out of here. Freya stopped weaving the hut and caught Katey's eye. She was one of the oldest. She'd know what to do. Katey addressed her.

'When's your birthday, Freya?'

Surprised at being selected to speak aloud in front of the whole group, Freya felt flustered but managed to say, 'March the third.'

'What month are we in now?'

'April,' said Freya, pulling an uncertain face.

'July?' guessed Donna, hoping to be the one who got it right.

'See what I mean? We don't know. We won't know when it's time for Freya's party. Or when it's anybody's birthday. We don't even know what today is.' Katey's voice trailed off. Her listeners exchanged glances, each hoping the other could fix this black hole that had sucked all sense of time and purpose into some other universe.

Time. Names. Numbers. Whatever separated one day from another day had gurgled the wrong way down the plughole. Katey sighed. She had done a lot of sighing recently. 'Don't none of you want no more birthdays?'

The Silent One pouted. Her shoulders sagged. She released a sound like 'flipping heck,' like a pony blowing a raspberry. Something mattered, yet nothing mattered. Her head shook slowly. Who cared about birthdays or any day for that matter? What was the point of a birthday without a dad or mum to wake you, all excited, with a gift or two? Back home people said Happy Birthday to other people, but the Silent One had only ever opened one card in her whole life - a home-made card from herself.

'To me. Happy Birthday. Love Gerald xx,' she'd scrawled. 'Gerald' because she hated 'Geraldine'. She'd tucked the card beneath her pillow ready for the morning of her seventh birthday. Or was it her eighth?

After her fifth foster placement broke down when she was almost twelve, Gerald had been moved into Blaze House to await a yet another family, well aware she was a lumpy, sulky, sullen, soon-to-be teenager with a flat disposition. Who in their right minds would pick her to join their happy family? Gerald dreamed about her very last foster mum, the one she'd tried so hard to love, who'd tried equally hard to love her back.

She thought of her foster dad who'd cried when he'd been made redundant because he'd had to relinquish his subscription to Sky Sports. She thought about his scruffy, foul-mouthed brother. When they were alone he'd grinned, 'See me as your foster uncle.' She could still feel the back of his hand on her cheek, smell his nicotine-stained fingers, see his dirty, chewed nails. She hoped he was dead in a ditch.

Gerald thought about the many meetings involving adults discussing her future. She'd slumped miserably at the conference table, while the big people smiled. They'd asked her opinion, 'Would you like this or that?' and she'd agreed *whatever;* a new foster home, a possible adoption, a long-term stay at Blaze House where she was apparently doing 'surprisingly well.' It was best to agree quickly because in the end you always said 'yes' to whatever they wanted. 'Yes' made meetings stop; 'Yes' made the grown-ups go away.

On the American fridge in Blaze House kitchen, the communal calendar had been marked with a red dot against which staff had scrawled, "*Geraldine – THP* - discuss." She'd agreed to sit at a table with all the professionals who supported her young life; Jan the tutor, Annie the nurse, Brenda, head of social services with Amena the note-taker, Sheila from the NSPCC, Lewis from CAMHS, Mike the ed-psych, and Mr Magsi, boss of Blaze House. This particular meeting included a special guest who turned out to be a pretty Australian lady called Lilian. It amused Gerald to observe the way they talked as if she was important. Acting like they were including her. They knew nothing. If they ever asked her, 'What's wrong?' she'd say, 'Nothing.'

'Geraldine, it's your choice to join the Transfer Hope Project - or not,' said Lilian. 'Nothing to worry about,' she was saying, 'Think of it as an honour to be invited. Twelve is the upper age limit, but we're offering you a place even though you've turned thirteen. You'll be the oldest girl ever accepted on our project. How special is that, Geraldine? My husband – Mr Cook - has agreed to include *you*, sweetie. How's that?'

The rest of the adults tossed their jolly words into the mix. Blah, blah, blah. Same old story. False hope followed by tense silence in which grown-ups shut up and nod their encouragement. The note-taker scribbles furiously. She's leaving space for Geraldine to speak. Emptiness hangs like a wardrobe without garments. Open the door, hear the hangers rattle. Come on, Geraldine, the Transfer Hope Project is a great opportunity. But hope hangs in the air like a stale egg sandwich. There's so much kindness in the room it could suffocate a girl.

'Yes?' The woman needed an answer.

Gerald had nodded. No need to speak. Silence did away with people quicker. *And don't call me Geraldine.*

'Great. That's that then. You'll have a whole new start. New friends, new family – a brand new country. Papua New Guinea.'

'Papa who?' she'd said. Oops, she'd spoken aloud like she'd puked in public. But it sounded so funny - *papa who*?

'Think Australia but smaller!' someone said,

and the adults around the table laughed with relief because they'd solved the crisis of what to do with this impossible child.

'*Papa who? Kangaroo. Who will I be? If only you knew.*' The poem invented itself in her brain. Gave her hope. She could start over. Like being born again. And no one would ever discover her secret. In that instant, Gerald knew that moving far, far away meant The Truth could stay forever hidden. 'Starting from now,' she vowed deep within her unseen soul, 'I'll never say another word.'

*

The crash happened so quickly, before Gerald could decide who to become. Her new self-to-be depended on so many things. If Ethan and Lilian Cook turned out to be mean and nasty, she'd be stroppy and nasty; if soft and kind, she'd be sweet and manageable. If school was fun, she'd work and learn. If they hit her, she'd hit back and run away. She didn't particularly care about having a fuss on her birthday, but then again, if the new staff turned out to be nice she might let *them* care.

'*Papa who? Kangaroo. Who will I be? If only I knew.*'

A clear, sure voice cut straight through her thoughts.
'Let tomorrow be the first day.'
It was Mizuki.

*

Mizuki rose up and stood behind Katey upon Hog Rock, managing (incredibly) to hold her head high, though in her weakness she could hardly straighten her back. Her legs wobbled like a new-born giraffe. Her skin was not her natural amber, but straw. She was barefoot, wearing a sleeveless iris-coloured top that was too short in the waist because it belonged to Melissa. Her own navy sweatpants that hung loose from her waist. She placed a hand on Katey's shoulder to steady herself.

The horrific sight of Mizuki, wafer-thin, with matted hair and ill-fitting clothes, silenced the girls. They strained to hear her speak above the jungle clatter.

'Tomorrow is "Day One". We must mark it by – I'll show you - see this nail varnish? Every day, starting tomorrow, we'll put a dot of varnish on that rock over there, but we can't all do it because we'll muck it up. Days must never get mucked up - so Freya, this is your special job. You are our Day-Keeper. One dot is the same as one day. Everyone agree?'

The children on the ground strained to read Mizuki's lips. They exchanged wary glances with one another before tentatively raising their hands.

'Vix went away,' said Katey.

'I know. I heard you talking about her.' Mizuki wobbled her head from side to side. Yes? No? Not sure what to do. She said, 'It's going to be dark soon so there's nothing we can do, is there? Let's talk about Vix in the morning. Shall we sit together? Does anyone know a bedtime story?' Mizuki held out her hand to Katey and together, slowly, painfully, they descended Hog Rock.

The girls gathered near one of the huts, pulling on their sweatshirts and tucking their knees beneath them for comfort and protection from bites.

'What about "The Ugly Duckly?" I like that one,' Joy suggested, but the others giggled so she stuck out her tongue at them.

'Ugly Ducker-ling!' corrected Pearl with a snort, 'but that's a baby story. I want Tracey Beaker.'

'TV stories are too complercated,' Katey said, but a thought came into her mind that this evening was no time to be mean. She patted Pearl's back and added, 'but you can tell us your TV stuff another night if you like.'

Beneath the moonlight Katey did her absolute best to recite The Ugly Duckling, and the others chipped in with their own versions until eventually, despite being outcast, despite being lonely and lost, despite the bullying, rejection and tears, the scruffy misfit stretched his pure white wings skyward to fly with the swans.

A bright star appeared, then a second and third, then thousands upon millions as the universe burst into star-fires to compensate for the absence of the sun.

4

Diggers and Searchers

Freya hardly slept a wink. Mizuki's words galloped through her mind like wild horses kicking up the waves along a beach. *A special job, my first ever, Mizuki believes in me.* In her imagination, Freya placed her hands upon the black rock. She heard the authority of her own voice striking the rock, *'You are the stone what marks the days. I, Freya of the Faraway Forest, name you, "Daystone."'* A bolt of lightning shot from her tongue, branding a crimson sun into the black rock. From behind the black rock, the sun rose. Smoke wafted out from its circumference so it seemed to Freya that the rock itself was on fire. She imagined angels crying, 'All power to Freya, queen of the Daystone,' until their cheering turned to clapping and the clapping was an engine roaring, rotor-blades clattering, helicopter jolting, branches smashing. The red sun shot out. Up, up, up it rose, then down it arced beyond the horizon, setting alight the earth where children groaning for salvation battled through the dust of their *Before*. Freya rose from the ashes, raised both arms to the sky and cried with great defiance, 'Let today be the First Day!'

On the actual morning of the First Day, Freya woke before the rest. The hungry pit in her stomach felt worse than her dad's broken promises. *I'll fetch you for the weekend.* This time he'll turn up. *I've got you a present.* This time he'll remember. Freya pressed her hands to her naval. Try as she might she could not squish that anxious, waiting-by-the-window, pit-in-the-gut feeling.

Barefoot, Freya crossed the firm earth to the Daystone. This was no dream. With fist and teeth, she twisted the sticky brush from the precious pot of nail varnish and, standing on tiptoe to reach as high as possible, created a single red dot upon the black rock. Freya replaced the brush, tightened the lid, then wedged the bottle into a narrow cleft in the rock. The Day-Keeper watched as the beautiful dot set hard.

'It is good,' she whispered. She placed her hands on the warm rock, thinking, 'I want to say something important,' but she had no idea what until it burst out with a sound so unfamiliar and confident, she shocked herself;

'Daystone.'

Alone Freya stood. A powerful woman blessing the beginning of time. 'There,' added the little girl, because a single word in itself seemed far too small for such an occasion. She reached up to place her hand where the red dot had dried, smoothing it over, feeling for the tiny, yet significant bump, then padded back to join the others waking up to their ordinary day.

*

Mizuki pressed her back against Hog Rock and sank down to the ground. This morning she felt too weak to climb again. The others sensed her fragility, but still they were drawn to her as, one by one, they rubbed the sleep from their eyes and gathered around her feet.

Donna spoke first, 'I was thinking to get me a banana.'

'And that's what we're gonna to talk about,' Mizuki managed to say, easing herself into a more comfortable position, taking a sip of water from a bottle. Hog Rock loomed behind her. 'We're gonna talk about food.'

Fungi, leaves, and what the girls called, 'spotty chickens' (disc-shaped birds more akin to guinea fowl than chicken) were not recognised as edible. *Before* chicken came wrapped in cellophane or breadcrumbs. The girls feasted on fruit, nuts, and fibrous roots or chewy bark or coconuts. Sometimes they shared their finds with Mizuki and the Silent One. Nothing was cooked because the children never considered making fire. If a microwave was even possible, where would they buy the ready-meals? If a freezer was even possible, where would they plug it in? And what was the point of Pot Noodles without a kettle in which to boil the water?

'But I always get me a banana. Plus, I ate nuts what gave me tummy ache.'

'That's 'cos you ate loads and loads, Donna's-a-Goner-Moore,' said Pearl, holding up six fingers, 'I only ate this much nuts and I was perfectly fine.'

'You saying I'm a pig?' Donna snarled, ''cos if you are, you's gonna get it. I'll smash your flippin' brains in.'

Mizuki shook her head wearily. The younger children glared at Donna to shut up. Donna sulked, shuffling closer to Freya, hoping her hate for Pearl was infectious and that Freya would catch it. Pearl counted her fingers, flicking them up and down, muttering about all the different ways they could make the number six.

At last Mizuki spoke so softly the children had to concentrate on her lips, 'Donna, you mustn't eat only bananas. We've got to try all different kinds of food or we'll get sick. Also, we need to talk about Vix. And Joy's lake. And toilets.' Mizuki sighed because the list was a burden and there was so much more but she didn't have the strength to say it all at once.

Pearl giggled, 'Toilets!'

Joy smirked, 'Pooey toilets. Yucky leafs.' Evie and Nadia nudged each other. They screwed up their noses because the bushes were getting shittier by the day.

Mizuki raised her hand for silence. 'Ever since we got here, everyone's done their own thing. Everyone's got into habits, eating the same food, checking out the same paths, collecting the same stuff just for you. You don't help each other. Except Freya who helps you weave. That's why I picked Freya to make the red dot, because I trust her most. She's going to do it every single day until . . . just until. You know.'

''Til the grown-ups get us?' Pearl grinned, knowing

she wasn't supposed to say that sort of thing aloud. It might upset the little ones. No one else grinned with her so she clamped her mouth shut.

Mizuki continued, 'Also, we need to dig a toilet so we don't go all over the place. Poo is dangerous. Germy. If you only wash your hands when it rains germs stick on you. Bite your nails, pick your nose, suck your thumb, you get to eat germs, right?'

Freya raised her hand.

Mizuki raised her eyebrows, Yes?

'If we dig a hole over there,' Freya pointed to the farthest side of Home Rock, 'behind those twisty bushes, then dig a ditch going away from the hole to where none of us ever walks, the rain will fall in the hole and go along in the ditch. Sort of like flushing a toilet.'

Pearl stuck out her tongue and giggled, 'No way am I digging nothing. Digging's too hard for me.'

Mizuki clapped her hands, 'Great plan, Frey. Everyone can dig a bit. We'll find things or make things to dig with. Don't use your bare hands because even teeny-weeny scratches in your skin can make you sick. We'll dig a hole and put sticks over to sit on, so no one falls in. And another thing, don't forget. Today is the First Day.'

Freya smiled because the red dot and the toilet idea were all her own work.

Mizuki continued, 'This is the first day when you find food and don't eat it yourself. Bring it back here. No more eating on your own. You can get your favourite food, but not too much or it will go bad.

Put it on that flat rock. Spread it out, then we'll eat breakfast together. That way no one eats only nuts - Donna Moore.'

Donna's lip rolled out in a smirking pout to show her pleasure and annoyance at the attention.

Mizuki added, 'You heard me. No one is allowed to eat only bananas or only berries.'

There was a flap of wings. An ornate fruit-dove with a golden head and a patchwork-coloured body settled on some nearby seed-heads, peck, peck, peck. The girls gawped at it. Nadia and Evie gabbled something unintelligible about fetching a notebook to make a drawing of the bird, but Mizuki was speaking and they didn't dare leave.

'After we've eaten, we'll split into two teams - Diggers and Searchers.'

'I want to be a Searcher,' shouted one.

'Me too. Me too!' echoed all but the Silent One.

'Shh!' Katey hissed, 'We're going to make two teams. Like in netball. Mizuki's telling us how to do it, aren't you going to tell us, Mizuki, go on, you tell us.'

'The Diggers will start digging the toilet. Freya, you lead that group, because you have the best ideas and toilets was your idea. I'll lead the Searchers to look for Vix. My group is, um, Joy, because Joy saw Vix last, and you Katey, because you're good at directions.' Mizuki read Melissa's anxious eager-to-be-chosen expression. 'I'd love to bring you with me, Mel, but Freya will need your help with the Diggers. So, I suppose we'll have to take Donna Moore.'

'Yes!' Donna pumped the air with a triumphant

fist.

Pearl jumped up, indignant. 'What about me? I wanna be a Searcher. You can't make me dig nothing!' She stormed off, huffing and folding her arms with as much drama as she could muster.

Mizuki shook her head. 'Frey and Mel will need Pearl's help because she's stronger than Evie and Nadia, and that girl,' she pointed to the Silent One, 'is useless.' Mizuki closed her eyes. Having said all she could, she lay back exhausted. Her world spun. She felt as if her feet were lifting off the ground and she was sliding backwards, head-first off the edge of the world, gravity-free, floating freely through the atmosphere. Star-light whizzed by like electrical wires.

Katey took charge, 'Come on you lot! You heard what Mizuki said. First, we hunt for breakfast.' She led the way into the jungle, leaping over twisted roots, swinging on familiar liana, scrambling over mossy rocks, and avoiding marshy areas. Behind her, most of the girls fanned out, heading for their usual haunts. The plan to gather and share the food was thrilling, if only for the moment. Nadia and Evie dipped into the shadows – they knew where to find honey. The site must have been recently abandoned because the only bees in the vicinity were drop down dead.

Melissa hesitated. She'd watched the Silent One wander over to her usual wonky rock and pick up a stick with which to jab the ground. Melissa snorted, 'What a slob. I'm glad I don't look like you.' The larger girl ignored her. She jabbed the ground again, so Melissa shouted, 'If you don't help find food you'll just have to starve. Your sort are spongers and I can't stand spongers.' Raising her nose skyward, Melissa tossed back her rippling brown hair and followed the others through the undergrowth.

*

Their first communal breakfast was a triumph. A low, flat rock had been allocated as the permanent dining table. Rules were discussed and agreed. 'No walking on the table. No spitting on the table. No wiping snot on the table. Everyone has to clear up.' The girls used moss and rags to wipe away bird-droppings or flick off insects before laying the food out.

'What a feast!' Donna's eyes lit up at the rainbow of berries, bananas and seeds, coconut milk and water. *Before*, she'd despised all fruit bar apples, and she'd only accepted bananas sliced in rings and soaked in custard.

Evie snatched a handful of nuts and wrinkled black fruits and was about to stuff them into her mouth when Mizuki took her wrist. 'Wait!' she said gently, 'First, can we be thankful?'

Donna smirked, 'Thankful? Ha! You're being a proper bossy boo.'

'She's not, 'cos Mr Blake says proper ladies always say please and thank you,' chirped Joy. She had her eye on the yellowest of the green bananas with the least brown marks.

Mizuki smiled weakly, 'Thankful is stopping, thankful reminds us to share. If we just grab, then

some will take too much, and they might get sick like
. . .'

'Like Donna's-a-Goner Greedy Moore!' Pearl
snort-laughed so much she could hardly stop. Pointing
at Donna, she chanted, 'Donna got sick 'cos she ate
too quick!' Nadia and Evie giggled. They nudged each
other, anticipating what would happen next. Donna
didn't disappoint. She flew at Pearl, snarling, lashing
out, swiping in all directions with her ragged nails.
Pearl fell backwards. Donna launched herself to sit
on top of Pearl, closing her hands around her neck,
shaking her and screeching, 'Vix shoulda stab-stab-
stabbed you when you nicked her food!'

Pearl's head bashed against the soft ground, her
neck flopping helplessly up and down, and her eyes
rolling white against her sweaty, brown skin. Melissa
and Freya rushed to intervene, but Donna's rage was
too heavy and too slippery. They couldn't get a grip.

Imitating the action, the three smallest girls, Nadia,
Evie and Joy, tumbled over one another, mock fighting
with delight.

'Vix shudda stab, stab, stabbed you!' Joy yelled,
and Nadia and Evie screamed with hysterical laughter.

As quickly as it had begun, it was over. Freya
managed to drag Donna back. Pearl hauled herself
up, rubbing her neck. Her eyes flicked daggers at the
snarling Donna. She looked to Mizuki. *'Defend me,'*
she begged with her eyes, *'You're the boss. Stick it to
Donna!'* but Mizuki had the energy of a ragdoll and
said nothing.

The little ones scrambled to their feet after their

71

fun scuffle. Evie high-fived Nadia and they both cheered because, through all the rough-and-tumble, Evie had clung on to the food she'd grabbed from the table. Crimson berry juice ran like wounds between her fingers.

Mizuki sighed, 'As I was saying, thankful is stopping. Thankful is making sure we all get the same - even the ones that *don't* help find food.' They all turned to face the Silent One. Their collective stare accused the girl, 'If being thankful means sharing with a sponger, then Mizuki can go play on a motorway.'

Mizuki raised her arm, palm up. She bowed her head and said, 'Thank you,' without any sign of embarrassment. Katey frowned, then shrugged, 'What the heck?' and she too raised her arm, bowed her head and repeated, 'Thank you.' She opened one eye to watch as the others followed suit, eager to fill their stomachs. 'Thank you!' they cried as they fell upon the food, snaffling it face first, grabbing the best for themselves. Mizuki quietly scooped up two handfuls of fruit and crossed Home Rock to where the Silent One sat alone. Mizuki poured the food out beside her. The Silent One briefly raised her head to nod her thanks. Mizuki smiled weakly before returning for her own breakfast.

*

The Searchers set off with only a bottle of water between them. Joy skipped ahead, unperturbed by thoughts of countless camouflaged creatures, from sage-blue spiders self-decorated in lichen to the wide-eyed mammals of the canopy. Mizuki followed, irritated that her trainers pinched her toes. Donna, over the moon to have avoided the dreaded digging, swung her diamanté-studded bag high and low. She skipped as she chattered incessantly about Before, about sweet shops, TV's Bake-Off competition, and missing school because when her mum got drunk she always forgot to wake her. Katey was comforted by Donna's rabbiting. It passed the time. Also, it reminded her that the Before was not some vague collective nightmare, but a tangible life. A real existence they'd survived. Shared memories were real memories.

Joy gasped. She stopped in her tracks and pointed at the foliage, her mouth and eyes wide open.

'What? What?' Donna elbowed past Mizuki fully expecting (and half hoping) to see Vix lying mutilated in the bushes like a murder victim in "True Crimes," Bradley's favourite programme.

'It's that black and yellow snake,' Joy said, 'but it's different because someone's chopped it into little bits.' Sure enough, the snake appeared to be in three separate pieces, curved over then under then over a slender twig.

'Is that all?' huffed Donna.

'I saw that snake after I lost Vix. This was our path from when we found the baby deer. It walked off that way. We followed it to the lake.'

Katey pulled back Mizuki's arm, 'Careful. What if it bites? What if it's pois'nus?'

Mizuki smiled. 'I've seen a couple of those already and I'm telling you that's no snake. It's three caterpillars trying to look like a snake. I bet they invented looking like a snake to scare the birds so much they don't fancy eating them, but you're right, Katey, we don't know if it bites or stings so we'd best not touch.'

They walked on a while until Donna stopped for no obvious reason. Opening her palms to the heavens she declared in her broad northern accent, 'A chopped snake. I just saw a real-life chopped up, mashed snake. No one in Engalund's ever gonna believe me.' She hit herself on the forehead with her fist. Some things were just too funny. 'Darn!'

*

Joy led the Searchers to the Flower Palace. As the older girls entered the beautiful clearing they gasped because, for a moment, the beauty overwhelmed them. An incredible sight with a powerful scent - an indescribable perfume of bursting blooms, eucalyptus and orange leaves. Huge bees buzzed louder than an electric box with by-passed wires. Massive black and green crickets chomped jagged holes into spear-shaped leaves, while other insects drilled, droned, or simply fluttered.

'Do you think we're in a film set?' asked Donna.

'If we are, you'd better not go on about murder and stuff,' Katey warned.

Donna smiled, 'Don't be stupid, there's no dead

bodies here. I mean a *nature* film set. Do you know something? Well, at Blaze House we watched Blue Planet.' Donna giggled because as soon as she said it she remembered that Blue Planet was about sharks and icebergs, so she added, 'but this nature film they're making here's not about water. So if you ask me, this is Green Planet.'

Joy squealed, 'Ooh, see what I found! Finders keepers!' She dived onto the grass and snatched at a delicate shiny object.

'More snapped-up mashed stupid snakes, I 'spect,' Donna sniggered as Joy skipped in circles, waving a fine, silver chain above her head.

Joy chanted, 'I got a necklace, a necklace, a necklace!' All four girls suddenly stopped stock still and looked up into the blue sky from where the necklace surely fell.

'Treasure. Give it me!' Donna rushed at Joy to steal the necklace, but Joy clutched it tight against her chest.

Joy turned to Mizuki, 'Put it on me, Mizuki. Do it up.' Joy bowed her head as Mizuki examined the chain before clipping it behind her neck. Behind Joy's back, Mizuki and Katey exchanged puzzled glances. *Strange. Very strange*.

Mizuki had a thought. 'Joy, did this necklace belong to Vix?' Joy shook her head. She was already scanning the ground for more jewels.

*

They heard the water before they saw it gurgling over massive plates of volcanic rock set over a quarter of a million years ago in the Pleistocene era. Where soil had long settled in the dips and fissures of the rock, the ground was soft and marshy underfoot. All around, mounds of moss created a spongy patchwork quilt of emerald, amber, red, with tiny white flowers or seed-heads. The children picked their way, trying not to get their feet wet until, to their amazement, Joy's lake came into view. A stunning expanse of water flanked by a seemingly endless curve of shingle.

Joy ran to the log where, only yesterday, she'd removed a splinter from her foot. The terrapins were back, sunning themselves. With a sweep of her arm Joy swished them into the water, then she jumped onto the log and stood staring out into the distance.

Donna craned her neck hoping to be the first to spot a floating body, suitably bloated and vile, but she knew better than to share her fantasies with the others. Instead, she fired questions at a bewildered Joy, 'You know them tortoises you chucked off the log - can I get one for a pet? Do you know what, there's a story about a tortoise spelt backwards? Did you ever swim without armbands when grown-ups weren't watching? I bet you and Vix did that. Did Vix drown and you saw but you're not telling?'

Joy shook her head. 'I jus' did this. . .' she said, sitting on the log, holding her foot leprechaun-style to re-enact the removal of the splinter. As quickly as she lifted her foot to her mouth, yesterday's terrors whooshed back and she jumped up shouting, 'Vix!

Vix!' then leapt into the water, wading out until the water was up to her thighs, 'Vix, where are you? Please come back to me!' But the lake was deep and wide and Joy's wails were lost in the cries of the jungle.

'There she is!' Katey pointed to the far trees that wrapped around the west side of the lake. 'Look! Over there - hey Vix! We're here! We've come for you!' and she set off running along the shore.

Mizuki and Donna had seen nothing but, abandoning Joy in the water, they raced after Katey along the edge of the lake, avoiding the fly-infested remains of a stinking catfish, until Mizuki bent double, hands on knees, panting. Katey stopped. She turned to Mizuki. In a trembling voice she said, 'Vix was there. For definite.'

Donna cried, 'See on that tree, there, look! A pointy stick. See that arrow? It's directions. A secret sign. Vix must've put it there so we'd know.'

Mizuki stood up straight, clutching her side. Pale and breathless, she struggled forward. Sure enough, a stick had been tied at an angle to the trunk of a tree. 'Secret sign, my foot. How would Vix have an arrow? Anyway, that's higher than Vix can reach.' Mizuki ran her fingertips along the length of the stick. One end was white. It had been sharpened with a knife.

'Atishoo!'

Everyone jumped. Shocked squirrels leapt from branch to branch above them; *Alarm, alarm!* Mizuki put a finger to her lips, beckoning the Searchers to follow. Joy had caught up, tracksuit bottoms soaked and feet squelching in her trainers. She reached for

Mizuki's hand. The four girls moved softly away from the arrow, melting stealthily into unfamiliar territory. In the relative safety of the undergrowth they froze, eyes scanning north, south, east, west, hardly daring to breathe.

Donna broke the silence. She whispered, 'Indians?' but Mizuki frowned and pursed her lips, holding up her hand for silence.

'*Shh!*' she mouthed.

A stick cracked like a gunshot. Then voices. Distant voices.

'Are we being saved?' Katey whimpered. Mizuki's fierce frown demanded silence. Joy, still clutching Mizuki's hand, scanned the shadows for her sister.

*

'Pick it up. Go on, move. Don't be such a baby.' Voices. Someone close by. Female. Through the leaves they saw the rear view of a tall girl shoving a smaller one in the back. The child fell to her knees. The tall girl spoke, 'Stop messing about. You did it before no problem, so we know you can carry it. Get up. Lift it, you lazy little cow.'

Donna flapped her hand in front of her nose, 'Phew, what a stink!' They all grinned, recognising the smell from the helicopter. It wasn't a Blaze House or Castle Care girl, but cheap body-spray used by one of the older London kids, the one with the big gob.

The Transfer Hope Project children were from all

over Britain. They'd met for the first time at a hotel in Heathrow. Perfume-pong-girl had stuck with her peers, talking loudly and a lot, but only to those she knew.

The tall girl, (not Perfume-Pong), had hair twisted on top of her head to form a tornado ingeniously held fast by two pencils. One of her extensions escaped down her back, long as a rat's tail. Her gaunt face, stained with engine oil, was unsmiling. She whined, 'I can't make her pick it up!'

'So? I told you what to do, didn't I? You smack her. I'm sick to death of telling you how to handle disobeyers. Go on, Claire, smack her!' The owner of the voice came into view, a broad-shouldered girl with wide-hips, and a bolshy, down-turned mouth. She marched over and slapped the child across the top of her head.

'Ow!' The child ducked too late.

'Vix!' started Joy, but Mizuki slammed her hand over Joy's mouth. They watched Vix, still on her knees, struggling to lift a paint-can full to the brim with shingle. Vix hauled it off the ground, swung and dropped it a few centimetres ahead. It spilled a little. Another slap. Another cry. Katey surged forward, but Mizuki grabbed her arm and pulled her back. *Shh, stay still!* Shaking with fury, Katey obeyed.

'That's how to train brats. Don't let me tell you again or . . .' The bolshy girl stormed off, leaving Claire sighing like any world-weary mother, but when the bolshy girl was out of sight, Claire shoved Vix aside and lifted the can herself.

'You owe me for this. I'll learn you another time, but if Jody comes back, you've gotta grab the can proper quick or they'll shave my eyebrows off like they did Elle-Marie's. And they'll do yours off if you don't stop acting like a baby.' Claire arched her shoulders back and stretched. She dragged her feet as she hauled the can of shingle deeper and deeper into the jungle.

Katey recognised Claire as the girl with hair extensions and thick eyebrows, the one she'd seen falling through the wreckage of the helicopter. When Claire and Vix were out of sight, Katey rounded on Mizuki, 'Why didn't we speak? We could've said "Hi." Donna could've smashed that girl in, easy.'

'But we don't know who else is with them? The guardian? Pilots? Strangers? We don't know them and we don't need them.'

'What about Vix?' Katey argued, 'We can't just leave her with them girls.'

'We'll get her, but not yet.' Mizuki's legs felt like jelly. All she wanted was to lie down, but she said, 'Okay, let's follow them, but tread soft. No stomping.' A fly landed on her cheek. She slapped it dead then examined its blood on her hand.

The Searchers moved lightly, their ears sharp, every sense intensified, alert to every glint of light, each new shape created by the shafts of sunlight sliding steeply through the canopy. As they walked they sniffed the air for Jody's perfume, listening out for footfall or muted conversation. Tracking was simplified by all the junk strewn along the way: plastic bottles, a cracked mug, a hairband, a once-white ankle sock, now stained brown, stuffed with wizened mushrooms.

The otherwise pristine paradise created a harmonious sound with rises and fades; the zing of insects and overlapping birdsong, alternating and interlocking caws and cackles, chirps and trills, gurgles and whistles, punctuated by unseen mammals that whooped and barked, yapped and squeaked, squealed and chattered. All manner of creatures swarmed over the land or up trees and ivy, across rocks and through sky. Creatures crawled and flew and dived and, never having encountered humans, were unafraid of the intruders.

Mizuki spotted a hollow space beneath a massive, bulging, web-guarded tree root. The tree had fallen long ago, but its once upper reaches rested precariously in the branches of other trees. 'We should stop here. Clear out this space while it's still light. It's a good place to hide.'

'Hide? But . . .' Donna winced at the grotty web.

'Because I can see the crashed heli and something feels wrong.'

'I can't see no heli. If something feels wrong then something is wrong. We gotta get back to Home Rock quick or them Diggers'll think we're dead or something.' Donna tugged Mizuki's arm, 'See that mega spider – that one there with the hairy legs – you won't catch *me* sleeping next to that monster. I vote we go back.'

'First, we save Vix,' Katey scolded. 'That's what Searchers do. You wanted to be a Searcher. You begged. I'd've chose Melissa, not you, but . . .'

Donna shrank back, 'Chill out, you're not my boss. I was only saying . . .'

'Show me Mizi - where's the heli?' Katey strained her eyes to where Mizuki pointed, but try as she might, she could hardly decipher the shape of it through the climbers and the woody strangler fig already shooting up the metal mountain.

'We stay here and watch. Hey, clear this space for me, will you?' Using twigs and trainers they swept the space as best they could. Most insects could be brushed away, some they flicked, others they squashed. Job done, Mizuki dropped down exhausted with the heat and effort of responsibility. Feeling light-headed, she closed her eyes and allowed her mind to drift backwards through the universe. Somewhere far, far above, she could hear the Searchers talking, but their voices were muffled.

'She needs water,' Katey decided. 'Donna, go and get water for Mizuki. Here, take this bottle. We should of filled it when we was back at the lake.'

Donna folded her arms, 'Mizuki said to stick together and not be by our own so I can't go to the lake. I'll get lost. You go.'

'Right, I will, but I'll take Joy with me 'cos she can't 'xackly look after Mizuki can she? See them berries, yes those, eat some if you're hungry, but don't crash about. If Jody catches you, scream lots and lots so we know.'

'But I don't want to be prisoned,' Donna squirmed. *Why did Mizuki have to be ill all the time?*

'You got to check and check that no one sees you

get them berries for Mizuki. They got juice inside what I think makes her better. Come on, Joy, you and me's going to get water for Mizuki.'

*

Katey turned to Joy, 'You're going a bit slow, aren't you? I can run quicker on my own. Stay here and wait for me or you can go back to Mizuki if you like.'

'But I'm hungry. I want Blaze House.'

'Blaze House closed down. Didn't you even know that? Melissa told me what happened. All the one's what wasn't already fostered or 'dopted got chosed for THP. It's why the most THP girls here are from Blaze House. You had bad staff there. That's why no guardians from Blaze House came here with you. They got tagged by the court and Mr Blake got took to prison.'

'He did not!' Joy stamped with her hands on her hips.

'Not everyone liked Mr Blake. Melissa said he was a stealer and a liar. Also, Melissa told me Tariq Magsi got prisoned too.'

Joy grimaced, 'Good, 'cos Mr Magsi was the scary boss. I hid from him all the time.'

'Melissa said everybody at Blaze House got 'vestigated and it went on TV.'

'I hope Mr Magsi got loads of time-out, but not Mr Blake. Mr Blake said . . .'

'Can we stop talking about *Before*? You have to

stay here all by yourself until I get back or go back to Mizuki. Which?'

'Go back to Blaze House.'

Katey sighed, 'That's just being 'nnoying. I told you stop going on about *Before*. Go back to Mizuki.' She indicated roughly in the direction of the sleeping Mizuki. After all, it wasn't far and the tree root was massive, sticking up big as a whale's mouth. After a cursory goodbye, Joy wandered back, roughly in the right direction as Katey ran confidently towards the lake.

*

Katey returned with a plastic bottle full of water to find Mizuki recovered, sitting up cross-legged, deep in conversation with Donna. Katey hesitated, her eyes narrowed and her eyebrows twitched. *Their heads are too close. I was with Mizuki first.*

Mizuki looked up and smiled, 'Hey!' She took a sip of the water, nodding her thanks. 'That's good.'

'Joy?' Katey looked about.

'What do you mean, "Joy?" Joy's with you, isn't she?' Mizuki tried to stand, but her legs wouldn't hold her. She grabbed hold of a root to steady herself.

'She was going too slow and I thought you were dying, so I asked her "What d'ya wanna do?" And she said, "Go back to Blaze House." So I told her to go back to you. I showed her which way. She wanted to . . .'

'You let her go alone? You're sooo stupid!' Mizuki's furious eyes cut deeper than words.

'I . . .'

'Yeah, that was sooo dumb,' Donna smirked, squatting as she wrapped her arm around Mizuki. She smiled at Katey with one side of her mouth. Donna offered Mizuki more water, tipping the bottle to her lips. As Mizuki gulped, Katey glared at Donna, turned her back and stormed off into the bushes.

Mizuki pushed Donna away. 'Go after her. Get that stupid kid back here!'

'But she's only running away for attention,' whinged Donna, 'she's just making a scene.'

Mizuki pushed the water bottle so Donna dropped it. Mizuki waved her hand weakly, 'Go.'

Donna threw up her hands in defeat. She trudged after Katey, whining her name, pleading with her to come back, yet hoping and wishing Katey would disappear forever. Get lost. Same as Joy.

*

A six-year-old wandering through a strange land with no home and no mother ought to be terrified, but to Joy this land was welcoming. Here was home. Joy had not cried for her mother since, well, maybe never. She shrugged happily. Right before her nose an iridescent butterfly with sparrow-sized wings settled upon the jagged lip of a trumpet-shaped flower. Sensing a nectar trap it lifted off, beating upwards, its indigo wings shimmering gloriously in a shaft of sunlight where faeries and unicorns capered and beckoned, '*Come, play in our magical garden.*'

Back at Blaze House, tiny, winged people were always waiting for Joy beyond the tangled buddleia and rhododendrons. A clanging bell would sound for meals from within the imposing red-bricked house, but Joy would ignore it. Staff would never let her go hungry. They'd come outside and shout her in. From beyond the undergrowth Joy could hear someone calling, not her name, but 'Katey! Katey!'

'Katey!' she heard, but it wasn't Mizuki or Mr Blake or even Mr Magsi. Only Donna's-a-Goner-Moore. So Joy tossed her hair, wrapped herself in a flowing gown of stardust and twirled and skipped through her magical world in greater safety than she'd ever known before.

*

Katey smacked the trees and yanked at every creeper that dared block her way. *What's the point of a mother who calls you stupid like Mizuki did? A real mother would never let another child wrap their arms around her like Mizuki did. A loving mother would never smirk in your face like Donna did.* Katey snatched a cluster of dark berries from a branch. She squeezed them furiously, staining her hands and her filthy t-shirt until the scent of the fruit overpowered her and she forced her face down into her cupped hands, gulping in the sour-sweet goodness. Small seeds caught in her teeth. She pushed against them with her tongue. She wiped her blackened hands through her hair, scraping her fingers through the tangles, relishing the pain of the tug on her scalp.

Far behind her, Donna's languorous voice floated unconvincingly, 'Katey! Katey, wait for me. Don't run so fast,' but Katey was more interested in watching her own feet move forward, fascinated by the ground moving between her feet; leaf, twig, stone, leaf, twig, stone. And as she marched, she snarled, 'I hate Mizuki. I hate Mizuki. I hate Mizuki.' Spitting out Mizuki helped her stomp.

*

From the start, the chase had been pointless. Donna huffed, threw up her arms dramatically and turned back in the direction of Mizuki, wondering what she'd tell her, how she'd explain that, not only Joy, but Katey had also vanished. Excuses and lies multiplied in her mind; *Katey ran back to Home Rock - Katey spat at me - Katey stuck her tongue out at me – I did find her but she refused to come with me so it's not my fault.* Donna giggled to herself. Mizuki's fury would be short-lived but worth it because, ultimately, she'd have her all to herself. Then she thought, 'What if Joy's returned while I've been away?' She pictured Joy snuggling into Mizuki's arms and sped up her pace.

Brown trees and brown liana, light-green and

dark-green leaves, scuffed channels where animals ran, everywhere was exactly like everywhere else. Butterflies and birds moved in all directions. Shadows shifted with the sun, lighting new paths and disguising the one Donna had just followed. She thought back to the time the Blaze House staff had taken the residents to the Steakhouse for Melissa's birthday lunch and she, Donna, had needed the toilet. Afterwards, she'd come out into the corridor and stood, bewildered, unable to remember the right way back. It was so baffling. Her heart beat faster and faster. Doors, corners, white wall, cream wall, this way or that way? On two doors were letters of the alphabet, big ones next to little ones. Donna knew they made words, but words and symbols were so confusing, jumping about and swapping places to trick her. She'd pushed a random door and peered in to see a man in a stripy apron, holding a huge knife over a mountain of vegetables. The man yelled, 'Oy! Says private! Can't you read?' Donna backed away in panic. She swung around and bumped into Nadia and Evie emerging from the 'Ladies.' They were chattering their usual gobbledegook. Donna let them pass, then trailed behind them into the clattering dining area where no one would ever know she'd been lost, and no one would mock her for being unable to read.

*

Sweat shimmered over Mizuki's forehead. She closed her eyes. Shrouded beneath the spider-ridden roots of the ancient tree, she drifted in and out of consciousness.

5

Rebel

High in a tree, overlooking the Helizone, Katey felt safe. She wedged her trainers into a space between the branch she was sitting on and a thick, hairy vine that gripped it. Attached to the vine, clusters of long leaves with ripple-edged fronds enticed insects or birds to pollinate their trumpet-shaped flowers. Without the stress of Mizuki fainting or Donna moaning or Joy being slow, Katey relaxed into a day-dream.

Mizuki's a big, fat let-down. She was supposed to be my sister or my mummy, but she beed sick, lying about all sweaty, 'specting to be fed, acting just like the grown-ups from Before. And she let Donna's-a-Goner-Moore creep up close to her when I wasn't looking. And . . .

Katey caught sight of a terrible thing. Below her were two dozen cobbled-together cages of varying sizes and durability. The flimsier ones had been constructed from bamboo canes interwoven with reeds. At each intersection, the canes were bound with elastic hairbands, string, cable or shredded seat-belts - the heli had regurgitated all manner of useful items. Several of the cages were crudely wrapped in mosquito nets, tied at the top like some bizarre gift. Each one contained a rodent or a bird that had been caught (tangled) in a crude net-trap: several spotted 'chicken-things', three doves, a parakeet, and a bird of paradise with a broken wing. One cage held a huge long-haired rat of the kind that, (to the delight of Nadia and Evie) regularly bumbled through Home Rock.

Behind the cages, a large pen had been constructed in a similar style but with stronger uprights driven deep into the soft ground, partly woven with rushes. The uprights had been sharpened at the top in the same way as the 'arrow' by the lake. This large pen was empty.

'A baby elephant could fit in, except for no door,' puzzled Katey.

The floor of the pen was strewn with reeds, plus a hotchpotch of materials, including a light-weight leather jacket that the guardian had worn. The roof was a patchwork of ripped mosquito nets from a consignment of two hundred that had been ordered by Ethan Cook for his project. He'd cut a good deal with the manufacturers after the original order was rejected by the Rwandans, the material packaging being too tough for their machinists to recycle. The nets folded into small hoops that sprang open to form protective tents.

Forty metres beyond the pen loomed the broken helicopter, its nose deep in the marsh. 'Wow, that is ginormous,' Katey marvelled, 'I'm not surprised it fell out the sky!' She remembered the pilot back at the airport, a cheerful guy with dark eyes and cropped hair, calling, 'All aboard the Super Puma. Next stop the Transfer Hope Project. Bring your picnics and crayons and don't worry about a thing. From now on, your life will be brilliant. If you lot do as well as the Aussie kids, fulfil your potential and don't make trouble, then you'll pave the way for many more.'

The rotor blades had snapped clean off. One was supported by branches, looking like it could fall at any moment and smash the head in of an unsuspecting child. Wrong place, wrong time, ouch. Another had speared the earth, with its end resting against the helicopter; a formidable playground slide. Around the base were scattered tissues, sweet wrappers, crisp packets and plastic bottles. Torn clothes and rags littered the bushes like flotsam and jetsam at low tide. Beside the mosquito nets, Ethan Cook had ordered a consignment of white paint for doing up the veranda and picket fences. The lids had burst off many of the cans and paint poured out, setting into other-worldly shapes. The body of a fly-infested mouse had stuck fast in a dried pool of the stuff. The battered cans contained rainwater and drowned insects.

From her perch, Katey could distinguish the marshy zones from the firmer ground. A crude path ran erratically across the marsh linking the cages to the helicopter. Various objects, such as rucksacks and boxes and of course, paint cans, acted as hardcore. Piles of shingle from by the lake had been poured over and trampled down. At the cage end of the path, a pyramid of shingle and litter rose knee-high, waiting to be shifted. With the slightest breeze the pong of rotten meat wafted up. '*Stinky stink*!' Katey grimaced, pressing her nostrils into her knees.

Overhead, enormous birds gathered, wheeling, black phantoms with tatty, storm-battered wings. Some descended to the marsh, out of sight behind the Puma. Katey listened as they squabbled over the remains of meat or bones. She peered over the edge of the branch and wondered, 'Where is everybody?'

They must have understood her question because all at once the caged creatures went crazy, squeaking and squawking. Birds flapped. Their feathers fluttered like snowflakes through the bars. A rat-like creature escaped, knocking over its cage before limping into the shadows. Katey could see the hole in the wooden bars where it had chewed its way to freedom.

What's that? Singing? A terrible rasping discord of a song from beyond the trees. Katey pressed her body flat along the branch and watched. Two girls appeared. They stood, one each side of the animal track and parted a curtain of foliage through which Bronwyn Bowen made her entrance. Bronwyn's wavy, auburn hair had been backcombed into filthy, stiff flames that fanned out in all directions. A makeshift crown of feathers was tangled in the mesh of hair. Bronwyn wore a shabby red t-shirt over her ripped tracksuit bottoms. (Despite the heat and the daily downpour, all the girls opted to cover up against mosquitos, spiders and the leeches they called "slug-suckers.")

Bronwyn swayed her shoulders and hips, staggering like a string-puppet, arms swinging awkwardly, elbows sharp as daggers, wrists loose. In her wake, four girls crawled on their hands and knees, tunelessly singing a vaguely familiar song. Katey craned her neck, moving her head from side to side like a curious owl, searching for spy-holes between the leaves.

'Louder!' screamed a blotchy-faced girl with one arm tied against her chest in a makeshift sling.

'Louder!' screamed another, 'Lydia and me ain't gonna tell you again.'

The four little voices rose higher, muddled chants from the *Before*: '*Too hot! Say my name. Don't believe me, just watch! Too hot! Say my name. Don't believe me, just watch!*' Behind them dawdled Claire and Elle-Marie, their eyebrows newly stencilled in the shape of traffic cones falling towards their ears. Each used a bamboo stick to tap a failed, funky rhythm onto a paint can while listlessly 'singing'. There was a brief pause, then a more confident rhyme, an army-style chant, '*We're the girls of Helizone, this is our land, get your own!*'

'Louder!' screamed Elle-Marie in a bid to impress her leader.

'*We're the girls of Helizone . . .*' they repeated with greater conviction as the terrified caged creatures flapped and pecked the bars. Bronwyn sauntered across the shingle path to the helicopter then hauled herself up through a space where the mangled door hung limp. She perched awkwardly on the wrong side of a seat as the underlings and slaves gathered to await instructions. As the music faded, the creatures in the cages calmed down.

'Slave One. Fruit!' Bronwyn beckoned an emaciated child, who stumbled towards a large suitcase that lay directly beneath Katey.

The child lifted the lid of the suitcase and let it fall open. A cloud of flies escaped the gaping mouth. Inside was a mouldy mush of melons, prickly pears, rotting mangoes, blackcurrants and coconuts. Slave One selected a coconut because the soft fruits were maggot-infested. She hugged it to her chest, struggling with the weight of it as she picked her way over the path towards her keeper. Bronwyn screamed over her head. The child jumped then ducked, but the scream was not for her.

'Slave Two. Water!' Bronwyn pointed towards a discarded bottle. The second slave scurried to retrieve it. She pressed the bottle into the marsh and the water flowed in. The solemn child cupped the bottle in both hands, raising it as an offering to Bronwyn. Bronwyn leant down, grabbed the bottle and screamed again.

'Slave Three. Meat! Kill me a chicken, quick.'

The tiniest slave leapt up, hands waving, 'I aint killing no chickies!'

Katey gasped. She almost lost her balance and grabbed the branch. The branch shook, sending leaves fluttering to the ground. Katey froze. She held her breath not daring to move, but she needn't have worried. Squirrels and tree kangaroos were always moving through the canopy, so a sudden shake of a couple of leaves alarmed no one.

'Vix!' Katey mouthed as the fearless six-year-old arranged her body in a well-practiced stance of defiance; hands on waist, hip to one side, shoulder lifted, mouth sneering up at Bronwyn as if to say, '*You aint never gonna make me kill nothing.*'

Bronwyn gripped the sides of the Super Puma until her knuckles turned white. She leant down towards Vix so her head seemed too big for her body. She sneered, 'You stupid, useless, disobedient, filthy little runt! Can't you even count? You are not Slave Three. You are Four. And when your turn comes, if I tell you to kill, kill – is - what – you – will – do,' Bronwyn jabbed her finger at Vix, 'or else.' Bronwyn drew her finger across her throat the way she'd seen in the movies then she settled back onto her throne.

Vix did not smile. Neither did she cry.

The real Slave Three had already loped over to one of the cages and was picking and pulling at the ties, loosening the bars until she could reach through and pull out a spotted chicken. The hapless bird flapped its pathetic protest, but it was too malnourished to cluck, let alone put up any kind of fight. The girl dragged it out but she clutched the bird so tightly its head dropped forward and it expired. Nevertheless, Bronwyn reached down to receive the offering.

Katey wondered, '*How's Bronwyn gonna cook that without no microwave?*' A second thought, '*I wonder what Asda does with all them chicken heads and chicken feet they chop off? Who keeps the feathers? I want some of them feathers. Do they put them in pillows?*'

With one hand gripping the chicken and the water bottle in the other, Bronwyn took a swig of water and immediately spat it out, 'Disgusting!' Furiously, she shook the rest of the water over the head of Slave Three, then chucked the bottle at Vix.

Vix did not flinch.

'Slave Four approach!' Bronwyn screamed, letting the chicken flop down by her side. 'Yes, I'm speaking to you, brat. Stop it with your dirty looks.'

'I can look how I like. I'm fed up with your stupid slave game. You can't make me do nothing.'

Gasps from the onlookers. Lydia rubbed her broken arm, caused by the crash, exacerbated by Bronwyn. The pain from the crash had been bad, but since Bronwyn twisted it up her back it had been agony, especially at night.

'Aaaapproach!' Bronwyn would have risen again, but it was difficult enough holding onto the seat with one hand and the feet of a chicken in the other. Instead she tensed her muscles and shook her head until feathers fell from her hair that shivered like snakes shedding their skins. She hunched her shoulders and once more leaned forward, reminding Katey of a crooning cartoon vulture, but this Bronwyn-vulture had nothing to sing about.

Vix stood, feet apart, refusing to move, though her legs were trembling. She'd been through worse. Grown-ups did that exact same leaning-down, looming-bully thing, pinning kids against the wall, and yelling. Vix stared directly into her captor's eyes, eyeball to eyeball, and there it was - she recognised it – that familiar flicker of self-doubt. Vix peered into Bronwyn's open mouth at a fascinating, wobbly bit that flip-flapped over Bronwyn's words as they tripped along her tongue.

'Aaaapproach, child. I command you, take the first bite. Queens and kings get slaves to taste stuff for them. I'm giving you this very important job so I don't get poisoned. You should be grateful.' Still holding the chicken by the feet, Bronwyn shook it.

From her lookout, Katey noticed how the dead bird's white spots shone like stars against its navy feathers. The sadness of such beauty stuck in her throat.

Bronwyn turned to her slave-trainer, the quivering Claire. 'Make your slave obey. She shall obey me.' Bronwyn swept her arm dramatically from Claire to Vix and back again. The chicken swung like a pendulum.

Claire glared at Vix and her glare said it all. *How dare you attract all this attention onto me? Don't you know to shut up when someone threatens you? Obey Bronwyn now. Can't you see it's me she'll hurt if you talk back?* Claire stammered at Vix, 'Go, b . . bite that chicken.'

'But it's not cooked proper,' insisted Vix, 'I'll get germs.'

Bronwyn threw back her head and laughed so raucously the caged creatures squawked and flapped. Jody, the wide-hipped girl who ruled Claire, laughed along with Bronwyn. Lydia forced a laugh, then Elle-Marie laughed hysterically but her ridiculous coned eyebrows betrayed her fear. Three slaves stood unsmiling, but Vix cocked her head at Bronwyn and grinned. *See if I care. What you gonna do about it?*

Bronwyn stopped sharp, her expression instantly deadpan. The fly-ridden air buzzed a warning. The sun stabbed daggers into the forest floor. No one moved. Bronwyn looked from one slave to the next, and with a terrifying grin she slammed the dead chicken against the helicopter. Bang! Everyone jumped. The bird left a greasy imprint on the metal skin of the helicopter. The creature hung limp in Bronwyn's hand as a thin string of sticky blood and slime oozed from its beak and slowly, so slowly, dropped all the way to the ground.

'I'll give you germs, you insolent little . . .' Bronwyn all but star-jumped off her throne. She rushed along the path towards Vix. As she ran, she swung the chicken above her head. Blood sprayed out like water from a garden sprinkler. The girls screamed and scattered in all directions. With head-feathers flying and a manic grin, Bronwyn rushed at Slave Four.

Vix turned on her heels and fled into the jungle.

A split second of uncertainty. Bronwyn hesitated. Then she screamed after Vix, 'Slave, obey your queen!' Bronwyn beckoned wildly to Jody, Claire, Elle-Marie and Lydia, 'Underlings, spread out. Circle round behind. Cut her off. Catch her. No one escapes Queen Bronwyn and lives.'

In the tree, Katey clamped her hand over her mouth. She watched Vix run, not west in the direction of the lake, but east, deep into an unexplored region of the jungle. If Mizuki was waiting in that tree root, Vix would miss her by a mile. Bronwyn stormed after Vix, screaming for help from her underlings, yet none followed. They were rooted to the spot, petrified, listening to their leader as she roared and cackled and crashed through the undergrowth.

*

In the interval between Vix running away and Bronwyn returning, dusk happened. In all that time no one had moved. No one dared run. In any case, where would they run to? Better the devil Bronwyn Bowen. Vix should have known better. The jungle's no playground for a six-year-old. When Bronwyn catches Vix she'll teach Vix not to be so stupid.

*

Bronwyn returned. She was not alone. Through the darkening leaves Katey strained to see Bronwyn dragging a tiny girl by the wrist, skipping and tripping in her effort to keep up.

'Am I being saved?' the child chirped.

Katey slammed her hand to her mouth, 'Joy!'

Bronwyn grinned. She beckoned the quivering Claire. 'Look what I found. This kid was playing faeries! I let Slave Four go. That one's too much trouble. Doesn't deserve to serve me. I was just thinking how to punish you for failing as a slave-trainer, then this daft bat turned up, so hey-ho what d'ya know - today's your lucky day. Here, take her. Your last chance to prove yourself. Don't mess up.'

Bronwyn, still clutching the chicken, pushed Joy into the arms of Claire. And darkness fell.

6

Darkness and Light

Katey stretched her stiff legs. She wished the girls would stop messing and go to sleep so she could sneak down, grab Joy and run back to Mizuki. A beam of light hit the Puma, throwing the wonky doorway into shadow, yet shining brightly on Bronwyn who was perched inside.

'How?' gasped Katey. Another light came on, then a third. Katey's mind raced, 'Fire? No, not fire. Proper lights like in England.' An eclipse of moths gathered around each glow, casting bat-sized shadows. Long, spikey claws rippled over the rough ground from the cage bars. The Helizone girls yawned and coughed, drifting one to the other, chattering and giggling, until Bronwyn called out lazily, 'Claire! Jody! Pen my slaves.'

The three original slaves didn't wait to be ushered, but quietly queued by the large enclosure. Katey wondered how they'd get in without a door.

Claire and Jody worked together. They rolled a small log off a battered sheet of metal, then lifted the metal to reveal a hole that led to a u-bend under the bars and up into the pen. The slaves took turns to lie flat on their tummies and wriggle down into the hole, emerging inside the structure. Claire commanded Joy, 'Oy, you! Get down there - act like you mean it, or . . .'

Horrified, Katey watched Joy willingly obey.

'This is very, very nice,' exclaimed Joy to her new companions as she squeezed in beside them. No one agreed, so she spoke again, 'Where do your big girls sleep? In Home Rock we got houses. We got . . .'

'Shush, or the demons will get you,' whispered one child, barely audible.

'What's demons?'

'Shh.'

'Monsters in the sky what you can't see,' whispered the child.

'Bogey men with red faces and horns,' added another.

'And fangs for biting your neck . . .' said the third.

'Oh.' Joy fell silent, but not for long - 'If you can't see monsters, how do you know they get you?'

'Shush! They got Freya 'cos she wouldn't scream Queen Bronwyn's special magic words, so they gobbled her all up and we never saw her again. QB did an offering called a sackerfice.'

'Freya's dead from sackerfice.'

Joy whispered, 'That's just being silly. Freya's at Home Rock. She was all white and scary so Melissa shouted, "Look out for the ghost!" We thought Freya was a ghost but she said, "I'm not dead," and she wasn't. Freya was alive. She showed us how to weave mats and make houses, and she put a red dot on a rock so we know when our birthday is. I still don't know, so I'm going to be six forever and I never have to be a grown-up.'

'Shut up,' hissed the slaves, unable to comprehend a world of mats and houses and breakfast and nail varnish and birthdays.

One slave whispered, 'I don't ackshully believe you. Freya did got ate up by demons, so don't talk no more.'

Two of the lights by the Super Puma went out in quick succession. The slaves froze, eyes wide, senses sharp, straining their ears to listen to what had become the familiar bossiness of Bronwyn. 'Claire, move your butt, sort the pulleys, I'm still reading my mag.'

Claire groaned. She'd half fallen asleep on her bed of junk, but she hauled herself up. If she didn't hurry, the third light would go out and she'd be forced to feel in the pitch black for all three pulleys. She levered her stinking, disintegrating trainers onto her wretched feet. She parted the mosquito net and dragged herself out until she was standing in the dim light, then picked her way over the path, avoiding metal shards that could pierce her soles.

Claire located a small sandbag that had been slowly sinking to the earth on a beaded pulley. She pulled a bead-cord, hand over hand, raising the sandbag-weight back to its starting position above her head. She let go and, as the bag very gradually descended, the friction caused the light to flicker back on. Claire didn't understand the mechanism of the drive sprocket and gear-train that drove the generator, but what she did know was that these lights worked without "wall" electricity and there were plenty more where these came from, boxed up inside the helicopter.

*

In the waiting room at Daru Airport, Claire and Jody had sat opposite a guy named Jim and in their usual, uninhibited way with strangers, begun to fire pertinent questions at him, 'What's your name?' and 'Where are you flying to?' even 'How old are you?'

Jim had been friendly, patiently answering every question, fascinating the girls and their guardian with tales of his special inventions, 'Me and my mate Martin developed something called 'GravityLight.' I've brought some of my stock over because Mr Cook - your Transfer Hope Project guy - has been one heck of a major crowd-funder in support of our company. Would you like me to show you how the light works? Ever seen the pulleys on a cuckoo clock? No, of course not, you're too young, but look I'll show you.' Jim had taken a mechanism from his rucksack and explained how it had to be fixed pretty high up, and the light wasn't that bright and it didn't last long, but it was better than nothing in some areas of the world. Most of the Transfer Hope girls lost interest, but Claire had been mesmerised, asking question after question. As Jim got up to leave, he'd patted Claire on the head and said, 'You've got an inquisitive mind, young lady. You're like me - an innovator. To be an innovator is to have a gift that cannot be taught. It's something you feel deep inside. Your mind is restless because you're not comfortable with the way life is. People like you can change the world.'

Claire clung on to these precious words, not daring to boast about them before or after the crash, for fear of being bullied. "Innovator," Jim had called her. "You're like me," he'd said. Whatever innovator was sounded so good. One day she'd find out what it meant. For now, innovator was something beautiful, a precious pearl to be treasured deep inside her troubled mind.

No one else had ever told Claire she'd grow up to be anything but a pain in the backside.

*

Bronwyn yawned as Claire released the pulley on the second light. They both watched as gravity did its work. The light cut through the darkness. Claire gave Bronwyn a double thumbs-up. Bronwyn feigned irritation. She clicked her fingers for Claire to do the same with the third pulley because the sand-weight had lowered to knee-level and would very soon reach the ground. Bronwyn turned the page of her grubby magazine, one of several their guardian had brought from the UK that had survived the smoke and damp. Bronwyn had found the magazines inside the belly of the helicopter, along with various paperbacks and useless DVDs. Most evenings she read one particular article with the headline, "Arsonist Daughter Sets Fire to House." The sensationalist story had been sold by a gaunt woman with weary, sunken eyes whose photo had been inset into a large image of the blackened house. Bronwyn pressed the photo to her lips.

'Night, mum,' Bronwyn croaked. She tucked the magazine into a plastic bag and stashed it deep inside her rucksack.

*

Eventually two lights flickered out and were not restarted. When the Helizone girls had stopped nattering and most were asleep, Katey shifted and stretched, checked the coast was clear, then inched down the tree. She dropped down the last metre with a light thud and stood still, holding her breath.

Bronwyn heard Katey land. She squinted beyond the third light, but seeing nothing she settled back into the helicopter, adjusted a mosquito net across the doorway, hugged her knees to her chest, and closed her eyes.

Katey tiptoed away from the Helizone, melting into the rustling jungle with no thought for snakes or spiders or humans. She no longer relied on light to guide her, because the familiar noises of the night were comfort enough. Silence was more scary than any snort or snuffle or trill. Katey shut her eyes to help her decide which way to go, concentrating on useful sounds such as trickling water that might guide her to the lake. She thought she heard a sniff. Katey opened her eyes. Another sniff, louder this time.

A pathetic voice whined, 'Somebuddy help,' followed by more sniffles.

Katey stiffened. Adrenalin rushed to her feet and fingertips, her heart raced, hairs rose on the back of her neck. Something grabbed her ankle. She squealed and stamped, 'Get off!' and whatever or whoever it was let go. Katey's eyes were used to the dark. She stared into the shadows until she deciphered a shape, a child sitting cross-legged.

'Donna?'

'Katey, it's you! Don't leave me. Stay. I'm a bit scared all by myself.' Donna leapt up and flung her arms around the smaller girl, 'I hate it by myself. I'm all bit to pieces and my face itches.'

Katey pushed her away, 'Get off me! Why did you have to grab my leg? And where's Mizuki?'

'She sent me to find you, then I couldn't find you. Then I couldn't find Mizuki. Then it went dark. I've been sitting here for a million years. Can't go back. She'll hate me if I don't find you 'cos really she likes you more than me.' Another sniff. Donna lifted her aertex and blew her nose on it.

Katey urged, 'You've got to listen to me. There's this horrid thing they're doing at the Helizone - that's what they call their place – Helizone. I heard them singing about it. The horrid thing's called "slaves," what are in a cage. There's chickens and rats . . . and stinky dead things. And they've got real live lights what go off and on.'

'How do you mean, slaves?'

'Them big girls make the little ones do all the work. Freya told us Bronwyn Bowen's got a gang and it's true. I saw them. Vix was a slave but she said "NO!" and ran away. Bronwyn chased her.'

'Vix ran away?'

'Yeah.'

'My brother ran away to London, not Dan what died, the other one.'

'Who cares about your brother?' Katey made a move to walk away, 'Bronwyn's got Joy and we need to snatch her back.'

Donna placed a hand on Katey's shoulder, 'Don't leave me. I'm dead tired. Can't we do Joy another time?'

Katey thought for a moment. Returning to the Helizone with Donna didn't seem the best idea. Vix could be anywhere, and Joy was happy enough being fast asleep in a nice comfy cage. Katey sighed, 'Okay, but we can't sleep here without Mizuki so we have to find her. I'm going to shout for her mega-loud.'

Rooted deep in the cleft of a tree, a trumpet-shaped flower inadvertently tipped and spilt rainwater down the back of Katey's neck. She squealed, 'That tickles!' then she took the deepest breath she could muster and yelled, 'Mizu . . . ki!' It was loud, but it fell flat. Dead flat in the darkness.

Again; 'Miz . . . u . . . ki!'

No reply.

'Shout with me, Donna.'

'What if Bronwyn hears?'

'Even if she does she won't find us. She doesn't

like blackness. She's jus' pretending not to be scared by making everyone else scared. Come on, Donna's-a-Goner Moore, shout with me - one, two, three . . .'

Katey grabbed Donna's hand and squeezed. Together they filled their lungs, 'Mizuki. Miz . . . u . . . ki!' They screamed until their throats were sore, shocking themselves into a fit of giggles until Katey fell serious and stepped away from Donna.

'You gotta promise me somefink.'

'Okay.'

'Mizuki is my mummy, not yours. She can be your friend, but she's not your mummy.'

'Whatever.'

'Katey? Donna? Joy?' Mizuki could be heard thrashing her way through the undergrowth towards them. Katey and Donna tripped over themselves to get to her first, crying her name and laughing hysterically, gabbling every detail of Katey's watching-place in the tree and Vix running away and Joy in a cage and chickens and dead things and real, live light.

Joy in a cage. It sounded all wrong, but the Searchers could do nothing more useful on this moonless night than sleep. Mizuki led Donna and Katey back to the tree root where they huddled together for the rest of the night only to be woken at dawn by Mizuki begging for water. She was shivering violently, talking all manner of rubbish, then falling back to sleep. Donna and Katey exchanged worried glances. There would be no saving Joy and no returning to Home Rock. After yesterday, the last thing they wanted to do was to separate.

It promised to be another challenging day.

7

One Will Die

Joy's tummy rumbled. During the sweaty night, her hair had stuck to her face and her t-shirt to her back. She stretched and yawned and opened her eyes. 'Stripy sky,' she smiled, forgetting where she was. 'Katey?' she tried to call, but her mouth was dry and no sound came out. One of the others groaned and turned over. Joy remembered, 'Not Home Rock. I'm at Bronwyn's house.'

Joy stared at the sleeping slaves, trying to recall their names from before the crash. Since the accident there were grey spaces inside her head, impossible to colour in with the right words. Joy wriggled her toes. She'd kicked off her trainers during the night. Her toenails had grown uncomfortably long. She picked at the dirt beneath them but soon gave up. She peered through the bars and saw the bigger Helizone girls sleeping in random places and, apart from Bronwyn, without shelter. She imagined the Home Rock girls collecting breakfast already and had an idea. 'I'll find them girls breakfast for a nice surprise.'

Last in, first out. Should be easy. Joy pulled on her trainers and set off, wriggling nose down through the earthy u-bend, then up. Her head bumped the metal sheet. Here, where it was dark and airless, she flattened her hands palms down beneath her chest, then forced them up under her face, expecting to push away the metal cover, not considering the heaviness of the log on top. After several attempts she gave up, exhausted, with no choice but to give up and back up the narrow tunnel.

Joy's elbows were wedged against her head. She couldn't bring them down. She tried to shuffle backwards but could not. Suffocating with panic, panting fast, her heart raced. She groaned, 'Can't . . . get . . . out.'

Something scraping. A chink of light. A waft of air. Joy gasped. Something rolling. Something shoving. A flood of light. Two hands held hers. She was being pulled by the hands. With a whoosh, Joy scrambled up and out of the u-bend to freedom. She brushed herself down, wiped her face with the palms of her heads, sneezing and spluttering dust. She opened her eyes to see her saviour - Bronwyn Bowen.

'Aha, my new pet,' Bronwyn grinned, 'Glad *someone* bothered to wake up. It's sooo boring when everyone's snoring. I'm a poet and I know it! Get it? Boring, snoring. Come with me, I've got something to show you round the back of the heli.'

'Water . . .' Joy gasped, sticking out her dry tongue.

'Here,' Bronwyn shoved an open bottle of water in

Joy's face, 'hurry up and drink. Not too much, greedy guts. It's mine.'

Joy gulped twice. Bronwyn snatched back the bottle, 'Mine!' She threw the bottle to the ground, not bothered that it spilt.

'I was going to get you breakfast,' Joy tried to say, but she was being dragged by the wrist.

'Breakfast, what's breakfast?' Bronwyn scoffed. She walked too fast for Joy, patting the helicopter as she negotiated her way around its vast body, dipping under the blade that rested precariously against it.

The sight of half-devoured human bodies happened too quickly. Bronwyn grinned, 'Ha! What d'ya think of that then?'

Joy yanked her wrist from Bronwyn's grasp and slapped her hand over her nose to mask the terrible smell. Straightaway she wanted to cry, but she couldn't.

'The pilot. The guardian. My bad, I know, but we nicked her jacket. And their socks too.'

'They're dead?'

'No, they're having a pint in a pub, stupid.'

'I don't like it.'

'Do'ya think I do? They stink! They're too heavy to move, so we're waiting for them to lose weight. Now there's not so much meat left on them.'

'Move?'

'We've got a dragging idea. When there's only bones, we're going to roll them in mozzy nets or sheets – we've got loads, then we'll tie the sheet in a big knot under their feet. My underlings will pull them through the jungle, far, far away. Dump them somewhere. But not yet. Today's about chilling out.'

The rags on the bodies twitched ever so slightly. Both girls fell silent, mesmerised by the flies and maggots doing their work.

Bronwyn coughed, 'I've got this great idea for a party tomorrow.'

'Is it your birthday?'

'Do I care? But I have a special task for you. If you do it I'll give you a massive breakfast. Anything you choose – porridge, toast, hot chocolate . . .'

'Hot chocolate!' Joy squealed.

'Shh, it's our secret. Don't tell the others. Can you trill?'

'What's trill?'

'Like this.' Instantly, Bronwyn threw back her head, arched her neck and rolled her tongue, releasing a high-pitched ripple that woke the Helizone girls, while across the forest in Home Rock, Nadia and Evie cocked their ears at the spine-chilling call of the jungle-rooster.

Without hesitation, Joy threw back her head and, despite her dry throat, imitated Bronwyn.

'Mega trill. High five!' Bronwyn slapped Joy's hand, 'Now, listen. This is what we're going to do . . .'

And behind the fallen helicopter, beside two disintegrating bodies, Bronwyn flattered Joy into agreeing to her horrific plan.

*

Next day, Bronwyn left the Helizone along the usual track, sailing ahead of those she called "Underlings", Jody, Claire, Lydia, and Elle-Marie, followed by the four slaves. This ritual happened most days, but it was the first time for Joy. It gave their day purpose, a reason to get up and go. Despite their hunger, they pressed on, moving a little faster than usual, encouraged by the promise of Bronwyn's special celebration, imagining a party with pizza, crisps and cake.

*

Mizuki, Katey and Donna watched until the Helizone troupe were out of sight. They emerged from the undergrowth into the abandoned camp. Katey rushed to demonstrate how the cage door worked, explaining how it took two underlings to shift the log off the metal, pointing out the "horrid hole" through which the slaves were made to crawl.

'Them birds is dead,' Donna pointed, aware she was stating the obvious but wanting to be first to announce the doom. Several of the spotted chickens, without food or water, had perished. Donna kicked a cage and the whole thing collapsed like pick-up-sticks to reveal an emaciated, maggot-ridden bird. Realising that some of the birds were still alive, Donna overcame her revulsion and rushed to open another cage.

'Help me,' Donna called to Katey and they excitedly snapped open the prisons, shooing several injured birds and small creatures to freedom.

The hairy rats ambled nonchalantly away as if nothing was amiss. 'Don't rush then,' Katey laughed. 'My mum says, "Watch out for Mr Nippy, 'cos our rats was so quick we never catched them.'

'English rats are small, that's why,' explained Mizuki. 'Come on, we best follow Bronwyn and rescue Joy.' They filled some empty plastic bottles by pressing them into the emerald moss that grew over the clearest water. The suitcase of rotten food lay open to scavengers, but the Home Rock girls gave it a wide berth. They understood how the forest provided enough for each day. Food was the least of their worries.

Mizuki led Katey and Donna over level ground, stopping every so often to listen for the chant of the Helizone girls. Even as the way became steeper and rockier, the girls moved quickly without complaint. The once pudgy Donna was wiry and strong, while Katey's legs were muscular for her age. Mizuki had always been lithe and, despite her recurring infection, she'd grown physically more powerful. She moved softly, graceful as a gazelle, her jade eyes sparkling and alert beneath her lumpy scar.

They paused at a place with fewer trees, where scrubby bushes and web-laden ferns provided the only cover. A mighty bird soared overhead, its wings fanning up and out, hang-gliding on the thermals. Mizuki smiled at Katey, 'Wow, we didn't get those monster birds back home, just loads of pigeons.'

'Up there!' Donna spotted Bronwyn's troop some way ahead, wending between the rocks towards a plateau the size of five football pitches, its vast expanse broken only by low-growing shrubs battling to survive in the heat, and a scattering of rocks.

'Let's keep going. Don't let them see us,' warned Katey. The Searchers hastened. The chanting grew louder as they gained ground.

'I know that song . . . I think,' said Mizuki.

". . . times supposed to heal ya, but I ain't done much healing. . ." [2]

Then, "Like a child . . . spirits running free she trapped me wild, oh . . ." [3]

'Cool, Mizuki! But where do you think they're off to?' Donna rasped with the thrill of the hunt, though if she'd shouted, the Helizone girls could not possibly hear her.

'Who cares? They got Joy,' said Katey, 'And stop whispering like that. You sound stupid. Talk proper.'

Feeling rejected, Donna rushed up to Mizuki and pawed her arm, 'Where do you think they're going?'

Mizuki shrugged and shook her head. She held her arms wide to stop Donna and Katey in their tracks because, not too far off, the strange procession had halted on the plateau. The terrible music stopped. The underlings fanned out in a semicircle behind their queen, with their backs to the Searchers and were made to wait.

Mizuki, Katey and Donna ducked down then crept, cat-like, to where two fierce rocks cut a steep V. From here they watched Bronwyn performing, stretching her body and arching her back. She stood on tiptoe, raised her face to the sky, flung wide her arms, flexing back her fingers like the wings of an eagle. So still.

Still. Still, until her body shook with the effort. She dropped onto the soles of her feet, lowered her arms and stalked away, clicking her fingers - a sign for only the slaves to follow. Each slave carried a bowl or a tin, cupped in both hands, one behind the other, solemn as a nativity.

A wispy, warm, orange mist drifted around Claire, Jodie, Elle-Marie and Lydia who hung back, together yet alone, on the vast plateau. They were grateful not to be one of those slaves, yet anxious for what their unpredictable leader had in store, what power she would wield, what excitement would soon be theirs.

From the V in the rock the Searchers saw the rising sun set fire to Bronwyn's feather-filled mane of back-combed hair. Her four slaves cast long elfin shadows over the ground, but which one was Joy? Bronwyn, followed by the slaves, walked to the boundary of the plateau where the slaves stopped. They placed their containers on the ground. Bronwyn shoved them into a row with their backs to the underlings, facing out across the vast sea of treetops that stretched away to the mountainous horizon. The four tiny girls held hands, a zigzag silhouette of paper dolls, cut out, folded, opened. Bronwyn paced up and down behind them pushing each one, little by little, closer and closer to the edge.

When she was satisfied they were perfectly positioned, Bronwyn turned to face the underlings, who had stayed obediently thirty or forty metres back. With an exaggerated gesture she beckoned Jody, Claire, Lydia and Elle-Marie, "Come closer."

The four approached cautiously, as if in a game of "Grandmother's Footsteps," stopping the instant Bronwyn raised her hands.

Near enough to see, far enough to be fooled. Keep your distance, underlings.

Once more she beckoned, 'Come closer my beauties!' then, when the underlings were less than fifty paces from the slaves, Bronwyn raised her hands and cried, 'See what you choose to see, believe what you choose to believe. Witness my great power.' Bronwyn opened her palm, sweeping her hand wide from one mute slave to the next. 'One will die, but which one? Only I, the most high, most fabulous Queen Bronwyn, will decide. Your future is in my hands!' Bronwyn skipped, crouched, then leapt up and danced for all she was worth, behind the backs of her slaves, a ballerina-marionette-cranefly against the early morning sky. Without warning, Bronwyn jerked forward as if to push the first slave over the edge. She laughed harshly. Unable to see her, the slaves stood motionless, submissive and unmoved, but the underlings gasped in horror.

Bronwyn's hand danced over the head of the second slave, then the third, then back again. As both hands hovered with flickering fingers, she glanced over her shoulder to gauge the reaction of the underlings. Good, good! Elle-Marie was clinging to Lydia. Claire was shaking her head in terrified disbelief. *No, no, no, no!* Bronwyn flashed a smile, taunting the underlings, screaming, 'Which one? This one, that one, the power is mine!' Her fists opened and closed. Her hands shimmered over the third slave - this one? Maybe? Maybe not.

Bronwyn's elbows eased back, she spread her fingers, rose on tiptoes, bent her knees, held her position. Six, five, four. She hovered over the fourth slave. Three, two, one. With all her might, Bronwyn pushed. The child stumbled and, without screaming, fell over the edge.

And then there were three.

Bronwyn threw back her head and cackled. She rattled her head viciously, so her hair shook, releasing an extraordinarily long, spaghetti-thin feather that whirled in the faint breeze like a shed snakeskin. Bronwyn cried, 'Underlings, approach! I have surprises for each of you, so many surprises you won't believe!' but Jody, Claire, Lydia and Elle-Marie did not approach. They were rooted to the spot.

At Bronwyn's command the three remaining slaves picked up their containers and trailed after Bronwyn, back across the plateau towards some boulders that had long ago been scattered by volcanic action, the usual gathering place of the Helizone girls. Bronwyn passed close to Jody and clicked her fingers. Jody nudged Elle-Marie and Lydia, 'Come, follow' and they obeyed. Only Claire hung back, tears pouring down her cheeks for the innocent, white-haired child who hadn't deserved to die.

On previous expeditions to the plateau, Bronwyn had lectured the Helizone girls with unplanned speeches, inventing terrible rules with deadly consequences that everyone forgot. On and on and on she'd ranted as her audience fainted from thirst or burned in the sun. On better days they taught one another song lyrics, or recounted personal stories of terror from Before, tales of starvation, abuse and neglect, of homelessness, new schools, bullies and nightmares.

The three slaves automatically queued one behind the other, with their full containers held out straight in front of them. Bronwyn leapt upon 'her' rock, the one they'd christened 'The Stage,' and she danced alone. Today there would be neither speech or story. Bronwyn had planned for them a more exciting thing.

'Did I not tell you this would be a celebration?' Bronwyn stopped to say, 'Come, take, choose cream, brown or gold!' urged the queen, as the underlings approached. The favourite, Jody, followed by Elle-Marie, Lydia, rubbing her elbow that had set at an awkward angle and blotchy-faced Claire.

'Smile! Party! Don't look so scared. Here, I got you this - looks like shit, tastes like honey. Close eyes. Taste. Tastes better than it looks. Lick a bit. Maybe you prefer gold? Here, eat. Crushed seeds, mmm – go on, try, eat. Hey, not too much, leave some for QB. QB loves gold. You prefer brown? Take some brown. It's only mushrooms, you know what a mean. The best - dried it myself.' The girls nibbled then swallowed because they were starving. Very soon Claire and Lydia fell to their knees, holding their heads, rocking. Elle-Marie curled into a foetal, rigid ball. Jody roared, clawing the sky with her daggered nails.

Satiated with success, Queen Bronwyn abandoned the underlings and stalked back to the edge of the plateau where she'd taunted the slaves. Facing the valley, she stretched wide her arms to the rising sun, swaying once more on tiptoe until, exhausted, she plonked herself down and dangled her feet over the edge. She made a listless effort to raise her arms, but they flopped back to her sides. Her head loped forwards. The party queen became still.

Very still.

Behind their rock, the Searchers watched and waited, afraid to break cover, awed by Bronwyn's power. Adrift on the plateau, among the scattered rocks, the three slaves wandered empty-handed, their tins and bowls fallen or snatched by the older girls and licked clean.

'Can you tell which is Joy?' whispered Donna, 'The sun's blinding me.'

'Joy!' cried Katey, suddenly overwhelmed with the enormity of the mission, 'Bronwyn's not looking - and them big girls are falling over - they won't see, and I don't care if they do, I'm going to get Joy.' Without waiting for Mizuki, Katey leapt up and ran boldly across the plateau towards the three swaying infants. From the V, the Helizone girls had seemed so far away, but Katey was soon alongside them, anxiously scanning their shocked faces, noticing the way they were streaked, not with tribal colours or elaborate cuts, but insect bites, scratches and utter exhaustion.

'Joy?' Katey looked from one slave to the other, 'J . . . Joy?' Tears welled up. She blinked them back. She bit her cheek and tasted blood.

The slaves flicked their eyes in the direction of

Bronwyn. Always checking.

'Water,' gasped one.

Katey unscrewed her bottle. 'A sip – hey, that's two, that's enough, stop.' Katey passed the water along, keeping hold of the bottle to regulate the drink, then she pulled it back, commanding, 'Come on, hurry up!' With her free hand, Katey grabbed a small wrist, preparing to run, but the slaves dug their heels in. 'Help me,' she cried to Donna, who'd caught up, her face puce and dripping with sweat. Together they pulled at the rags on the scrawny bodies, but the girls flatly refused to budge.

Katey stamped her foot, 'Stop being thick. Bronwyn Bowen *killed* Joy what's called *murder!* You saw her do it. And she'll do you next if you don't come with us right now!' She stamped again. The slaves didn't flinch.

Donna glanced nervously over the plateau to where Bronwyn still sat facing the valley, alone in her private world. Donna hissed, 'If you don't come with us this minute, I'm gonna shove you off a cliff!'

'What do you think you're playing at?' yelled someone, 'Get off our land or . . .' Katey swung around to be faced with Jody, the broad, scary girl who'd made Claire smack Vix. Jody's unblinking eyes had sunk into her round face exaggerating a historic scar on her cheek and a new scar, pus-yellow, on her neck. Her dirty-blonde hair, which, back in England, had been cut into a neat, layered style, hung unevenly over her shoulders. Her eyes blazed like a crazed parent on the brink of losing control of a child.

Katey's legs turned to jelly. She backed away,

wanting to run, but her feet felt like they didn't belong to her.

The slaves simply stood and stared. Jody launched forward until her chin was millimetres from Katey's forehead. With a terrifying grunt she raised her chin for a headbutt, then slammed down her head, just as Donna rushed, shoulder-first, into Jody's arm, knocking her the ground.

Donna stood astride her, raging, 'It's not your land, it's everybody's. You gotta share. No one tells the Home Rock girls what to do!' Her lip curled as she snarled, 'Yeah, you heard me, push off you great bully! Leave them little kids alone. Go! Go! Go!' Donna flapped her hands in Jody's face as Jody struggled punch-drunk to her feet. Jody staggered, raising her right fist to thump Donna, but without warning her face drained of blood, her eyes rolled back, and she fainted.

Jody sprawled uselessly over the parched earth. Donna felt no pity. She'd expected (and hoped for) a full-on fight with biting and scratching and tearing of hair, culminating in a victory cry for Home Rock but . . .

'Let's go!' Katey cried, looking round for Mizuki who was nowhere to be seen – Katey assumed she'd taken ill again. Most likely burning up, collapsed in the shade of the V. Still the slaves did not move. Katey took a deep breath. She went for a gentler approach, 'What're your names?'

'Roxy.'

'Stephie.'

'Yanita Skovgaard, what's called Sparrow.'

'Which resi you from?'

'Me and Roxy's frum Leaf Lane Care and Sparra's frum 'mergency placement,' Stephie said, pushing her thick wavy hair from her eyes. 'And do you got more water?'

'Yanita Skovgaard? What kind of name is that?' Katey peered askew at the skinny kid with translucent skin and thin lips, as she handed the water to Stephie.

The child replied, 'I'm Yanita from Denmark. My 'mergency placement foster dad Joe called me Sparrow 'cos I fell out of a nest.'

'Sparra's a bird's name,' Donna huffed, 'Is that why he put you back? Did he get fed up of calling you by a bird's name?' The child looked more like an emu than a sparrow, with her bulging, lopsided eyes, buck-teeth and patchy pale-gold hair.

Sparrow didn't take offence, 'He said I gotta stop hitting his kids, but it weren't my fault if they made me proper mad.' Sparrow coughed dryly, then added with a grin, 'I did do bad stuff too. Chucked his beer down their toilet, spat on the TV, wrecked my room. Joe belted me.' She giggled, then flung her arms wide to emphasise her next words, 'My 'mergency placement got finished dead quick and I got picked for Transfer Hope, and staff said . . .'

'Well,' interrupted Katey, noticing that Bronwyn had slumped over where she sat, 'My name's Katey with a yer. I'm actual staff at Home Rock and I say you have to make anuvva new start by coming with us. We got really, really nice houses woved by Freya. Guess what! Freya can be your foster mum. Remember Freya before your lot made her into a ghost? Now she's a Digger. You'll like them Diggers making a toilet specially for when we get back.' Katey shuffled backwards, her eyes pleading, beckoning Stephie, Roxy and Sparrow. At last, they followed. Right behind them, Donna gurned whacky faces, rolling her eyes wide to demonstrate her surprise at Katey's success.

Katey spotted Mizuki, no longer resting in the V, but walking on the far side of the plateau, heading for Bronwyn. Instinctively Mizuki turned and waved, flapping her hand, signalling 'Go on back to Home Rock, I'll catch you up later.' Katey nodded, though Mizuki could not have seen this. Mizuki would return soon enough, and if Mizuki had a different plan, Katey chose to trust her.

*

Katey, Donna and the rescued slaves walked quietly, occasionally pausing to pick fruit or sip warm water from the bottle. Stephie stopped in her tracks. The skinny, blonde waif released a long, loud sigh, 'Joy got pushed off.' She sighed again, shuddering the way adults do when the world overwhelms them. When there is no space or time for tears.

'I'm sad about Joy too,' agreed Katey, 'Bronwyn is a bitch.'

'I'm sad about the other one what runned away,' added Roxy, 'She had red hair like me.'

'You mean Vix? Don't keep going on about stinky

things,' Donna snorted, slapping her itchy bites. She was scared to scratch since Mizuki told them scratching caused 'fections, and infection had almost wiped out Mizuki. A striped possum scampered across the track, closely followed by a second and a smaller third, but no one commented because possums were like rats; they happened all the time.

Passing through the Helizone, Katey and Donna refilled their water bottles close to where five spotted chickens were nonchalantly pecking the ground. The girls shooed them into the jungle.

'They're so stupid not to be spooked by Bronwyn Bowen,' said Stephie. 'Them chickens don't be scared of nobuddy.'

'Yeah. QB's gonna grab 'em by the neck and stick 'em in them cages if they don't get outta here quick,' said Sparrow.

'Them cages make me want to get out,' Donna said, anxious to get going, but realising she couldn't remember which way led to Home Rock. Not daring to admit this she blurted, 'And this is a shitty place without no wheelie bins,' which did the trick because her words reminded Katey that they were hanging about in a hell-hole while the Diggers at Home Rock were waiting for news.

'Yeah, let's get moving,' Katey said.

Stephie, Roxy and Sparrow knew the way to the lake - they simply followed the gravel trail, the paint cans and arrows tied to trees.

8

Resurrection Queen

Mizuki approached with caution.

'Bronwyn?' The name stuck inside her throat. Mizuki coughed and tried again, 'Bronwyn? You okay?' Mizuki peered over the edge of the plateau, afraid to see Joy's body far below, bloodied and battered on some wretched, inaccessible ledge, but the drop was nowhere near as sheer as she'd assumed. It was steep, yet every kind of shrub grew in thick clusters and saplings sprung from every fissure in the rocks.

Bronwyn's shoulders slumped. Her head hung forward and her chin dropped almost onto her chest. Mizuki risked one step nearer. Another step. Her slender fingers tentatively reached out to touch Bronwyn's shoulder. She fully expected Bronwyn to suddenly turn and scream at her, or leap up and attack but, close-up, with her tatty clothes, broken feathers and dry, sallow skin, the Helizone Queen looked more like an abandoned pet than an evil dictator.

Mizuki considered shaking Bronwyn but her light

touch was enough. Bronwyn sat bolt upright, twisted round, raised her hands in self-defence, but seeing only a girl, only Mizuki, Bronwyn cupped her hands over her face and gulped deep, agonising tearless gulps.

Mizuki edged still closer. She sank down until she was sitting shoulder to shoulder with Bronwyn.

No words.

It was Bronwyn Bowen who broke the silence, though she could hardly speak. 'Wh . . . when . . . when you touched me, I thought you . . . you were my mam, but you're ju . . . just that girl off the helicopter.'

'You know me. I'm Mizuki.'

'I thought you were my mam.'

'No one here's got a mum.'

'But I thought you were my actual mam.'

Mizuki wrapped her arm around Bronwyn. Two twelve-year-olds acknowledging the truth, the heavy reality, that from here to the horizon, in all the vast expanse of forest, there were no mothers.

'What happened to your birth mum?' Mizuki asked.

'Prison.'

'Same here.'

'*Your* mam's inside?'

Mizuki nodded, 'Mm-hmm. She can't see trees or stars like us. Only walls. What did yours do?'

'Mam didn't give us no food never. Next door told social, silly cow. Social 'vestigated, asked nosy questions, said we can't live with our mam ever again. But us kids wanted to live with her, even with no food. We said we can get our own food, but social said, no, you got to eat. My little sister had bendy legs with bad pain from bad food. They put her in hospital. After that, they gave my sister a new mam, one what I never met. I went to foster care in Wales where they had boys older than me. Those boys were trouble.'

Silence.

Mizuki thought, 'Should I stroke her hand?' but she could not. The distance between them was too great. Instead, Mizuki dug her nails into the back of her own hand, to calm herself. To be still and wait.

Below and beyond, the amaranthine jungle released a flock of whistling, chirping parakeets. A sign of hope. A bright green flutter of acceptance. The birds were so glorious, Bronwyn reached out her arms towards them and, in her mind, flew with them, splashing the skies with their colourful song of freedom. Bronwyn dropped her arms and exhaled a long, long breath, because Mizuki hadn't butted into her story. *Mizuki proper listened.*

Bronwyn spat, 'I hate them boys.' A furious sob forced itself up inside her throat. She swallowed and burped. "I jumped on a bus. Ran away to Cardiff, to my old house where I lived with Mam, but I panicked and got off the bus too soon. It got dark, so I slept behind the shops.'

'Outside?'

'Not exactly outside. I found a wheelie bin with cardboard in. I went under the boxes in the bin. It was dead cold, but better than fighting boys at the resi. In the morning, someone squashed a whole load more boxes on top of me, but I never moved 'til they'd gone.

I couldn't get out. The bin tipped - I fell out . . .' here she giggled and rubbed her knees. 'I went in the Co-op to nick food and guess what?'

Mizuki shrugged, 'What?'

'I saw my face on a newspaper. All fuzzy. Didn't look nothing like me so I didn't care. It said I was missing, but obviously I wasn't. Do you know the Brink Estate?'

'Nope. I've never even been to Wales.'

'I had a quid in my pocket, so I bought custard creams. Yup, I paid for biscuits just so I could ask the Co-op guy, "Where's the Brink Estate?" and he said, "Just up there!" I *knew* I was close but I'd never been on that road before. I'm not thick you know. You don't think I'm thick, do you? For getting lost?'

Mizuki shook her head.

'I found my house. Number 47. Same but different. No junk in the front garden. It was dead tidy with grass in the middle. It had curtains, open ones, blue with white flowers all over. I thought, "Mam's got new stuff, so maybe I got a new bedroom." I knocked on our door. I knocked and knocked but no one came. I sat on the doorstep waiting for Mam to get home. That smelly cow, Julie Slingerland from next door came sniffing round. She snitched on us to social, so I hate her. Hate her face. Hate her guts. D'ya know what? She *eeeven* kicked her own dog and they *eeeven* let her keep it. Anyway, Julie said, "No one wants your lot round here. Get flamin' lost." She said, "That's not your house no more. Your Mam and Da's caged so it's good riddance to bad rubbish. Get stuffed!" Julie slammed her door in my face. I wanted to ask, "What prison? Where?" but I couldn't, so I went and got some matches off some boys I knew from St Teresa's juniors. They gave me some petrol and rags. I said they could only watch if they gave me some wacky-baccy. It was *so* funny. I'd planned to burn down Julie's place, but her dog barked, so I had to do Mam's house instead. Why should anyone else get to live in our house? I lit a fire on our doorstep. It burnt mega quick. Stupid door melted like snot.' Bronwyn smirked. 'Loads of people came outside, shouting, pointing at me. Fire-engines came, lights flashing. Julie Slingerland screamed in my face, "You little shit, Bronwyn Bowen, what have you gone an' done?" I spat on her slippers and she battered me round my head. I laughed in her face. She was mad as heck. The house burned crazy hot. We had to back off. My face hurt from Julie Slingerland battering me. She gave me a black eye, and who got put into care? Not *her!* I told everyone "Julie battered me," – the social, police, resi staff, but no one did nothing except sent me to a diff'rent resi, not in Wales. It had security doors for stopping runaways. Five weeks. Yawn. I got called into the office. This woman said, all posh, "We think you're the perfect candidate for the Transfer Hope Project," so I said, "But I haven't got no sex disease!" She just smiled.'

'Candidate's something about government, I think,' Mizuki said.

'I know that, d'ya think I'm dumb or something?'

Bronwyn's sudden aggression reminded Mizuki to ask about the girls on the plateau, collapsed in a heap, out for the count in the beating sun.

'What did you give those kids? I mean that stuff in the bowls?'

'I dunno. Who cares? You can't get done for anything here, so I'm not exactly fussed, am I? Seeds and mushrooms mostly. I collect all sorts of stuff. The slaves check it out for me. If they chuck up, I don't give it to the underlings. Today, they got the good stuff. Fully tested. Party time, raaaa!' Bronwyn giggled while pressing her palms hard into her eyes. No tears allowed. Not for QB.

Mizuki said, 'That's drugs. You could kill someone.'

'No, I couldn't. Eating one of them leafs makes you proper alive. You should try one yourself. And for your information, no one died.'

Mizuki sighed, 'No one died?' The conversation was exhausting.

Bronwyn shook herself, 'I s'pose you came for your kid.' She nudged Mizuki away and stretched her arms.

'Joy's not my kid, but I did want her. I also want Vix.'

'That runt with the red hair? She legged it.'

'Vix ran away? She must have been scared stiff of you. I saw what you did. Everyone saw. You killed Joy.' Mizuki looked down at her hands. They were shaking.

Bronwyn smirked, 'Just 'cos I set fire to a house doesn't make me a murderer. You're the same as the rest, making me out as bad when you don't even know me.'

'Me and Katey and Donna saw you push Joy.'

'So?' Bronwyn raised her eyebrows. She rose to her

131

feet then, without explanation, she arched her back and rolled her tongue, trilling as gloriously as any bird of paradise. The powerful sound carried down the mountain and over the canopy. Bronwyn paused. She was about to repeat her display when they heard an echo that was not an echo but a similar trill, higher pitched and weaker. It stopped short. The air hung empty and expectant.

Mizuki strained her eyes, searching for – she knew not what.

In one place, the tops of the bushes rustled. A small creature was pushing its way up through the undergrowth, panting and sniffling. As it approached it peered up from beneath a mat of filthy hair. Its face had been torn by thorns and smeared with earth and its black eyes sparkled sharp as a fox cub.

'Joy?' Mizuki's instinct was to rush forward and grab the little girl, to cling to her, to save her from the Helizone, but she caught a flash of understanding between Joy and Bronwyn, a mere flick of an eyelash, enough to make her hesitate. Jealousy stuck in Mizuki's throat as she watched Bronwyn reach down to haul the child up over the edge. Joy stood barefoot, in shorts and t-shirt, shivering in the sunlight, her grubby knees jutting awkwardly from her stick-thin legs.

'We planned it, didn't we, brat?' Bronwyn nudged the girl. 'I tried to teach all my slaves to trill, but they were rubbish. This one got it first time! When I said, "Fall over when I tell you, act dead and don't move 'til I say," she obeyed. Because of her, those underlings will fear my power. Watch. They will see this slave come back to life before their eyes. They will believe what they already want to believe, that I, Queen Bronwyn, am all powerful.'

Bronwyn beckoned Joy who trailed after her towards the groaning pile of bodies, all trying to shield their eyes from the glaring sun. Joy's tongue stuck to the roof of her mouth so she couldn't speak. She longed to run to Mizuki, but instead had lowered her eyes and ignored her. She knew how to play big people's games, to be subservient, to do precisely what they demanded. To obey is to keep out of trouble. To be mute is to survive. So Joy walked in Bronwyn's footsteps, with her nose close to the small of Bronwyn's back.

As Bronwyn approached, the girls scrambled to stand before her. Before they could work out what was going on, Bronwyn screamed, 'Slave Four, I give you back your life!' The underlings jumped out of their skins, squealing hysterically and clinging to one another. Bronwyn stepped back, whirled sideways and flung open her arm as if welcoming a famous star to the red carpet then, with their very own eyes, the underlings witnessed the incredible resurrection of Joy.

'I am your leader!' Bronwyn shouted, 'Power to me. Bow down - yes, you! You shall bow,' and the Helizone girls fell on their faces.

But Mizuki had seen enough, 'Stop grovelling and get up! Bronwyn's not God. She's not even a queen. She's just a girl, same as you, same as me.'

Jody chanted, 'Bow to Bronwyn, bow to Bronwyn, Bronwyn Bowen is our queen. Bow to Bronwyn, bow to Bronwyn, Bronwyn is our queen.' The others pitched in until the sound bubbled up and boiled over. When Bronwyn closed her eyes to absorb the adoration, Mizuki took her chance. Snatching Joy by the wrist she dragged her back across the plateau to the shadow of the V.

Mizuki glanced back, surprised that Bronwyn wasn't chasing them, but dancing and chanting zombie-style with her precious Helizone girls. She hadn't even noticed the disappearance of her original three slaves.

Mizuki guided Joy through the V, down the animal track towards the Helizone. To keep up, Joy half-ran, half-dragged her feet, all the time fighting sleep. Despite her own weakness, Mizuki scooped her up and cradled her in her arms. Joy slept as Mizuki trekked all the way to Home Rock.

9

Invasion

Nadia and Evie squatted in the shade of a rock, weaving a mat as best they could, hoping to make it into a fence to defend their precious zoo from marauding chickens and rats. Their zoo comprised of an assortment of bugs and beetles, some trapped in school lunch-boxes, others housed in assorted tins, even Evie's musical jewellery box. Evie turned the key on the box. The silver barrel turned, the mechanism tinkled a tinny Für Elise, as fat woodlice clustered around the base of a twirling, pink, plastic ballerina.

Just before sunset Katey and Donna burst into Home Rock with their new friends Roxy, Stephie and Sparrow. Nadia and Evie ran over to greet them, laughing and tugging at Katey's arm.

'Can lu!' Nadia beckoned.

'Luk Zu!' Evie pointed to their collection.

'We can't understand them,' explained Katey to the newcomers, hoping she sounded important like a proper Home Rock resi-staff, 'but it's okay, 'cos they know essackly what we say.'

'Come and look, look at our zoo, is what they said,' Stephie translated, 'Easy-peasy-lemon-squeezy.'

Donna rolled her eyes, thinking, 'That's all we need, a know-it-all newcomer.' She hoped Mizuki wouldn't be too impressed. Where was Mizuki anyway? She was taking ages. She should have caught up with them by now. Donna joined the throng who were curiously gawping at the 'zoo', amazed by the variety of bugs and insects clinging to twigs or crawling under leaves, displayed in boxes, cups and bottles. More fascinating still were two notebooks crammed with primitive sketches, some coloured, most labelled with random letters of the alphabet, upside-down and back-to-front, that pointed to 'antennae', 'hooked feet', 'wings', 'eyes', and so on.

'I've never been to a real zoo,' said Sparrow, but no one listened.

Freya greeted Katey and Donna with a shy wave. Her hair had been twisted into a pleat and fastened with a stick which made her appear very grown-up. Katey wanted to hug her, but she held back for fear of being rejected.

Freya asked, 'Where's Mizuki? And Joy? And Vix?'

'Mizuki's coming when she's ready. Joy's dead. Pushed off a cliff by Bronwyn Bowen.'

'Joy's dead? No way! That evil bitch.' Freya's eyes filled with tears.

Donna added, 'Vix ran off by herself. Bronwyn chased her but she missed so Vix is prob'ly eaten alive by lions or else starved to utter death. Mizuki went to find Vix, but she jus' couldn't. I sort of thought Vix would come back here by herself, but this is one big, ugly jungle and she's only little. Lions must've got her. Definitely, lions got her.'

'B.I.T.C.H.' Freya spat out each letter as a curse on Bronwyn, then she wiped her mouth with the back of her hand. She pointed at the new arrivals, 'I know them slaves from before I got kicked out of the Helizone, but not their names. Bronwyn Bowen called them, "Slave One, Slave Two, Slave Three." Bronwyn said using their proper names would make us go soft in the head. She said, "Don't let them make friends with you or they won't work right."' Freya cleared her throat, 'Bronwyn slaving, Joy murdered, Vix scoffed by lions.' She forced a weak smile, 'At Home Rock with no slaves we dug a really good toilet. We wanted two toilets, but it's too hard. Digging with hands takes ages to make even a little, bitty hole. Pearl helped at first. She dug and dug, but she got fed up. We need more Diggers.'

Freya led the way to the luxury toilet. She showed them a small mound of earth, stamped and patted into firm wall intended for privacy - as yet too low. Other earth piles had been dotted sporadically along the drainage lines, ready to be added to the wall. The all-important hole for the toilet had been modestly positioned behind the wall – as yet too shallow. From this, a wonky channel gradually deepened into a narrow groove that ran (somewhat impressively) into the jungle.

Freya explained, 'Got to dig deeper or it'll never

work. If the toilet doesn't drain prop'ly it will stink. Over there, the earth is softer so mostly we dug with our hand; but look here - we made spades!'

They'd spliced bamboo by bashing the end with small, sharp rocks. All this work had reddened their hands, causing blisters but not drawing blood. 'We've almost finished one drain, so we can start using the toilet when the pipes are fixed.'

'Pipes?' said Donna.

'We tried to make pipes to bring water down from the moss-place because the water from there is better. You know how we collect it in tins for drinking or washing, well, we thought how great it would be if we don't have to carry it all the way. We tried our best, but they don't work. Not yet, anyway. We can't stick them together right. We found a sort of stream, a soggy place covered with moss. Me and Nadia and Evie squished along it and found out where it goes,' Freya pointed, 'then further up the hill we found a waterfall and a swimming pool.'

'How far?'

'Too far for now. We can go there tomorrow if you like.'

Pearl appeared from behind one of the rocks. She grinned, 'Tea time!' Her skin glistened from washing in the new-found water, 'Ev'rybuddy gotta wash hands.'

Katey exchanged raised eyebrows with Donna. *Pearl, of all people, washing her hands without being asked! Pearl bossing them, but in a good way. So much had changed so fast.*

Freya explained, 'Pearl's in charge of the kitchen.

She was terrible at digging so I asked her to collect food. When you was gone we dug like Mizuki asked, but Pearl got fed up so I got an idea to give her another job - as long as she does some digging every day, just for a bit. Anyway, so we did a deal that Pearl does some digging, but she's has to fetch and prepare most of the food by herself. Nadia and Evie helped us dig a bit, but they're too little. They look after the zoo, like you know.'

The rock table had been spread with the usual fayre, not haphazard as before, but neatly laid out. In the centre, a thick bunch of grasses and seed heads poked up from a paint can. The girls gathered to eat. They stood or sat on the ground or perched on the edge of the table, depending on the rise and dip of the rock. The contrast from the chaos of the Helizone overwhelmed the newcomers and they could hardly wait. Stephie grabbed a handful of dark berries and stuffed them into her mouth, but Melissa held up one hand, 'First we say thanks, like how Mizuki showed us.'

Stephie scowled at Roxy and Sparrow, thinking they'd agree that thanking was a just some stupid Home Rock joke, but Roxy and Sparrow fixed their eyes on Melissa, eager to imitate her and get on with the business of eating.

Melissa held aloft a handful of food, Freya raised a bottle of water, and both chorused, 'Thanks!' The rest raised a hand and echoed, 'Thanks.' Roxy and Sparrow mumbled 'Thanks,' as Stephie glared, not comprehending. Then one Home Rock girl turned to the next, offering the first choice of food, because that was their rule to prevent grabbing and selfish snaffling.

The children ate, chattering stories of their day. Introductions were made, exaggerated experiences enjoyed, all but the Silent One, who slouched on the ground between Nadia and Katey, nibbling whatever came her way.

When the last morsel had been devoured, Pearl swept the table clear of twigs, cores and seeds, using a stick onto which she'd tied slender grasses, looping them round and tying them securely. Job done and Pearl set the brush upon another rock, stood back to admire her first ever invention with its very own place in the world.

'Check your beds and meet back here soon as you're done,' Melissa called.

'Check beds?' Donna screwed her face into a question mark – another new thing since she'd been away.

'Checking helps us sleep. Look for snakes, centipedes, millipedes, spiders, beetles, lizards, frogs, ants, whatever.' Melissa headed for her own ramshackle hut over which she had overlapped giant leaves for shelter from the regular downpours.

'We don't kill the bugs we find,' Freya explained, 'we take them to the zoo, but if Nadia says they've already got one like that, we throw them into the jungle and shout, "*Don't come back or else!*"' She giggled as she tossed a millipede into the bushes, 'There's loads of these long brown things with wiggly legs. And don't pick ants up with your fingers, they bite bad.'

Pearl added, 'Freya's going help us weave more mats, but we didn't want to go to the lake and anyway, the toilet's got to be done first. After that, bigger huts, better beds. You know how bamboo is good for building? Well, we're also using leaves off those skinny trees with leaves what stink of mouthwash.' Pearl laughed and skipped a little, happy with her own success.

'At Helizone we slept in a cage,' said Sparrow, 'The big girls made it with a special door. I was scared to go in, but they pushed my head down the hole, "*Get in there, dog!*" Jody kicked me, so I had to go. I cried lots, but it turned out a good thing because the big girls couldn't get in with us! Stephie and Roxy got kicked in too. We was squashed. Then Jody and Claire catched Vix and pushed her in with us.'

'Then Joy came in and talked and talked,' added Stephie.

'But only after Vix runned away,' Roxy corrected, doing the maths on her fingers. She watched as Pearl scooped up a praying mantis then rushed over to the zoo to show Nadia. 'Also, we got no hut here, so where're we gonna sleep?'

Like a guillotine, darkness fell. The Home Rock girls crept into their huts. Roxy, Stephie and Sparrow sat down beside Katey's lean-to and huddled miserably on some scruffy matting, missing the protection of the Helizone mosquito nets and cage bars. They listened to the familiar sounds of the night, the barks of distant creatures, raindrops drumming on huge leaves, distant waterfalls, until they fell into a fitful sleep.

*

Katey woke to the sound of footsteps and whispering in the camp.

'Mizuki's back!' Katey, overwhelmed by a surge of happiness, sat up. Melissa and Freya were all right all things considering, but Mizuki was the best. Mizuki had smashed her way into her heart. Since the age of three, Katey had dreamt of having a mother as wonderful as Mizuki. She was The One, and she had come back to her. Katey eased herself out of her hut, stood up somewhat stiffly and looked about, straining her eyes in the dark. The whispering stopped.

'Mizuki?'

Someone stifled a snort, 'Shh!' Another squeaked. Someone giggled, 'Shh!' A muffled scream, then, 'Belt up, I said!' Silhouettes scuffled through the navy night. A command, 'Now!' The invaders attacked, moving quickly, trampling the huts, stamping on sleeping bodies. With the playground holler of conquering Indians, their voices rose and fell with terrifying effect.

Melissa, Pearl and Freya were quick to react, slapping and biting and tearing the hair of whoever came near. Cries for help came from some of the Blaze House girls being hit with sticks. Katey flattened herself against Hog Rock. She didn't know how to help anyone without getting battered herself.

'Anyone find a slave?' Bronwyn Bowen's unmistakeable voice.

'We got us a fat one!' someone cried, possibly Jody.

Bronwyn again, 'One slave is all I ask.'

'We got one. We did the bag over her head, like you said.'

Behind the rock, Katey's mind raced. F*at? No one here's fat. What are they going on about?* And whoever they'd captured wasn't crying for help.

'My tooth's knocked out!' Donna stumbled towards Katey's flattened hut. 'I knew we should never have brung them slaves back. They're bad luck. Everything was fine 'til they had to come 'n spoil our game.'

'Shut up, Donna, they'll hear you!' Katey warned in a half-whisper.

Donna swung round, 'Where are you?'

'Hog Rock, shh!'

Somewhere in the darkness Nadia and Evie were wailing.

Pearl shouted, 'Who smashed my bed? Ouch, my knee hurts.'

Bronwyn Bowen's voice cut through the dark, 'You're right, this one's really is chunky! One of her makes up for those useless skinny brats we lost. She can help us drag the bodies. Yup, we'll take her. Look what a pathetic slob, so stupid with that bag on her head. Get the rope. Let's get her to the Helizone.'

Katey longed to save whoever was being dragged away but her legs felt like jelly and her heart pounded with such violence it stole all her decisions.

A new voice boomed out, deep and authoritative, a strange voice coming from above, 'I'm watching you, Bronwyn Bowen!'

'Who . . . who's that?' Bronwyn looked this way

and that.

'You'll go down for this one, Bronwyn Bowen.'

Everyone looked up but they saw only sky-shapes between branches. The sing-song voice, deep and magical yet sinister, echoed so many scary movies the children should never have been permitted to view.

'Well, what do you know?' Bronwyn laughed, but her bravado was betrayed by the unusual high-pitched tone of her voice, 'Some joker's playing spooks with us. Come on, underlings, get a move on. Obey!' But the Helizone girls feared the unknown more than their queen. Still hung over from the day's antics, half-starved and exhausted from the effort of the invasion, they dithered in the dark.

'I'm watching you, Bronwyn Bowen,' repeated the voice with eerie effect.

'Shut your mouth!' Bronwyn snapped, but her voice wavered. This further unnerved the underlings who began to shriek and yelp.

'What are you doing, idiots?' Bronwyn yelled.

'Something stuck in my arm!' Claire shouted.

'And my tummy!' squealed Lydia.

The echoey voice continued, 'We know all about you, Bronwyn Bowen!'

'Aargh, my leg!' Jody screeched, dropping the rope she'd been using on the 'fat slave.' She turned tail and ran crashing through the jungle, with Claire, Elle-Marie and Lydia close behind. Only Bronwyn remained.

Drawn to the strength of Hog Rock, the Home Rock girls found Katey. They stood with her and made no sound.

'How do you think we found you? We smelt you! Call yourselves Home Rock? I say Home Stinks!' Bronwyn shouted 'though she couldn't see a soul, 'We'll be back. No one sleeps until my slaves are returned. I'm warning you, if you don't leave them tied to the arrow-tree tomorrow, I'll burn down your houses!'

The trees trembled, the ground grumbled, a mighty dragon raged from the bowels of the earth. Hot lightning cracked the sky. Thunder threatened through the trees. Black mountains zigzagged against the white sky. The earthquake subsided. Bronwyn Bowen had gone.

'To the table!' Freya shouted. The girls hastened to gather where they'd eaten not so long ago. They huddled together in the heavy night air.

'Everyone okay?' Melissa called, 'Shout yes to your name. Pearl?'

'I gotta sore knee.'

'Jus' say yes.'

'Katey.'

'Yes.'

'Nadia, Evie, Freya, Donna, Stephie, Roxy . . .' One by one they answered in the affirmative. Katey prompted Melissa; 'What about Sparrow?'

'Yes, me, I'm here.'

'It's okay, Katey. Everyone's here what should be,' said Melissa.

'Where's . . ?' Katey strained her eyes. She could not find the Silent One.

'She's here with us. Bronwyn tried to kidnap her

but . . .' It was Mizuki, standing among them, and with her a small white-haired child. Shuffling between them, clutching her stomach, was the Silent One.

'Mizuki! So that scary voice in the sky was you?' cried Katey.

Mizuki explained, 'No, not me. Bronwyn tricked us about killing Joy. I sneaked her away when Bronwyn wasn't looking. I carried her and she fell asleep, but when we got to the Helizone I had to put her down for a bit. She woke up. Joy showed me Bronwyn's amazing light thingy. Bronwyn had three or four, so I pinched one.'

'Them lights don't need no 'lectricity,' boasted Katey, because she'd seen how they worked when she'd perched on the branch, 'and I know how to work them.'

Roxy chipped in, 'Yeah, we've had them ages. Us slaves aren't allowed to touch.'

Mizuki continued, 'They aren't Bronwyn's to keep to herself. She'd tied this one really tight on the heli door. It was hard to get off. We heard the others coming back, so we hid. They were mega sick, holding their tummies, collapsing, crawling. Bronwyn made them drink water. Me and Joy sneaked round the back of the helicopter, but they saw us and chased us. It was marshy and . . .'

'. . . I was sinking up to my knees,' Joy added.

'. . . I knew the only safe way was back through the Helizone, over Bronwyn's path, with everyone watching.'

'She carried me again, didn't you 'Zuki?'

'I had to – we made a dash for it. They could see us 'cos they turned on the lights, but they kept tripping over.'

'So Bronwyn shouted at them to get up,' Joy grinned, eyes wide with excitement.

Freya growled, 'Evil witch. I warned you about her. She thinks up bad stuff and makes you do it. Why do you think I never went back?' The ground trembled, a weak aftershock from a distant epicentre. The girls instinctively placed their hands upon the rock table to steady their fear.

'We got away, didn't we Joy? But they beat us to Home Rock so they must know a short cut. We were walking quite slowly, then we heard them arguing. Bronwyn was telling them to attack Home Rock. So we thought up a plan, didn't we, Joy?' Mizuki patted the child on the top of her head.

'Yup. First, I got a sharp stick,' said Joy, 'and next I climbed high in the tree. I've climbed that one before, for fruit, but not in the dark. It's got lots of branches. I looked down and said all spooky, *"I'm watching you, Bronwyn Bowen!"* Bronwyn's scary, but she scares easy. I did my best acting like at school, *"I'm watching you, Bronwyn Bowen!"*'

Everyone giggled. Joy continued, 'When them Helizone girls was proper scared, I sneaked down and poked their legs with my stick, like this, prod, prod!' Now everyone was laughing, especially Freya. Joy nodded towards the Silent One, 'But I didn't poke her because she's a Home Rock girl and they was trying to steal her for a slave.' Mizuki touched Joy's arm reassuringly. Thunder rumbled long and low, but no one flinched.

Mizuki added, 'I took the bag off her head so she could breathe, and I untied her. Joy was really brave to help me. She hid in the bushes, poking those big girls with bamboo 'til they ran away.' Lightning filled the sky in a huge white sheet, then again, leaping from east to west and back again. In every flash the girls caught sight of one another, ashen-faced but smiling. Comrades. More than comrades – family.

'Mizuki?' Katey cried, overcome with relief. Thunder clapped and cracked without rain.

'What?' shouted Mizuki.

'Will you be my mum?'

'I can't. I'm only twelve.'

'I know, but . . .'

'I can be your sister. Your big sister. But I can't be your mum.'

'Thanks 'Zuki. I never had no big sister before.'

*

Stuff cannot be fixed in the dark, so the dregs of a restless night were spent hunkering down beside the wrecked huts. Dawn broke. Nadia and Evie's first thought was to inspect their zoo which, for obvious reasons, they'd constructed well away from the huts. To their immense excitement, their precious notepads were still in their bag, wedged in a cleft in the rock, and the zoo was intact. The little girls clasped hands and skipped around the praying mantis, the beetle and the roach. Only the Whistling Spider, a beast as large as a woman's hand, had escaped, but she was always doing that - climbing out of her carton and scuttling back to her natural home, a tunnel she had dug deep into the soft earth.

10

A Dead Good Looker-Afterer

Days passed. The Home Rock girls rebuilt their homes, not without anxiety. *Be alert, take care, don't wander alone. Bronwyn might burn down your house or steal you for her slave.* Since the terrible night invasion, Mizuki had taken turns with Melissa and Freya to guard the camp while the younger ones slept, but Katey was restless. She'd taken to watching the Watchers.

It was Mizuki's shift. In the moonlight, Katey saw Mizuki stand up. Katey's hackles rose, 'She's going again, I know it. Why does she walk off by herself without telling no one, like she owns the whole jungle?' This happened too often - Mizuki sneaking out of Home Rock, leaving the camp vulnerable, forcing Katey to feel responsible for everyone's safety, feeling like she had to fight sleep, stay awake, to be on guard. The slightest rustle or squeak or earth tremor unnerved her, but then she'd wake and it would be morning and she'd feel guilty because she'd fallen asleep after all, and Mizuki would be there, serenely moving through Home Rock like she'd never been away.

Day followed night followed day.

During one particular breakfast the Home Rock girls were, for no obvious reason, listless and in no hurry to get going. Freya drifted barefoot across the camp to mark the Daystone with the varnish. She'd done her best to keep the row of dots straight, using a bamboo cane as a ruler, but from the start she'd been anxious and excited to begin a second row. Mizuki had told her, 'Yes, but only after one hundred dots.' Freya counted to one hundred. Easy. Marking one red dot every day for a hundred days – agonisingly slow, so if no one was looking, Freya added an extra dot (or two), justifying this to herself because 'what about them days between the crash and Day One?'

Freya returned to the table just as Mizuki walked up the track that led into the camp by the zoo. Mizuki sauntered over, raised her hand half-heartedly, mumbled 'Thanks,' and sat down without making eye-contact.

Katey scowled, 'You're late.' It was unnerving. A big sister should never leave the family without explanation. What if Mizuki never returned? How would they know where to search for her? What if she was killed by lions or tigers or bears? Or crocodiles, snap, snap! Even a baby knows never to smile at a crocodile, yet Mizuki was appearing and disappearing like she couldn't care less. Anything could get her. Thankfully she had returned. Ignoring Katey's accusation, Mizuki slowly peeled a miniature banana then nibbled it as if it were the most important thing in the world.

Freya thumped the table with her fist, 'Where the hell've you been going all these nights?'

Mizuki paled, said nothing, shrugged. She scanned the table for water.

Freya repeated, 'I said, where've you been?' All eyes were on Mizuki as she poured water into her cup. She drank it noisily, to demonstrate her presence, that she was still in charge. She paused to catch her breath, throwing Freya a brief, sarcastic smile.

'Where's you been?' chirped Stephie, imitating Freya, but missing the signs of danger.

'Where's ya been?' echoed Roxy and Sparrow, giggling, hoping to get in on the joke.

Nadia and Evie echoed, 'Ya bin you? Ya bin?' and nudged each other.

Mizuki neither laughed nor frowned, but Katey saw how Mizuki's jawbone clenched and the muscle beneath her left eye twitched. Katey recognised the same ominous expression she'd seen on her stepdad's face when he'd crawled home in the early hours. Many a night she'd sat on the top stair as the front door clicked open. It banged shut. Her mum leapt up from snoozing on the sofa, instantly interrogating, going on and on at her partner, tightening the tension on his jawbone until – snap! Without a word, he'd lash out. Her mum should've kept her mouth shut.

'You better tell us,' Freya said, forcing a gentler tone, but she was pushing the boat out and she knew it. Mizuki clenched her teeth. A muscle twitched in her eye-socket. Danger. Danger.

'Yeah, tell us!' Roxy was dancing with excitement, with no idea why she was dancing or what she was asking. Nadia and Evie chipped in, then Stephie and Sparrow, chanting, 'Tell us! Tell us!' On and on they chanted and danced.

Mizuki straightened her back. Her swan-neck lengthened. Her eyes closed. She inhaled a long, slow breath. Katey clamped her hand to her mouth. The voices stopped. Every eye widened, every foot pressed hard against the earth. Brake! Brake! Then they were skidding on the wet road, aquaplaning, swerving, scraping helplessly along the crash barrier.

Mizuki smashed her fist down hard onto the rock. She swept her arm over the table, scattering the remains of breakfast in all directions. She screamed, stretching her jaw until her fine bones shone through her sallow skin and the sinews in her neck pulled taut as piano strings and her glass-green eyes glared from one child to the next, without seeing.

'How dare you question me? I can do what I like. I can go where I like. I can eat what I like. I can sleep where I like. You are not my dad. You are not my mum. You're just a bunch of flaming useless kids. You have no right to question me. No right!' Her voice pitched higher and higher. She slammed her mouth shut.

The children froze. Mizuki breathed fast and heavy. Her nostrils flared like dragon's as her breath went in and out, faster and faster.

Katey's instinct was to drop to the ground behind the table, to shield herself from Mizuki's sight, but she dared not move a muscle. Nadia's lower lip wobbled and her eyes filled with tears, but she refused to let them fall. Evie sucked her thumb and reached out to take Nadia's hand. Melissa cowered, aware she was shaking but she couldn't help herself. Donna's shoulders hunched lower and lower as she muttered her vanishing spell under her breath, 'Invisible, invisible, not my fault. I didn't do nothing.'

Mizuki towered over them all, a scarecrow from a horror film with her shredded tracksuit and dark, tangled hair. She raised her sharp chin and all was still. When she spoke again, her voice was perilously calm, like a grown-up from *Before*, 'Everyone expects me to do this and do that and look after everybody and decide stuff. Well, you can stop expecting. I'm not in charge. I don't want to be bothered with you, see? I'm sick of the lot of you! You don't need me. Go dig your toilets. Get your own food. Find your own water. Play your own games. You want to know where I've been? You really wanna know? I walked over there,' Mizuki pointed east 'and it goes on forever. And the other night I walked miles and miles over that way,' she pointed west, 'where the forest gets darker and thicker and scarier - too scary for any of you wimps. Another night I crept past Bronwyn's helicopter. It's sinking. I cut my foot on a bit of metal. Anyway, you can't go that way because the marsh gets too deep. And you can't go up the waterfall back there, behind us, because it's too high and gets too steep, so I went to that flat place again, where Bronwyn pushed Joy. It's only flat for a bit, then it goes up very steep. I climbed higher where none of us have gone before. I looked all over the place for a way out. You know what I saw? You wanna know? I bet you do. Well, I'll tell you what I didn't see - no houses, no people - not even a single jungle person. No paths, no roads, no signs . . . no answers.'

Once more she swept her hand over the table, slower this time, with less conviction, but Freya's flowers went flying. A giant moth broke a wing and fell to the ground. The children watched it struggle, helpless to intervene. Mizuki cleared her throat, 'So stop thinking I can be your mum or your sister. You're stuck here forever. I can't save you. Do you hear me? I tried, you know I tried, but I can't save anyone. No one can save you. No one is looking.'

A mantle of hopelessness descended. Mizuki pressed her palms against her temples. She stroked the scar along her forehead. The Super Puma was falling, falling, falling, its lights flashing off, on, off, on, as the world spun like candyfloss with only the trees for brakes.

'I can't save you,' Mizuki whimpered. The littlest ones' mouths wobbled. They looked to each other for reassurance, fighting back tears.

Katey spoke softly, 'But we don't wanna be saved no more. We like it here. This *is* being saved.' Nods and murmurs of agreement all round.

Mizuki dropped her arms. She looked from one to the other in disbelief. 'You actually *like* it here? But there's no TV, no phones, no proper music - you'll never see X-Factor ever again, no games, no films, no dancing. Nothing.'

'But we don't need no phones. We talk,' said Freya, 'when we see each other.'

'And even if my Galaxy worked I wouldn't be speaking to no Bronwyn Bossy Bowen!' Melissa smiled. She high-fived Freya.

Mizuki sank to the ground, with her back to the rock table. She shook her head, 'But we can't stay here for ever. There's never going to be no birthdays here. No parties. No school. No boys.'

'Yucky school,' Roxy said, 'I got kicked out in reception 'cos I bit Jack's ear.'

'No boys,' whooped Stephie, 'I'm saved. High five!' She raised her hand and Roxie hit it with a loud 'Yay!' A giant hornet dropped by to check out the black fruit juice staining the table.

Donna looked into her trembling palms, 'But what if we need a real live hospital? I'm only a pretend nurse didn't you know?'

'Yeah, you don't have to tell us you're a fake, Donna's-a-Goner-Moore. We all saw who really mended Mizuki's gunky head - Melissa done it,' Pearl said, dabbing her own forehead, mopping the sweat. She pulled her best 'disgusted' face, recalling Mizuki's maggots and the stench of sick.

'So what if Melissa did be the nurse.' Donna shook her fists at the wasp. It was a monster, far bigger than any measly Blaze House wasp. Sparring with it, however feebly, helped Donna feel superior.

Mizuki rested her forehead on her arms as the others debated whether to stay or leave the jungle. Nothing out there was likely to be better. Nothing here was worse than before. Their words tumbled together without logic, muddied with emotion. Mizuki struggled to her feet and stumbled towards the privacy of her freshly renovated hut. Melissa had done a great job. This hut was bigger. Comfier. A leggy spider hesitated on one of the gigantic leaves that criss-crossed the flat roof, but Mizuki ignored it. She dived into the shelter and collapsed dizzily onto her rush mat.

'*Whoa, I'm floating. There is no gravity.*' Her whole being felt weightless, not from lack of food, but with her new freedom, a mind-blowing escape from the impossible responsibility that had been her personal burden ever since the crash. The attitude of the Home Rock girls puzzled her; *How can they be so chilled out?*

Her mind whirled as she released the mantle of saviourhood and drifted into a deep, deep sleep; the peaceful sleep of a child whose mother has read her a bedtime story and said a prayer and kissed her goodnight.

*

Mizuki did not emerge from her sleep until well into the next day. The others had eaten and were busy digging the drain or washing the table or weaving bedding. Freya had marked a red dot (or three) on the Daystone and was scouring the area for the perfect girth of bamboo to slot inside another one, thinking of ways to fix it so water could run from one length on another without leaking. She hoped, eventually, the whole system would flow into the toilet just like in England, but so far her efforts were as haphazard as a game of Marble-Run.

Freya took great pleasure in accumulating an assortment of tools, a combination of objects from *Before:* scissors, blunt knives, bent teaspoons, vicious shards of helicopter metal, nail-files, string, hair grips - and from *Now:* stones with jagged edges for chipping or bashing, bamboo, threads of liana, strips of leaf, feathers and their latest discovery, bones harvested from dead animals. Several days after the repulsive discovery of a disintegrating tree kangaroo[5] infested with flies and maggots, the girls returned to retrieve its clean skeleton. Freya collected the bones for sorting, scrubbing, and drying in the sun. They made brilliant hairgrips, jewellery, or toothpicks to get the seeds that stuck in their teeth.

Evie and Nadia had lugged in a ribcage, identity unknown. After illustrating it in their notepad (eight or nine lines curved over a 'stick' labelled DNS - *bones?*) they donated it to Freya's "tool-shed". They'd been battling to erect some sort of lean-to for their zoo, but the structures invariably collapsed under the force of the daily downpour. They trampled the ground around the zoo to firm it, then swept it clear of leaves and twigs. Visitors were permitted to stand in this clearing so they didn't accidentally knock over the containers or squish one of the live exhibits. Crawling insects which ventured onto this arena were easily spotted, captured, sketched, labelled then tossed back into the jungle.

Mizuki moseyed over. Nadia glanced up anxiously, but Mizuki's face was calm. In fact, she was smiling. 'How would you two like to come swimming with me?' Nadia and Evie exchanged glances – *she safe?* Safe, they nodded. Mizuki winked, 'Okey-doke, back in a tick.' She sauntered over to where Roxy sat chatting to Melissa. Melissa was coiling strips of fibre around a feather to attach it to the end of Roxy's long plait, already decorated with red and black beads.

'Where did you find those beads?' Mizuki reached out to stroke Roxy's hair.

'At the bead shop,' Roxy answered because Melissa had a mouthful of hairclips, 'Freya and her over there,' – she nodded in the direction of the Silent One who was, to Mizuki's amazement, scooping dirt with a length of bamboo to add to the toilet wall - 'they soak seeds in fruit juice. Black fruit makes black beads. Red fruit makes red beads. But,' she sighed, 'yellow berries don't dye the seeds yellow. They don't work for colouring stuff. Yellow is a problem. We've been looking for more colours. Steph's going to try mashing those purple flowers to get the purple out.'

'Bead shop?' Mizuki wondered how and when she'd missed this development.

'Yes, Steph's just started to run the bead shop for Freya. She opens in the afternoon. We give Steph something we found - a bone or special food - and she gives us beads. Evie and Nadia got beads in their plaits to make them pretty. Freya's the best at doing plaits. They stay in for ages. Ouch!' Roxy ducked to protect her head from Melissa's tugging.

'Oops, your hair's so tangly!' Melissa spat out the grips. 'Over there,' she added, pointing to the Silent One, 'she makes brilliant jewellery. She's going to open her own shop when she's got enough to sell.'

'*She* told you that?'

'Don't be daft, you know she don't speak. We gave her the idea to have her own shop when we saw her make necklaces. She's brilliant at threading beads. All of us is going to get all kinds of businesses.'

Mizuki blinked. She cocked her head to one side, 'Why didn't I see it before?'

'You were busy being a Searcher and a Fighter and looking out for us. You weren't a Digger or a Trader.'

'I'm not a Searcher any more. And I'd like a trade, but I'm rubbish at making stuff.'

'What do you like doing best?' Melissa ran her fingers through the final length of Roxy's hair, separated it into three, plaited it and fixed the end with an elastic band.

'I don't want to carve tools or dig or dye beads or weave hair.'

'What I think is this. You're a dead good Looker-Afterer,' Roxy said.

'But that's not a shop, is it? Not really.'

'Roxy's right. You're a good thinker,' said Melissa, feeding a string of natural and dyed beads through the last plait, 'We can come to your shop when we don't know what to do and you can tell us. We'll pay you with beads or a new mat.'

'But you don't need me. You already know how to do everything.'

'Not true. We don't know loads of stuff, like, what to do about rain? Problem is we need better cover, a roof that won't blow down in a storm. We know how to use them big leaves, but someone needs to think up a better cover than leaves.'

'I'm not sure...' but Mizuki was already considering the solution. 'Would you like to swim later? Or would it mess up Roxy's hair?'

'When I've done this, let's all go. Her hair is weaved tight. It will stay in. The beads are stained so the dye can't wash out. Even if it does wreck, we can do it again.' Melissa fixed a silver feather behind Roxy's ear. 'There,' she said, 'you look amazing. Off you go. Tell Sparrow I'll try to fix her hair after we've been swimming.' Melissa explained, 'Sparrow's hair is a real challenge. It's patchy. Some's long, other bits are bald, but I want Sparrow to feel proper pretty.'

*

'Bronwyn's not fussed about us any more,' Mizuki reassured the Home Rock girls, 'especially not in daylight, so come on, I'll show you my secret track up to the pool.'

No one chose to walk barefoot, but their footwear had seriously deteriorated, so some had cut holes in the toes of trainers to make room for their growing feet or fastened ragged soles on with string. Anything was better than nothing.

Mizuki led the Home Rock girls up a steep incline.

They moved confidently without complaint. Long before they caught sight of the pool they heard the falling water. Here the rocks levelled broadly, like hardened treacle. Millenniums ago, boiling liquid had bubbled up from the earth, cooled, then set. Now a shimmering curtain of water fell from a great height into the pool. On each side of the waterfall, myriads of flowers flourished, attracting a confetti of butterflies, dragonflies and iridescent beetles.

Footwear piled up as, in t-shirts and ragged shorts, leggings or worn tracksuit bottoms, they tested the beautiful water. The younger ones splashed in the shallows, but Melissa, Mizuki and Katey dived where the waterfall had chiselled a deeper pool, their long hair, plaited or loose, streaming out behind them. Afterwards, the girls sprawled over the rocks, chatting, singing or snoozing. High above them, two Harpy eagles spread wide their grey-brown wings and soared effortlessly on the rising thermals.

*

The dots on the rock multiplied. Without a word to Mizuki, Freya counted, 'Ninety-eight, ninety-nine, a hundred!' The hundredth dot meant more to Freya than time itself. Then, at last, 'A hundred and one,' she announced, placing this extra dot exactly below. Freya stood back in triumph. 'I done good,' she said. The Day-Keeper had accomplished her goal but no one took a blind bit of notice.

11

The Shock of the Trade

Evie and Nadia approached Mizuki's 'Thinking to Help' shop with an offering of a pale-green pear-shaped fruit. (Freya had told them it was a pear, [4] although it didn't taste like one. It didn't taste half as good as it looked). Evie and Nadia squatted down. They spread out several dog-eared notebooks.

'Or gone done.' Evie's eyes filled with tears. Her bottom lip wobbled. Nadia took her hand.

Seeing their distress Mizuki sat cross-legged. She patted the ground, 'Sit down properly Evie, Nadia.' Mizuki beckoned to a girl who was dragging in yet more bamboo for Melissa, 'Hey, Stephie, I need you.'

'What for?'

'Translate for me.'

'Or gone done. Manibles cano more.'

Stephie smiled. 'All our books are full. Can't draw animals no more.'

Mizuki shook her head, 'You mean we've run out of paper? Nobody has a notebook left? Have you checked everyone's bags?'

Nadia and Evie shook their heads then nodded their heads. Evie reached out to caress the soft pages of her favourite book, 'Runt ow.'

'Run out. Obvious really,' Stephie smiled. Nadia held up a couple of stubby colouring pencils.

'Dem near or out.'

'They're nearly all run out.' Stephie added, 'The biros dried up ages ago. The sharpeners are blunt. Also, our clothes are shrinking in the rain. There's no plasters left in the first aid kit, and . . .'

'Okay, okay, I get it. We're running out of stuff. It's not like I can magic new drawing paper for you. I can't go into town to buy you clothes – and they're not shrinking, it's you that's growing taller. Be thankful the light works and we can see to go to the toilet in the night without treading on snakes.'

'Another light would help . . .' Stephie started.

Mizuki thumbed through a notebook, marvelling at the infantile sketches of frogs, stick insects and ants, and countless other creatures, mainly unidentifiable. Nadia and Evie's efforts at labelling were admirable, jumbled letters remembered from year one, and scribbled arrows pointing to HEAD, HAND, HAIR, BODY, ARM, LEG, FOOT, PINCERS.

Mizuki nodded, 'Wow! You've done very, very well not to let them get wet. I know you use plastic bags to keep them safe, but these drawings are treasure, so I want you to take super care of them.' Mizuki smiled weakly. The girls seemed a little cheered, but still their eyes implored her for more notebooks and pencils.

Mizuki shut her eyes to think about how she could make the impossible possible. She shut out the sounds of the jungle. She shut out the songs and shouts of the Home Rock girls as they worked and played.

A woolly rat poked its nose around the corner of her "stall" and sniffed Mizuki's ankle before bumbling over the clearing and vanishing into the undergrowth. Mizuki opened her eyes, 'I can't make promises but . . .'

Freya interrupted, 'Something terrible's happened!' This from Freya, the girl who hardly ever panicked. Mizuki waved Nadia and Evie off and, uncrossing her legs, she stood up gracefully without using her hands. Stephie dithered within earshot. *Did she say something terrible happened?*

Freya thrust two empty bottles of nail varnish into Mizuki's hands. The brushes were stiff as pencils. 'We've run out of days,' she said.

Mizuki shuffled her feet because she'd completely forgotten about Freya being the Day-Keeper. And birthdays weren't a thing until the other evening when Katey had asked, 'When's Jesus' birthday?' and 'Do jungles even do Christmas Day?' The question triggered a lively discussion on debt and drunkenness, affairs and fist-fights, random strangers snoring on the sofa beneath a lop-sided, plastic, present-less tree.

That evening Katey had shared her story, 'You know what? I got two uncles, Uncle Lem and Uncle Dylan. Christmas Eve they brung home a 3D flat-screen, big as a table. Uncle Dylan went crazy 'cos Uncle Lem dropped the remote back in the alley and he forgot to put plastic bags over his boots. Uncle Dylan said them "ruddy great footprints" will lead the cops to my house so he smashed Uncle Lem's nose in. I runned upstairs and hid under my bed, wishing and wishing for the cops to find them ruddy footprints and bash down our back door and stop the fight, but they never did."

Mizuki rolled the varnish bottles over and back over the palm of her hand, 'Oh, Freya, I should have told you already, we don't need to do dots anymore now we're not getting saved. What difference does it make what day it is?'

'To know.'

'Know what?'

'How long our life is,' Freya sighed.

'We're born, we live, we die. That's it. Why count days to death when we only need days to live? But,' Mizuki clicked the bottles together, 'if it makes you happy – and I'm not promising – I'll see what I can do.'

'That's really it? We're born, we die?'

'Well, maybe Heaven after – what thing do I know, there's no dots in Heaven.'

*

From her sleeping mat, Katey watched Mizuki slide into the undergrowth without so much as a rustle. Mizuki had confessed that she'd stopped searching for an escape yet every few nights she stilled slipped away. Darkness intensified the smell and feel of things, which intensified the sense of danger, but Katey knew Mizuki was hardly afraid. With a thudding heart, Katey pulled on a pair of trainers that Donna had outgrown and crept out after Mizuki with the utmost stealth.

A huge, blotchy moon patrolled the sky and a billion stars battled to outshine it. Mizuki picked up the pace, cutting a leggy, marionette figure between the trees. Small creatures scurried through the undergrowth - a silky cuscus, a ring-tailed tree kangaroo, a brown mouse with a long, white tail - but nothing slowed Mizuki. It was obvious to Katey she'd walked this way many times.

At the lakeside, Mizuki crossed the shingle with a delicate crunch, crunch, crunch. Moonlight cast a rippling path over the water, its light broken only by a fallen tree trunk and patches of reeds. Mizuki stopped, cupped her hands to her mouth and blew a low, hollow sound through her fingers. Katey crouched on the forest fringe and waited, eyes wide, straining to see.

Mizuki blew again, a higher note, sharp as a dawn bird, ending on an eerie rise, then she scanned the shingle for somewhere to sit. She chose a rock and perched on it, drawing her knees up to her chin and wrapping her arms about herself. The lake lapped rhythmically. A fish broke the surface, creating expanding silver hoops. Deer drifted through the shadows, elegantly sniffing the air for signs of danger.

A movement. Someone was at the far side of the beach, close to where the arrow was attached to the tree. Katey made out a gangly, hunched figure, checking left and right, then stepping out into the open. She thought, 'That's like Bronwyn, but it can't be because we hate the Helizone girls.'

Mizuki looked up but otherwise made no signal of acknowledgement. She waited for her guest to cross the shingle and sit beside her then, wordlessly, she withdrew something from her pocket and handed to the visitor who snatched the offering and shovelled it into her mouth.

The two conversed so softly that Katey could not eavesdrop. She was forced to inch closer, crawling on her hands and knees, cautiously lifting a limb then placing it down on the shingle, acutely aware of the slightest sound, hardly daring to breathe. Katey avoided the moonlit areas, keeping to the shadowed gulleys until she was within earshot. The visitor was whining, protesting something.

Mizuki spoke, 'At least trade with us. You've got stuff we need.'

'Like what?'

'Pens, paper, pencils, sharpeners, maybe a sharp knife?'

'Yeah.'

'Yeah you got them? Or yeah you'll get them for us?'

'Got 'em.'

'We need nail varnish or paint. Actually both.'

'What do we get in exchange?'

'I dunno. What do you need? Food? Jewellery? Hair decorations? We make all sorts of stuff.' A colony of bats fluttered over the lake, their translucent membranes stretched into delicate wings. They emitted the tiniest of squeaks as they devoured mosquito, moth and beetle on the wing.

The visitor made a sound like she was choking, but she was only scoffing food too fast. Katey's eyes widened, 'That is Bronwyn!' She listened harder.

'We make our own headdresses, eat our own chickens and their eggs, raw. We don't need your stuff,' Bronwyn rose unsteadily to her feet, 'Except . . .'

'What?'

'You know what we want. I told you the other night.'

'And I told you, no way.'

'You stole our workers. You owe me my slaves back.'

'And I told you they're just useless little kids.'

'Useless to you maybe, but I had fun with them. Send them back and I'll get as much of your gear as I can.'

'But what will you do with them?'

'None of your beeswax. Five slaves and you can have all the paper you want.'

'Five?'

'Okay, four. Keep the one that legged it. She was a right pain in the backside.'

'Vix? She never came back. I swear on my gran's grave, we haven't got her. And you can't have Joy. She's a Home Rock girl.'

Damp seeped through Katey's tracksuit as she lay in the gulley. It blew her mind to hear Mizuki, of all people, talking so meanly. Katey was tempted to stand up and yell, but Bronwyn Bowen terrified her. The way things were panning out, Katey was beginning to think Mizuki might even exchange her for a piece of junk from the helicopter. She wished she hadn't followed. She wished she didn't know the horrid truth about Mizuki, and yet she needed to know. Someone had to know the truth.

'Okay,' said Mizuki, 'I'll give you Sparrow. She's a good worker. Less chatty than Stephie and Roxy. A bit weedy, but she's getting stronger. She helped Freya dig our toilet and tie the pipes together.'

'Toilets? What d'ya mean? How did you get toilets? Are they for real?'

Mizuki rose to leave, 'Toilet. Only one. A hole in the ground with a bit of an earth wall. Hard work for the Diggers. Better than nothing, but we still can't use it. Not finished yet.' Mizuki took Bronwyn's hand and pulled her to her feet, 'Right, you win. Not tomorrow but the night after is my watch duty. Bring all the pencils and notebooks from your personal bags. Don't forget the nail varnish – someone will have some stashed away. Otherwise paint will have to do. I'll bring Sparrow. If you fetch enough stuff to make me happy, we can trade again another time.'

'Whoa! Hang on a sec - one slave for all that?'

'You're only giving us stuff you don't want. A slave is worth more than a few pencils.'

'How will you make Sparrow go with you?'

'Not your problem.'

'Send her with food.'

'Deal.' Mizuki high-fived Bronwyn. To Katey's amazement the two girls slapped one another on the shoulders and hugged briefly before parting. Bronwyn dipped down to scoop a handful of lake water into her hand and smacked it against her mouth, slurping noisily.

Mizuki called out, 'You shouldn't drink straight from the lake, it'll upset your tummy. The water in the moss pools is purer. That's what we think anyway. No one gets sick drinking that. Never drink from the marshes. That's the worst.'

Bronwyn splashed her face and neck. She dried herself on her sweatshirt. 'Helizone girls are tough. Drink from the marshes all the time. No one's died.'

Katey shut her eyes. 'Got to go,' she told herself. Fighting exhaustion, she mustered what little strength she had and stumbled after Mizuki. Every now and again, Mizuki turned around as if she sensed she was being followed, and Katey instantly dropped her chin to her chest and stopped dead still.

A cloud defaced the moon, plunging the jungle into utter darkness. Even so, Mizuki raced back to Home Rock, her footfall soft and sure as any deer.

12

One Birthday for All

The 'Thinking to Help' store was the only one with a hand-written sign:

手伝

The girls crowded in to admire Mizuki's handiwork. She'd used black fruit juice combined with beetle blood and applied it with a stick onto sand-coloured bark.

Roxy asked, 'What does them sticks and lines mean?'

'Thinking to Help,' Mizuki said. She stood back from her handiwork and cocked her head. 'It's the name of my shop. Actually, it just means "help." I don't know much Japanese so I might've got it wrong.'

'Beautiful,' Melissa smiled, 'but you should clean up a bit. Look, there's flies all over.' She pointed to the 'Thinking to Help' floor where a creature, half-kangaroo, half teddy-bear lay crumpled and dead. Insect-infested spaces where the eyes had once been.

Melissa said, 'Whoever moves it has to wash their hands ten times.' Everyone giggled, knowing no Home Rock girl would dare touch anything so obviously infectious.

Freya plonked herself down cross-legged beside Mizuki, 'Did you solve my nail varnish problem?'

The others overheard, which set them talking nineteen to the dozen.

'What about that paper you promised for Nadia and Evie?'

'And what about my tummy ache?'

'I want pizza.'

Mizuki laughed, and the little ones laughed with her without knowing why they were laughing. Maybe because their leader looked so pretty when she smiled, what with her white teeth and her dark hair pinned up, decorated with beads and feathers. Mizuki held up her hand for silence, 'Okay, okay. My shop is 'Thinking to Help', not 'Father Christmas,' so don't all shout at once. I'm not a magician. You know-know that pizza is a no-no.' Mizuki waited for them to get her joke. She tapped the side of her nose, 'But paper . . . I have plans for paper and paint, and maybe, just maybe, nail varnish for Freya.' Mizuki winked. The little ones jumped and cheered.

Katey fixed her eyes on Mizuki's mouth, trying to sort truth from fiction. From infancy she'd learnt not to trust adults who talk and smile at the same time. They'd say, *'We'll see,'* and smile to make her believe they were saying *'Yes,'* when they meant *'Not on your life.'* They'd say, *'Of course you can watch TV – whatever you like, princess,'* when they really meant, *'Watch CBeebies all day and all night for all I care, while I get smashed.'*

Mizuki grinned again. 'You know how I said there'd be no birthdays here?' The crowd fell silent. 'Well, I've got a brilliant idea. Me an' Freya are going to organise a birthday party with food and games and dancing and . . .'

'But who's it for?' Roxy asked.

'Who for? Who for?' cried the others.

'Everybody! That way, we can all be one year older at exactly the same time.'

'So I can be seven!' Stephie squealed, 'QB wasn't letting us be seven ever!' She caught both Sparrow's hands in hers and the two spun circles, their hair streaming out behind them. 'We gonna be se-ven, we're gonna be se-ven,' they chanted, 'Happy Birthday to us!'

'How old will you be next, Katey?' asked Mizuki, 'Come on, cheer up. I'll get you a pressie!'

Katey's eyes narrowed. *You're up to somefink. I'm on to you. I've just got to figure out a way to mess up your plans.*

'Cheer up glummy dummy.' Freya tweaked Katey's cheek, 'Are you ill?'

'I'm nine and I'm staying nine, and I don't want no present.' Katey's lower lip wobbled. She turned her back and stormed off to hang out with Nadia and Evie in the calm safety of their zoo.

'No digging today!' the girls cried as they fetched water and gathered the fruit and nuts for the breakfast table. In the centre of the table, instead of the usual tin of flowers, Freya carefully placed Donna's scratched, blue bag with the diamante design. Nadia and Evie nudged each other, jabbering in YaYa.

'Zatfa?'

'Nuno you?'

Stephie interpreted, 'What's that for? I don't know, do you?'

Mizuki pressed her palms together, creating a space between her thumbs then pressing the gap to her lips. She blew hard. Only a squeak. She adjusted her thumbs, blew again, an owl-like sound, first mellow, then piercing. The others tried to imitate Mizuki, with varying degrees of success and much hilarity. Mizuki picked a length of grass and fixed it between her thumbs. She blew again, squeezing her palms together, raising and dropping her fingers to play a distinctive tune, 'Happy Birthday to you.' Her audience clapped.

The Silent One joined the group, sliding down with her back to the rock-table. She stuck her legs straight out in front of her and, groaning, clasped her hands over her stomach. Nothing athletic to boast about there. If anything, she was becoming lazier and more ungainly.

'Happy birthday everybody!' Donna yelled joyously, pushing the shoulders of the nearest girls, 'and happy birthday to me!'

'Tomorrow Freya will do two dots to make up for no varnish today,' Mizuki said. She beckoned Nadia and Evie, 'Let go of those poor bugs and come to the table.' Mizuki raised her hand only to waist level, palm outwards as a blessing.

'After thanks and before you eat, Melissa wants to say something.' The group imitated Mizuki, raising their hands. 'Thanks' they chorused, then eyed Melissa impatiently; *Hurry up, be quick, we're hungry.*

'Right. I want to say this. Right, um, we are a family,' Melissa frowned, concentrating on choosing the right words, 'but Mizuki and Freya and me was thinking, "Are you happy at Home Rock?" and we had an idea for our birthday. Everyone has to say your name and your work, and something else, I forget . . .'

Freya rescued her, adding, 'Say one thing about why you like it here.' A picture of the nail varnish flashed across her mind. The very important job. The joy of being trusted. 'But I botched it up,' she thought. She resolved never to add an extra dot again, starting from tomorrow, and from now on she'd use bamboo to keep the days straight.

'That's right, we're going to say what we like about being here,' Melissa nodded.

'That will take for absolutely ever and ever,' moaned Donna, licking her lips, 'Why do we have to do it right at this utter exact, precise minute?'

'Because it'll be fun. Tell you what, you go first!' Melissa said.

'Humph! What I wanna know is why's my bag in

da miggle of da table?'

'Don't talk babyish, Donna. Just get on with it.'

'Me, me, lemme go first! My name's Pearl and I'm a Digger and I'm a very, very good food finder. And . . .'

'Stop boasting. They said for me to be first. You're not the best food finder, fat face.' Donna blew a raspberry.

'Hoy! No being mean on our birthday,' Melissa scolded, but Nadia and Evie giggled at Donna and Donna smirked back.

Pearl parted her shaggy, black ringlets from over her face. She lifted her nose into the air so her hair would hang back and stay back. She looked to Mizuki for encouragement who nodded impatiently. *Will someone just get on with it.*

'And I . . . um. . . I like it here because there ain't no school.' Pearl's contribution gained enthusiastic applause.

'My turn! My turn! My name is Stephie. I mash dyes. And I help Freya in the bead shop and I know YaYa. I like being here because I hate Jody and Claire and Bronwyn and Lydia and . . .'

'You shouldn't say bad about them Helizone girls. They can't help being mean. It's 'cos they're sad,' said Joy, sighing with the effort of defending an enemy with whom she'd only shared a few breaths, 'My name's Joy and I'm six – oops – seven,' she giggled, slapping her hand over her mouth, 'and I was really brave hiding, poking the attackers in the night. Bronwyn Bowen pushed me off . . . I hurt my knees. And when I grow up I want to be a swimming teacher.'

'That's not a shop,' Donna pouted, 'You're supposed to tell us your work at Home Rock.'

'I'm Melissa. I'm a hairdresser. I like it here 'cos you're all my forever family.'

'My name is Donna. I'm a nurse. Now can we eat?'

'You aint no nurse!' Pearl mocked Donna's reaction to blood and gore, '*Ugh! That is sooo disgustable!*' then collapsed into fits of laughter.

'I don't care what you think,' Donna growled, ''cos really I'm a Searcher. I like being here because . . . I just do, bersept when a certain someone makes me out to be stupid when I'm not. It's good here because stinky Bradley is far away. And stinky Bradley's dad.' She snatched a fistful of berries and stuffed them into her mouth, 'and we're gonna die of utter starvation if you lot don't get on with it.'

'I'm Sparrow. I make fairy cakes,' said Sparrow, blinking her bulbous eyes, hoping she'd said something acceptable.

'Mud cakes more like,' Donna mumbled through her mouthful. She rolled her eyes at Mizuki to hurry up and put a stop to this nonsense.

'I'm Freya. I teach mat-weaving, roof-making and bug disposal. And sometimes I run the bead shop. I like being here because it is Home Rock, and Home Rock is mega. Also, Evie and Nadia run a brill zoo. They never moan or cry. And you,' she pointed (not unkindly) to the Silent One, 'got the special skill of making jewellery. You poke holes in seeds and stuff and thread them on string, right? And you make dyes. You're s'posed to be a Digger, but you don't dig much considering you're an actual Digger.'

Mizuki stood up with ballerina-like grace. 'I'm Mizuki. I'm a Searcher and a Thinker-Upper. I like being here because people aren't s'posed to live inside bricks, not seeing their neighbours. Before, I thought jungles were dangerous but none of us have been attacked here. Not by animals. Okay, you can eat now.'

Everyone fell on the food. Everyone, that is, except Katey and Roxy who nudged each other. 'They forgot to do us,' whispered Katey.

Roxy smiled. She leant into Katey's ear and whispered, 'My name's Roxy and I like being here because I don't have to do no slave stuff for Bronwyn no more.' She reached over for a sweet banana; 'It's okay, Katey, I don't mind not saying my thing to all of them girls. It's only been a fun kind of a game for our birthday.'

But Katey wasn't smiling. She was watching Mizuki's every move.

As soon as they'd finished eating, Freya jumped up onto the rock, avoiding the crumbs and dribbles of fruits. 'And now, ladies and gentlemen, now for the grand opening of the magnificent, the wonderous, the brilliant - birthday presents!' She lifted Donna's bag above her head, 'You must be dying to find out why this bag is the star of our table, so here comes the big reveal. Ta-dah! Stand up - not you, Donna Moore, you . . .'

The Silent One heaved herself up, then exhausted, dropped her arms to her sides. Sweat trickled down her forehead onto her flushed cheeks. She hated every day being a sick day. She guessed it was cancer like her aunty had, eating her insides, making her want to throw up or curl up and die. She prayed to God for a doctor to parachute in and give her chemo like her grandma had. Melissa cared the most, but she couldn't give chemo even if she'd wanted to.

Freya was saying something. 'One for each of you - because our friend,' she pointed to the Silent One, 'made all these jewels.' Freya pulled necklace after necklace from Donna's bag, like magic. Stunning, unique strings of bead and bone, feather and fur, shiny, matt, mottled, natural colours or dyed. Gasps from each child who bent their neck to receive their gift.

'Awesome!'

'My favourite thing ever.'

'Happy birthday to you,' repeated Freya, solemn as a priest. Little by little the Silent One edged backwards, to stand in a less conspicuous place.

When each creation had been admired and some had cried with joy and vowed to keep their special gift for ever and ever, Roxy couldn't help squealing. She rushed over to the Silent One, flung her arms around her neck and clung on, whispering, 'Thank you, thank you.' One by one the others stepped forward to hug the creator of their gift. The Silent One stoically bore the ordeal without pushing anyone away or returning their affection. It stole her breath to be shown such love.

The sun burned overhead. 'Let's go swimming!' someone shouted. Nadia and Evie rushed to check that their bugs had plenty of shade and water before joining the troop skipping and singing, joyful for necklaces, joyful for family. Birds of paradise flew overhead while all around, butterflies, bees and dragonflies busied themselves. The splash of falling water promised a glorious afternoon ahead.

*

At the pool, the necklaces were removed to be hung like trophies on a bamboo stick that Freya fixed horizontally between two branches. Those that could, swam, while the others splashed and ducked and somersaulted and kicked the blue-green water.

In her dirt-streaked t-shirt and off-cut tracky bottoms, Mizuki lay back. As she was wondering where the atmosphere stopped and the universe began, a tiny speck moved through the sky. A flash of sunlight hit it, diamond on sapphire. Inside the speck would be pilots, stewards, businessmen, parents – most probably social workers, guardians, carers. 'Can they see me lying here so far below them?' she yawned. Mizuki stretched as she stood up and dived into the water. The shock of the cold caused her to gasp and shoot to the surface.

That guy said in assembly, "Never swim in reservoirs. The shock of the cold can kill you, even when you think you'll be fine." She hauled herself onto a warm rock to recover as the others splashed in the shallows, pushing their faces under, blowing bubbles, gasping, screaming, chasing. She searched for the diamond, but it had vanished without so much as a farewell contrail. Those passengers would soon disembark, greet families, friends, colleagues, all hugs and handshakes, then home to hot food, showers and beds with clean, white sheets.

The afternoon consisted of Blind-Man's-Buff and Hunt-the-Thimble. Then charades, or gymnastics with cartwheels and handstands. The girls danced and sang and acted. They were judges on Strictly, giving points and reasons, arguing, flouncing, sulking, cheering like real TV stars.

All except Sparrow. That scruffy little oddity daydreamed her life away, stamping her wet feet onto the hot stone, fascinated by how fast the sun stole her footprints. And Mizuki observed Sparrow with her oversized, odd-coloured eyes and tufty hair. Sweet, but different. A fair exchange.

13

Gifts from the Skellington-ghosts

After the party, the trek home seemed like a marathon. Mizuki's long legs set the fastest pace. After retrieving their necklaces, she'd rushed ahead, holding Sparrow's hand. The emu-child skipped along beside her singing nursery-rhymes in her own little world. The rest followed at various distances; Melissa, then Freya with Katey, Roxy, Joy, then Stephie. There followed Nadia and Evie, holding hands, gabbling intensely to each other as if they were the only humans on earth. The stragglers were Donna Moore, then the Silent One. Way, way behind, Pearl dragged her feet.

Pearl, wrapped in her own world, tugged her black locks until her skull stung, while singing 'Somewhere Over the Rainbow,' and 'If You're Happy and You Know It Clap Your Hands' as loud she liked with no one to tell her to shut up. 'I've just been to my first ever birthday party for me,' she told the butterflies, 'and, see this necklace? It's the best present in the whole wide world!' Yes, some bitchy insect had bitten her bald patch and yes, she'd scratched it to bleeding, but her euphoria was such that she'd hardly noticed. Something wonderful had happened inside her skin and she relished the feel of it.

'My tummy's laughin' but my lips aint movin',' she said. 'I love bein' with my forever family, us all walkin' home after a looong day in the sunshine. The sun sinkin' down down like a slooow yoyo what's gonna smash on them spiky mountains and bust in a billion bits, and all them bits is gonna bounce right back up into the sky. Whoosh! And when the sun gets bust, it splats all over that big sky making itsy-bitsy-baby stars, then some poor guy's gotta sit up all night puzzling out how them star bits fix back together to make one big sun again, right in time for breakfast.'

'Oomph!' Pearl crashed into the Silent One, knocking into her, nearly pushing her over. The Silent One reached back and grabbed Pearl's hand to steady herself. She would not let go and clung on for dear life.

Two skeletons had been dumped across the track. They were splayed out face down on a disgusting sheet, crossed over each other, their clothes ripped and blackened, their bone-white ankles and feet sticking out at awkward angles. Pearl shuddered. Drops of sweat rolled down her back. Her hand in the older child's felt clammy. Both girls gripped on tight. Neither dared move.

Then deep in the undergrowth something huge rustled. Branches rattled. They heard feet running, loud breaths panting, a shushing, shush, shush sound like sea on shingle.

'Lions,' gulped Pearl, imagining sabre-toothed tigers snarling, with vicious, curved teeth. Shoulder to shoulder the girls pressed against each other. Whatever it was was moving away, trampling heavily, snorting, tittering. Then nothing.

At last Pearl whispered, 'That there's the pilot.' She pointed at the skeleton in uniform, 'so that other one's gotta be the guardian.'

The Silent One was no longer interested in the bones, but in a grey, plastic box with handles each side, and a lid. Pearl looked around for a grown-up to help, or at least Mizuki. Why hadn't the others stopped for this? How come they'd walked on? How come they'd missed seeing it?

'Not funny,' Pearl called into the jungle. Her strength returned. 'You think this is some kind of a sick joke? Well, we aint pissing ourselves just so you can have a laugh. Shove off, shove off, whoever you are. Go, crawl home to your ratty flea-pit hole where you belong.' Prising her hand from the Silent One, Pearl side-stepped the bodies and bent down to investigate the box. It smelt noxious, like tyres set alight on the common. On the top of the box was a magazine for girls with the words, *'Animagic with Free Gifts!'* The cover design was of a white rabbit splattered with shocking pink hearts. Pearl stumbled over the words, 'A free hedgehog puzzle for you to cut out and keep. Wow!' She hugged the magazine to her chest, 'Mine,' she said so no one would snatch it away.

The Silent One was in no mood to compete for a magazine aimed at infants. She unclipped the lid of the box. Inside were two packets of biros, pencils with rubbers, a multi-pack of sharpeners, several ring-bound notepads, two mosquito nets (unopened), a box of blackcurrant-flavoured Dioralyte, and one bottle of bright red nail varnish.

'Treasure!' Pearl licked her lips. The Silent One replaced the lid. She tried to lift the box but it felt awkward against her tummy. She signalled to Pearl to help her. Pearl reluctantly placed the magazine onto the lid and grabbed a handle. Between them it was a light and easy load.

As they walked, Pearl considered the find, voicing her theories out loud, 'If you ask me, the pilot and guardian were looking for us Home Rocks all over, doing their responsibility. They brung us presents for our birthday, but when they couldn't find us, they got hungrier and hungrier 'til they dropped utterly dead and their skin fell totally off.' Pearl contemplated this for a while, then, 'Actually, they wasn't real skellingtons, they was skellington-*ghosts*. They spied on all them girls passing, then quickly lay down to stop us so we'd see this present. They'll go back to haunting, see? Getting this birthday stuff to us was pretty good considering they're dead. Did you know, skellington-ghosts can fly back to England in five seconds without an actual aeroplane?'

By the time Pearl and the Silent One arrived at Home Rock, supper had been spread on the table beneath the soft light, and the girls were gathering round. Pearl and the Silent One plonked the box at Mizuki's feet.

Pearl said, 'Here's a birthday pressie from the skellington-ghosts and I've bagged the mag with a hedgehog puzzle for just me to cut out and keep.' The Home Rock girls piled in, squealing with delight, but Mizuki simply smiled.

'Now,' Mizuki said, 'can someone please pull the light or it'll go out.' Melissa reset the mechanism. Huge insects with clacking wings bounced off it as a million moths danced. The light shone on the sun-browned children, catching the whites of their eyes and teeth.

Mizuki beamed, 'Great day?'

'Yes! Yes!' they cheered.

'As you see, a brilliant thing just happened. I wonder, who asked for notebooks and pens?' Evie and Nadia waved and jumped up. Mizuki winked, 'Later, later. Tomorrow these will be yours. Freya, the nail varnish is for you. Pearl, you get to read the magazine first because you found it, then *you* can have it,' Mizuki pointed at the Silent One who was, for the first time ever, sitting at the table and eating with the group, 'then everyone gets a turn. Keep it dry. All of us should read this every day, or else when we get saved, *if* we are ever saved, we won't know how to read, and Ethan Cook will say we're stupid and send us back to you-know-where.'

'Where's Sparrow?' Roxy asked, looking about.

'Toilet,' Mizuki said, quick as a flash.

'Can I have a blackcurrant thingy?' Donna asked, eyeing the Dioralyte.

'They're only for if you're sick, having a runny tummy, but maybe we could share just one between us – you know – have a little lick for the flavour, as a birthday treat before bed. The mozzy nets are for sleeping under. They ping open easy, and you crawl in through a flap. There's not enough so take turns, or else you can squash in and share. Up to you.'

Later, when the others were asleep, Katey decided to confront Mizuki. As she approached Mizuki's hut, she hesitated because Mizuki was standing alone, wiping her face with her hands. Was Mizuki crying? Hard to tell in the semi-dark. Katey cleared her throat softly.

Mizuki turned on her a little too quickly, 'What now?'

'That stuff's from Bronwyn Bowen.'

'Don't be a noodle. Bronwyn doesn't give nothing to no one.'

'So where did it come from? And don't say ghosts or skellingtons, 'cos I don't believe in them.'

'Who cares what *you* believe. At my Thinking to Help shop they told me what they wanted. I got them what they wanted. Everyone's happy.'

'Not everyone's happy.'

'Trust you to be a moaner. If you're jealous you should try asking for something for yourself.'

'I don't want nothing, bersept one thing.'

'What's that?'

'You have to keep your promise.'

'What promise?'

'You promised you'd be my big sister forever.'

'I only said it to make you happy.'

'Liar. You was being real when you said it, but

you're not my sister 'cos you don't treat me special no more.'

A large bird swooped low over Home Rock. Mizuki felt the breeze of it, but when she glanced up it had gone. Wings. *If only we had wings.* Mizuki sighed, 'The sister thing was for one day only. I never promised forever. And I warned you not to trust me.'

'Right then,' Katey huffed, 'tomorrow morning I'm telling on you.'

'Say what you like.'

'I'm telling about Sparrow.'

'You know nothing. Sparrow makes her own choices. She wanted to go, so there's nothing to tell.'

Katey hadn't banked on Mizuki being so matter of fact. It was confusing. *Had Sparrow decided to go back to the Helizone of her own free will?* All the same, tomorrow the others would hear all about their perfect, precious Mizuki, then they'd hate their plastic-box-birthday-presents and only love their necklaces. A mosquito whined too close for comfort. Katey slapped her own head hoping to kill it. She checked her hand for blood, 'You 'sposed to be guarding us tonight?'

'No. It's Melissa. Go bother her if you want to gas all night. She doesn't stay awake, but it's up to you. Do what you like. Try her. She knows as well as I do there's no point guarding Home Rock if we're never going to be attacked again.'

'How do *you* know no one's going to 'ttack us?'

'I told you, it's Melissa's turn to guard, so shut up going on and on at me. You don't have the foggiest. Buzz the hell off. Go!'

189

'I'm never going to let you be my sister again. You and me's divorced. Dee Eye Vee Orsed. Forever. I hate your guts. I hate you! I wasn't going to tell the others 'bout Sparrow, but I am. I will. You've got no chance never again with me being your sister. Buzz the hell off your stupid self.' Katey stomped to her bug-ridden bed and threw herself down with as much drama as she could muster. She raged and sobbed but Mizuki didn't follow to offer any sympathy. Katey yelled, 'I always knew you hated me!' She slammed her mouth shut and listened, eyes wide, for any kind of response. Nothing. Nothing. Nothing. Even in the jungle, apologies and forgiveness were the stuff of daydreams and fairy-tales.

*

Breakfast, but not as usual. A heavy atmosphere hung over the camp. Even the morning mist was slow to lift. Katey wished she could be bothered to blurt out 'Sparrow's missing!' but it seemed like too much of an effort. In any case, Sparrow wasn't the only one absent from the table.

The Silent One had crossed the expanse of Home Rock, up and away from the toilet to the mossy area. She knelt down, pressing her palms into the springy greenness, relishing the cool water soothing her puffy hands, then she ambled back to her hut which had deteriorated into a mess of bamboo and twigs and layers of leaves. She sunk onto her nest, holding her stomach, rocking and groaning.

Also, Freya had a fever. She'd been shouting in her sleep but now she'd gone quiet and no one could wake her. Mizuki sat on the ground, leaning against a rock, peeling the knobbly skin off some fig-like fruits. Katey mooched about, giving Mizuki the evil eye, but Mizuki never acknowledged her presence.

All at once, Pearl and Donna stood up together as if they'd planned it (which they had). Pearl opened her mouth, but she was giggling so much that Donna was forced to speak for her.

'First of all,' - Donna raised her voice to make them listen - 'it's been raining too much what's making us ill, and so me an' Pearl want a proper roof. We *demand* a roof, don't we Pearl?'

'And walls,' Pearl tittered nervously. She glanced at Donna who nudged her, *go on, keep going!*

'And proper hot chicken for dinner,' Donna blurted, licking her lips.

'Roast potatoes!' Pearl rubbed her stomach in circles and rolled her eyes. 'Mmmm.'

'Apple pie and custard!' shouted Stephie, because something was fun again.

'Burger and chips!'

'Ice-cream!'

It hadn't been Donna's plan to let the whole wish thing run away from her. She cut in, 'And guess what? You'll never guess, so I'm telling you and this is actually true. Pearl thinks Sparrow's been snaffled by them skellington-ghosts and I believe her. Them spooks got Sparrow right good and proper, don't you know.'

Mizuki's lips tightened. Her chin lifted sharply. She stiffened her back. Katey read her body language. She sat bolt upright to watch for more signs of guilt. The others looked this way and that for Sparrow, shaking their heads, believing, yet not believing, then believing again. Even Roxy and Stephie, who hadn't bothered to double-check on Sparrow last night, rushed over to their shambolic hut and, too right, Sparrow was nowhere to be seen.

Melissa said, 'She was with us all day yesterday. Who walked back with her?'

Donna shifted uncomfortably, 'She was up the front with Mizuki. I was on my own behind. I'm sure Sparrow was with Mizuki the whole time.'

Roxy said, 'We never seed her go to her bed. It was too dark.'

Stephie tried asking The Silent One, 'Have you seen Sparrow? Did the skellington-ghosts get her?' but speaking was futile. The girl simply curled more tightly into herself. Nadia and Evie shrugged. They had stuff to do. Creatures to check on. A day to enjoy with new notebooks and pencils to love.

Katey's words cut into the conversation, five words, stubborn as truth, 'Mizuki sold Sparrow to Bronwyn.' There. Said it. It felt good to hear everyone gasp.

'No way!' Pearl shouted, 'I saw them skellington-ghosts by my very own eyes. They was dead bodies with no hair on, only clothes like what pilots and guardians have, and with claws for feet. They snaffled Sparrow and flied off!' She flexed her fingers, twisting them to show she was remembering yesterday for real, that this was no lie.

Katey jumped up, 'Where do you think we got all that stuff? Do you think them notebooks landed from outer space? What about the nail varnish? Does Father Christmas go in the jungle when it's not even Christmas just to give kids nail varnish? No. He only does snow places like Lapland and England. Bronwyn Bowen wants her slaves back. *Bronwyn* gave Mizuki that stuff off the heli.' Blank faces all round. They didn't get it. They couldn't believe what they had not seen with their own eyes. Katey took a deep breath, 'Mizuki sold Sparrow to be Bronwyn's slave.'

Mizuki tutted loudly, shaking her head in open denial, asserting her leadership. The owner of the 'Thinking to Help' shop that rarely opened, the one with all the answers was shaking her head. Mizuki's word was her bond. When Mizuki said she could solve a problem, she'd been good as her word. Her word was truth.

Katey's eyes narrowed. Her shoulders dropped. She lowered her voice, 'I followed Mizuki in the night. I overheard her and Bronwyn Bowen talking. Deciding stuff by the lake . . .'

Slavery and betrayal. Too heavy to handle. Heavy is for grown-ups. The little ones could not, would not, understand. Nadia and Evie left the table. Roxy and Stephie resumed their conversation about food. Melissa wandered Home Rock, lethargically calling Sparrow's name with no sense of panic. Mizuki stretched and yawned. She stood up with a smile, and ruffled Katey's hair.

'You've been having nightmares, little sister. It's tough out here. Be careful little ears what you hear. Be careful little eyes what you see.

Three days later, Freya had fully recovered from her fever. The Home Rock girls once more trekked to the waterfall-pool to swim. Pearl rushed ahead to show them the place of the skeletons, but the trees and shrubs had changed, or else she'd been dreaming. Pearl found not a shred of evidence to prove she and the Silent One had seen 'skellington-ghosts'.

*

The new varnish dried up. 'You stupid, stupid stuff!' fumed the Day-Keeper, stabbing the brush violently against the rock. The splayed dregs looked more like fading dahlias than days. Mizuki had upset Freya, refusing to admire her second row.

'But I'm doing it perfect!' Freya insisted, 'Dead straight. One dot for one day like you asked so we'd know how long . . .'

'Don't you get it? We're stuck here forever. What does it matter how long we've been here? Or how old we are? Who cares? Not me.' Nothing mattered any more, least of all time. The rhythm of Home Rock spoke for itself: eat, work, rest, play, fight, forgive, story, sleep. Past, present and future were constructs from Before where a red dot on a calendar signified an appointment at a contact centre, followed by disappointment when the parent, instead of playing with their child, flicked through their iPhone or hung about outside smoking.

Nadia and Evie obsessed over their zoo, frustrated yet entertained by the unpredictability of their livestock. Some creatures bit others - devoured them even - while others cannibalised their own species. It was normal to discover several bugs or small creatures maimed or dead. The girls learnt that caterpillars had to be fed the right leaves, eating only the kind they'd been found on, and that snakes easily escaped from every container, and that rats were happy to stick around if left to their own devices. These docile rabbit-sized rodents generally appeared after mealtimes to clear the scraps.

Melissa, Mizuki and Freya concentrated on building huts that were a massive improvement on the originals, because a girl could stand up inside and move around, while the rest of the Searchers and Diggers worked together on the bamboo pipeline imagining, hoping, believing that eventually this would successfully flush the toilet. They split bamboo with blunt knives and nail-files, splicing the ends then inserting a metal shard, striking this with a stone until the bamboo split lengthwise. By trial and error, they fit one length of half-pipe into another, tying them tight, laying them on upright 'posts' with a shallow drop from one to the next. When it rained the water flowed, but when it poured the channel overflowed.

Teeth-cleaning. They chewed coconut flesh or tasteless, stringy bamboo then spat it out. Nadia, Evie and Stephie lost milk teeth, but to their dismay no tooth-fairy visited Home Rock and their tiny teeth were lost.

'Tell stories!' cried Roxy and Stephie most evenings. Donna or Pearl especially relished themes such as 'The Horriblest Person You Know,' or 'The Scariest Monsters You Ever Saw.' They'd all talk at once, sharing anger, confusion, fear of abandonment, laughter, tears, hatred. Stories helped them sleep despite the sound of distant drumming, intimidating screams or terrifying yells from across the jungle. Stories helped young minds handle the Helizone, a terrible place to where, inexplicably, Sparrow had chosen to return.

*

Roxy disappeared.

Mizuki said, 'Listen up you lot, Roxy says she misses you but she missed Sparrow more, so she's gone to live with her. She hopes you don't mind but she's taken the grey box with her. She says Bronwyn's not as bad as you make out and Home Rock's boring. Helizone girls have more fun, chanting and marching and partying. And the cage isn't a prison, but a safe place to sleep.'

'But why didn't Roxy say good-bye to me?' Stephie wailed.

'Because she knew you'd do exactly that. Cry. You'd be sad. She knew you'd try to stop her. Cheer up, kiddo,' Mizuki wiped Stephie's eyes with the back of her hand, 'I've got some special treats for you. Here look, loads and loads of string. Useful for all sorts.

And safety pins. And even more amazing – follow me!'
Mizuki led the way into the undergrowth and pulled
on a piece of rope. Whatever was at the end of the rope
weighed a total ton.

'Help me, Katey!' Mizuki laughed, but it was Pearl
and Donna who rushed to her side. With all their
might, they tugged until they fell backwards in a heap.
From the undergrowth, they'd dragged a length of
khaki-coloured tarpaulin that Mizuki, with the help
of Lydia, Claire and Jody, had hauled little by little,
night by night, along the short cut to Home Rock.

'It's waterproof!' Mizuki announced proudly.

'Where . . ?'

'Ask no questions, tell no lies . . .' Mizuki tipped
the side of her nose with one finger.

'Put it back,' Katey pursed her lips. 'I know what
you did to get that. We all do. You traded Stephie's best
friend for that smelly piece of junk. We don't want it.'

Mizuki, lithe and strong, loosened her hair and
leapt nimbly to the top of Hog Rock, 'Let's take a vote.
I'll count to three and shout "vote." If you want dry
nights under a proper shelter plus a waterproof roof to
collect rain, jump up and down and shout "Yes!" but
if you want to help me drag this thing all the way back
to where it came from, say "No!" Altogether, one, two,
three, vote!'

'Yes! Yes!' squealed most of the girls. Mizuki cocked
her head and raised her eyebrows at Katey. See?

Katey stamped her foot. 'No!' she cried, 'Bring
back Roxy. And I vote for Sparrow.'

Mizuki said, 'But you can't force them to live here if

they don't want to. That's just being cruel. And there's, um . . . there's a reward for those who voted yes.' Mizuki held something high above her head. They couldn't work out what it was. A plastic package full of shiny orange, yellow and red rods. Mizuki tossed down the package for the girls to squabble over.

'Lighters!' Pearl squealed.

'Duh, we don't smoke,' muttered Donna, disappointed that it wasn't sweets.

'But we do like fire,' said Mizuki, sitting down with her feet dangling over their heads. 'You asked for roast potatoes? How about cooked fish and those potato thingies the Diggers dug up, that aren't real potatoes, but nearly are. We can cook those and see how they taste! So, no, I haven't been sneaking off to meet Bronwyn or whatever porky-pies Katey wants to feed you, I've been out with Melissa. We've been fishing in the lake with the mozzy nets. We trapped some massive fish, then built a fire at the Flower Palace. It's all ready and we're going to cook fish. Come on little sisters, let's have some fun!'

Most of the girls, visualising breaded fishfingers, chased after Mizuki. Katey trailed behind, unwilling to be alone - and she was curious. She'd never seen a real fire, not even on bonfire night. At Castle Care resi, fishfingers went under the grill, and no children were ever allowed in the kitchen because sharp knives cut. Watching the Home Rock girls cook their first hot meal wouldn't hurt.

*

The audience grimaced and groaned as Mizuki stuck each fish through from mouth to tail with a water-soaked splinter of bamboo as if she'd done it all her life. Some fish were slimy and brown with flat faces and bulging eyes, others were smaller fry with green scales, pointy fins and triangular tails. They'd suffocated on the beach, tangled in mosquito nets, attracting hoards of flies before Mizuki wrapped them in a sweatshirt and lugged them to the Flower Palace.

Mizuki lit the wood fire. It burned fast and smelt sensational. The unpredictable sparks and crackles were as scary and brilliant as a house on fire. Mizuki piled on larger twigs and insect-ridden rotten wood. The girls gathered in the sunlight, fascinated by the smoke as it whirled skyward. Mizuki twirled the fish on their skewers to prevent the bamboo burning. Everyone had a go, apart from Nadia and Evie who were wary of the flames.

'Ugh!' Donna tittered, 'See all them eyes going white.' A fish eye popped out and fell into the embers, hissing to nothing. The younger girls squealed and clung to each other, wondering when the fish would morph into a battered brown blob from the Hungry Haddock. Instead, their scaly skins blackened and blistered.

'Turn, turn!' Mizuki shouted, 'Lift them off the flame. Hold them up in the hot smoke!' As the fish cooked they fell apart and were dropped onto flat stones or large rubbery leaves. Even without breadcrumbs or batter, they smelt divine. No one had thought to gut them.

Donna was the first to pick at the overcooked flesh, careful to avoid the heads and tails. Her eyes almost popped out of *her* head with the dizzying shock of saltiness and mouth-watering flesh bursting with flavour. Everyone fell upon the fish, picking with their fingers, stuffing hot, white flakes into their mouths and blowing out the smoky heat. They ate until only one fish remained.

'Mizuki did this for us,' said Melissa quietly, 'and I love her.'

Katey's mouth watered, but she held back. It felt wrong to be excited about food when Sparrow and Roxy were crying in a cage or fetching gravel and being slapped by Jody and Claire. She imagined them calling, 'Katey, Katey, set us free!' She felt the same powerlessness as she had at Castle Care, watching TV ads about starving children, thinking, 'I'm a kid with no money and no mobile phone to text 'FEED.' X-Factor came back on; Katey was expected to forget crying babies and decide who was the best singer. Staff never discussed starving children or refugees. Katey wondered, 'Don't they care those poor little babies are dying?'

Katey gulped on a mouthful of saliva. She glanced at Mizuki, *'I'm not being part of your filthy deal.'* Their eyes locked. Katey's eyes narrowed. Mizuki shrugged. She bunched her fingertips against her lips, mouthing, 'Eat.' Katey shook her head and pursed her lips all the more tightly.

'It's okay,' Mizuki soothed. *Eat, eat, it won't hurt.* Katey gulped again. Under the sun, sweating beside the fire, she couldn't take her eyes off the hot food and betraying her longing.

Melissa dropped the last fish onto a stone. It split open, spilling its steaming white flesh in all directions. The smell oozed deliciousness. Everyone, including the Silent One, had had their fill and were wiping their fingers on their clothes and flapping away flies.

Katey stepped into the steam, closed her eyes and inhaled. Plunging both hands deep into the body of the fish, she scooped out the flesh and crammed it into her mouth, accepting the blistering pain as punishment for her failure to resist. Strength flooded her body, goodness rushed to her fingertips and down to her toes, and she experienced an overwhelming 'out-of-body' clarity. The leaves on the trees were greener green, the sky bluer blue, and the colours of the birds and flowers popped like fireworks. *Before*, in England, nothing, nothing, nothing had ever tasted so perfect.

'Soon,' announced Mizuki, 'we're gonna have a real party and not just us, there's going to be guests.' Everyone laughed. She was joking, right? Guests? Just joking like a grown-up promising stuff that never comes true. But Mizuki was different, better than any mother. She could be trusted to keep her word.

14

手伝 Only the Dead Miss Parties

The 'Thinking to Help' store was open for business. Mizuki stood, arms folded, beside her fading sign, watching the others washing, braiding and beading hair, or swapping ragged clothes to wear as protection from bites. Across the clearing, Stephie and the Silent One squished seeds and berries and petals with stones, experimenting to create pure colours instead of the usual shades of sludge.

'If anyone wants anything shout now or I'm going swimming,' called Mizuki, 'Use me or lose me.'

'You know what?' said Pearl, self-consciously preening her freshly-braided hair. Pearl's wiry hair stayed intact for the longest time. Dark stubble was growing in her previously bald patches. She constantly stroked this new hair, checking it was still there, fearful it would fall out in her hand.

'Do I know what, what?' Mizuki slapped at a tormenting fly.

'I want . . .' Pearl hesitated - *Mizuki can get anything.*

Mizuki works magic.

Pearl's eyes glinted, 'I want . . .' Suddenly she was shoved sideways with such force she put out an arm to break her fall. Katey had rushed and pushed Pearl with all her might and now she stood, a furious referee, piggy-in-the-middle between Pearl and Mizuki. Katey looked from one to the other.

Pearl lowered her shoulders, her nostrils flared, 'I said, I want . . .'

Katey yelled in Pearl's face, 'No, no, no! You want nothing, do you hear me? You want nothing.'

'But I do, see. I want a pretty dress to go with my hair. I never had a pretty dress, and now you've bust my arm.' Pearl grimaced, twisting her face to exaggerate the pain. She massaged her shoulder and when, for a fleeting moment, Katey showed concerned and seemed about to apologise, Pearl edged towards Mizuki. *My Mizuki. Mizuki and me. This is between us, not you. Mizuki is the Thinking to Help person and you can't stop her.*

Katey screamed, 'You want a dress? What for? What if one of us disappears just 'cos Pearly-Whirly wants a stupid dress? What if Mizuki says, "Here's your dress," but then you look for Stephie and she's gone? Or Melissa? Or Freya even? Pick someone. Who, out of all of us, would you sell to Bronwyn Bowen, just so's you can get your dress?'

Mizuki shook her head at Katey, tutting like an exasperated school-teacher or a long-suffering parent whose wayward child refuses to 'get' it. Pearl stood side by side with Mizuki. She took a deep breath for an

203

unplanned speech, but she'd always struggled to form important sentences. Pearl flapped her hands, shooing Katey to shut her up, as her mother had done to her when she was small. Very small.

The last time Pearl saw her mother, the huge woman was flapping in her face and scratched her cheeks. *Shut up shut up shut up shut up*. The toddler tried to please but opened her mouth and talked gobbledegook and woke up in hospital.

Here in the jungle. Pearl had plenty of words to say. Grown-up words to keep herself safe, 'You shut your flamin' fat face, Katey, stupid know-all. None of us is gonna disappear, but if anyone's gonna get sold I hope it's you. I'm sick of your dripping about, being mean to Mizuki, making us miserable. Moan. Moan. Moan. That's all you do. What do you ever give us? Nuffin. Totally nuffin. I hope Mizuki sells you forever.' Pearl reached out to touch Mizuki's arm. *It's me and her against you. This is us. Mizuki an' me.*

Mizuki stepped away.

Instantly Pearl dropped her hand, hoping no one had noticed her trying to win the heart of the bigger girl. Pearl shrugged off the rejection. *What do I care? Everyone knows Mizuki's not a real mother.*

*

Mizuki stood on Hog Rock to summon the Home Rock girls. A couple of fowl and a rat were scratching around the base of the rock, cleaning up after breakfast.

A flock of parakeets dipped and screeched overhead, then vanished. Cicadas stridulated, scraping their forewings against the back of their heads.

Joy popped out from beneath a mass of towering leaves, holding a miniscule, iridescent beetle. 'Evie, Nadia, see what I've found for you!' and they rushed over, pencils and notebook at the ready.

Freya, loaded from arm to chin with freshly stripped bamboo, dumped the lot by a dilapidated hut. 'Your turn for a new roof, Donna!' she called cheerfully. The reconstructed huts were almost waterproof, with tightly-bound canes and neatly overlapping leaves.

Melissa was sweeping bugs from the huts with a bunch of twigs tied to a cane, when Mizuki called. 'Coming?' she asked Donna, and everyone congregated at the foot of Hog Rock.

Everyone apart from the Silent One, who languished alone inside her hut. She'd commandeered a mosquito net to herself, despite the agreement to take turns. Inside the net, she clutched her belly and rocked and groaned. No one, not even her fellow bead-dyer, Stephie, could console her or coax her out of her misery.

'Today's the day,' Mizuki announced. No one interrupted. They knew they'd be given their say; it was how things were done at Hog Rock. 'I promised you a party with guests and today's the day. Going to be mega fun. But first there's work to do. If you do well, lots of great stuff will come your way.'

'Great stuff? Huh! She means a dress,' Katey hissed at Pearl.

Pearl grinned, 'Yay!' She clicked her fingers, pointed and winked at Katey.

'Okay, so food is the number one thing we'll need, but don't collect any until after the rain stops or the fruit will go soggy. Bring food in lunch boxes, but if you don't have a box, use the rush baskets Freya's been making. I've already set the nets in the lake so there'll be fish, but if we catch any of those massive brown ones, we'll chuck them back 'cos their skin's a bit thick. You liked the smaller ones more. Pearl, Melissa, Donna – you're going to rustle up some great pressies for our guests to take home. Pick out the best necklaces, bracelets, anklets, earrings and stuff for hair braids. Freya, bring that clever sleeping mat, the one that rolls up. Can you trim the edges a bit? And shake out the bugs. How did you get on with our new idea for a fish-holder? Remember what you did before - a branch with three sticking-outty bits, like a big fork? Pull the ends together, and weave little sticks between. A bit like a tennis racket. You made three already? Brilliant!'

'I soaked them in the marsh, like you said, to wet them so they won't burn over the fire.'

'Good one, Freya. Right, Nadia and Evie – here's a challenge for you. I want you to take a mozzy net, pop it open and fill it with as many butterflies as you can. Be super gentle with their wings. I don't want them hurt. You can do it. I trust you.' Nadia and Evie's faces lit up.

'Nim com elpus?' Nadia gabbled to Stephie as she grabbed Evie's hand. Mizuki shook her head. 'Sorry, Stephie can't help. She's going to collect flowers to put in a vase . . .' Seeing Nadia's crestfallen face, Mizuki added, 'but when she's done maybe.'

'What about her?' Melissa gestured to where the Silent One was sighing, moaning, retching.

Joy whispered, wide-eyed, 'Is she gonna die?'

Mizuki shrugged. Her dad had died of cancer but that didn't mean she knew what to do about it. Death usually happened on flat-screens where it couldn't be smelt or felt, where it could be switched off and ignored. Plus, the grown-ups on the heli died and turned into skeletons and it was as if they'd never been real people. 'If that girl is dying she's taking ages about it. Today's about living!' Mizuki punched the sky, 'Katey, come with me. You can help build the fire.' Mizuki sprung down the rock sure-footed as a mountain goat.

Katey followed, but she fumed under her breath, 'I'm gonna wreck your fun.'

'You didn't ask if we've got any questions,' piped Pearl, ''cos I've got one. Who's the guests, then?' The others laughed because they knew Mizuki was only joking about guests. Guests were pretend.

'Bronwyn, of course - and her friends,' said Mizuki. She wandered over to Stephie's shop to find some dye to use as make-up. Pearl rushed after her, whining, 'But they attacked us. I peed my pants. You didn't know I did that, did you? And they put Joy in a cage. What if they kill us? I'm not going to no party if Bronwyn's coming. You're not listening, 'Zuki. What

207

if them guests stab us or something?'

Melissa and Freya exchanged terrified glances. They'd managed to ignore the Helizone out of existence. Now, not only were they talking about their enemies, they'd soon be hanging out with them. 'Bronwyn Bowen's coming,' they whispered.

But a party! A real, live, being-invited party with real guests. Who in their right minds would miss that kind of fun? Only the dead miss parties.

*

On the shingle beach, Mizuki and Katey built a low, circular wall with pebbles and small boulders. Katey refused to speak, channelling her fury into the sweat of the work. The regular daily downpour signed off with swirls of warm mist evaporating from the lake. A fish jumped clean out of the water and landed with a splash. The girls looked up to see only ripples. A heron stalked the far edges of the lake, jabbing at frogs and small water-birds.

The girls gathered sticks and leaves for the fire, avoiding spiders, "snippy" bugs and hairy caterpillars that made their skin itch. It occurred to Mizuki that green moss didn't burn, so she'd thought of using a layer of moss as a kind of grill-pan on which to place the fish. She selected half a doormat-sized rectangle of moss and pulled it from its roots. It ripped easily from the ground. She rolled it up. 'Now for another wedge to go on top of the fish, like a lid. See how that goes.'

*

The Home Rock girls gathered tentatively on the shore of the gently lapping lake. They laid the fare on some rocks, covering it with leaves as protection from insects, birds and rodents. The usual terrapins cooled themselves just beneath the water, sticking out their scrawny necks and flaring their nostrils like nosy neighbours.

Mizuki muttered, 'We need music. I miss music. One thing our guests will bring is music.'

The girls scanned the jungle, checking for humans. Unlike the party in the Flower Palace, where the cooking of the fish had been fun, they felt exposed and vulnerable. Katey glared at Melissa, 'You're all going to pay for not believing me about Roxy and Sparrow.'

'What if . . ?' Melissa turned to Mizuki, 'What if Bronwyn kidnaps one of us? What if she's tricking us and this is a trap?'

Mizuki stiffened. Her head shook a warning, *Ssh! No sowing doubt and fear.*

Melissa continued, 'But will they be . . . all right with us?'

Donna overheard. If Melissa of all people was worried, there must be something to worry about. She edged closer, hoping to overhear more, to be the one to initiate an open discussion about the risk of the guests, but unsure of what she'd get away with. Mizuki might bite her head off.

Nadia and Evie went in search of mini-beasts. They

209

squatted by the lake, turning stones and snatching up anything that scuttled. Not long ago, everyone wore trainers to protect their feet from cuts or stings but Nadia and Evie's feet were bare. Nadia's toes gripped the stones for balance. Evie's body had grown strong and lithe. They flashed their eyes at one another to signal a direction, or to communicate shock or puzzlement, excitement, even pain from a bite.

'Mind-texting,' marvelled Katey, who'd been watching them nearby. Instinct told Katey to look across the top of the unlit fire. Her eyes met Melissa's. Melissa held her stare and Katey understood her imperceptible nod, a softening of her cheek muscle, a flick of her eye in the direction of Mizuki then back to Katey. Aha! Katey smiled the faintest of a flicker so only Melissa would catch it. Melissa knew all about Mizuki's nasty game and, at last, Katey did not feel so alone.

When every task was done, from food, to butterflies, to seed-heads poking from the plastic-bottle vase, Mizuki spoke.

'Gather round, make a circle, come over here. Evie, Nadia. Stephie - what you up to? Join in. Everyone hold hands.'

Donna giggled. Mizuki's seriousness made it hard not to snort, 'Funny in my tummy.' She snorted in her throat, but no one giggled with her.

Freya glanced around, checking the fringes of the jungle for signs of Helizone aggression.

'Peace,' Mizuki began, reaching for the hand of Joy to her left and Stephie to her right. Another giggle from Donna. Stephie squeaked like a mouse then tittered. Donna said, 'Tee hee,' but Mizuki remained solemn. Donna sucked on her tongue, smirking, pretending to fight for self-control, wishing they'd laugh at her.

'I've been thinking,' Mizuki cleared her throat, 'that there's us at Home Rock and there's them in the Helizone which is all the people in our world. You've got to stop hoping to be saved if you see an aeroplane, because anyone inside is so high up they may as well be from another planet. They can't see us. To them, we're tiddlier than ants.' Flies buzzed around, attracted by the fishiness of Mizuki's skin and clothes.

Mizuki dropped hands with Joy and Steph, 'We're itty-bitty, tidgy-widgy midges.' She clapped her hands at a passing fly and killed it. 'We're nothing. No one's coming to get us.'

Freya shuffled uncomfortably. 'But, Mizuki,' she coughed a little, hardly daring to speak, 'That's okay, 'cos we don't want to be saved, not by no one.'

'But what about stinky toilets? I want proper toilets with flushing handles and soft toilet paper,' Donna grinned. *Finally, a proper argument.*

Melissa said, 'We all miss the toilets from Before, but remember what we did when we first arrived? We hid in the bushes. Had to check for snakes. Got nipped by ants? But we Diggers made it better. Our toilet is mega, compared to . . . and the rain fills the green tarp . . . tarp . . . what d'ya call it, that catcher thing?'

'Tarpaulin,' said Mizuki, holding hands again.

'Tarping helps the toilet flush. We don't get germs when we've been, because we know to wash hands and not bite our nails.'

Donna inspected her chewed nails. She folded her arms and tucked her hands under her armpits, but no one noticed. No one ever cared what Donna did.

'Forget toilets, what about burgers?' said one.

'What about them?'

'I miss burgers with cheese.'

'Yeah, but not salad.'

'And soft pillows on your bed.'

'And cake.'

'And shopping.'

'What about TV? Who misses Corrie?'

'Stop!' Mizuki's raised her hand. 'I warned you. See what happens when you start missing stuff? You drop hands. Look how you've let go of each other. Letting go makes us broken up and sad.' The girls looked at their hands as if it was a great surprise to see them waggling independently on the ends of their arms. Mizuki sighed, 'We are a team, like in netball. We're all made different, but we need each other to win the game.'

'But there's two teams in netball,' Joy said, self-conscious about adding her very own sounds into a big conversation and making grown-up sense.

Mizuki hit her own head with the flat of her hand, 'Exactly, Joy. You've hit that nail. Yay! Two teams, twice the fun.'

This sparked a new debate, all speaking at once.

'Sometimes one side wins and sometimes the

other.'

'What about the referee?'

'Mizuki's our ref!'

'What about rules?'

'We don't need no rules.'

Katey interrupted, 'What Mizuki's being sneaky about is the Helizone being the other team. She wants a party with our 'ttackers, them ones what we hate.' Katey pointed her finger at Mizuki, 'She invited them Helizone girls.'

'Who else did you expect in this dump? Father Christmas?' Melissa spat.

'Can we hold hands again? I want to hold hands like before,' Joy wailed.

The circle reformed. Katey pouted, but held hands with Freya and Pearl, taking her lead from Melissa, who believed Mizuki was selling slaves but still chose to be in the circle without causing trouble.

Mizuki spoke again. 'Bronwyn's coming to our party, plus Lydia, Claire and the rest. They're girls, same as us. Not enemies. Just on a different team. We can't be scared of them forever. That's why I said, "Peace." I invited them. They'll bring music. And gifts.'

'My dress!' Pearl did a jig. *Mizuki's magic.*

'Don't be daft,' snorted Katey, yanking Pearl's hand to stop her, 'You're not getting any dress, but we can get you a smelly tracksuit what's too small for you, or a pilot's clothes off a skellington-ghost.'

'Patience,' Mizuki mouthed to Pearl, and she winked. 'Now,' Mizuki raised her voice, 'when I light the fire it's a sign for the party to begin. The fish are swimming in the trap we made. It's good - stones piled up under the water with a net fixed inside. The water goes in through the gaps, but the fish can't find their way out. One jumped straight out like this,' she dropped Joy's hand and imitated the arc of an escaping fish, 'so we quickly put some mats on top of the trap. Fish like shadows.'

'I wondered what happened to those mats?' said Freya, 'You never asked me. I made them for roofs.'

'Are the fish alive?' Joy asked.

'I just told you. They're swimming in the trap, staying fresh 'til we need them. Last time, some died. We left them on the grass and maggots ate them.'

'Poor fish,' said Stephie.

'Poor fish.' Joy made a "sad" mouth by pushing out her bottom lip.

'Yummy fish!' grinned Donna, licking her lips, 'Yummy, yummy, in my tummy. Hope we don't get rescued before we get to eat them fishies!'

Mizuki knelt down to light the fire using a lighter, 'Don't worry about that, Donna Moore, 'cos no one's coming to get us. Not ever.'

*

The fire was a ravenous dragon, devouring stick after stick. Heat upon heat, the sun swelled, lowering into the lake, a magnificent mirror-ball flashing against a Blackpool-blue sky.

As the smoke rose a lone figure emerged from

the jungle. A small girl lugging a familiar grey box, struggling to keep it under her chin. Two huge eyes fixed directly ahead. Bare feet feeling their way over the stony beach, step by tentative step.

Katey's heart leapt. She couldn't help screaming, 'Sparrow!' and rushed to greet her, but Sparrow kept plodding.

'I'll carry that for you,' Katey offered. Without so much as a blink of recognition, Sparrow continued until she came face to face with Mizuki.

Mizuki took the box, bowed her head and stepped back.

Sparrow fumbled inside her clothes and pulled out a shred of bright red cloth, thin as a sari. She turned to face the way she had come, then lifted the cloth high above her head so one end hung over her face and counted, 'One, two, three, four, five.' On five, Sparrow dropped the cloth. It landed like an open wound upon the shingle. Sparrow set off back, passing an astonished Katey before vanishing into the foliage.

Katey brushed her tear-filled eyes with the palm of her hand, confused because Sparrow hadn't cried, 'Help me!' or run into the arms of the Home Rock girls.

The Helizone girls arrived. First, Bronwyn, flanked by Claire and Lydia listlessly making dull thuds by bashing sticks on paint cans. Behind them, Elle-Marie and Jody clapped in time. Taking up the rear, Sparrow and Roxy shook seed-filled bottles.

The guests chanted, '*Too hot! Say my name. Don't believe me, just watch! Too hot! Say my name. Don't believe me, just watch!' And, 'We're the girls of Helizone, this is our land, get your own!'*

Bronwyn's sun-damaged face was smeared with mud, streaked with smears of green sap and spotted with white paint. Her tangled hair was shot through with feathers, her broken nails painted white, and her body covered in tatty cloth strips with long grasses flowing out behind. A string of bones, interspersed with chicken claws, hung about her neck. She carried a bow, a sapling moon, tied taut from top to bottom.

Seeing the heron motionless in the lake, Bronwyn stopped. The 'music' stopped. Everyone stopped. Fixing her eyes on the bird, Bronwyn beckoned for Roxy to come quickly but quietly with a bamboo arrow, one of a dozen tucked under her arm. Bronwyn set the arrow against the bow and pulled the string, forcing back her elbow until her whole body quivered with the strain. She took aim and released the arrow. It rose in a wobbly arc, stabbed the sun with its silhouette, then dived into the water. Up it popped and floated lazily on the surface. The heron eyed the stick with suspicion, jerked its beak at Bronwyn, folded its neck against its cumbersome body, and flap, flap, flapped its wide wings low and away over the lake.

Bronwyn tossed the bow to one side. She spat a gob at the feet of Elle-Marie. 'These bows you made are pathetic!' she screamed. She shook her head so furiously that several feathers broke loose, then once more she set off walking to a renewed beat and lethargic chant from her underlings and slaves.

The Home Rock girls cowered behind a shroud of

smoke.

'Let's run for it,' Donna whispered loudly.

'I can't run fast like you,' whined Pearl, 'Don't leave me.'

'What if Bronwyn Bowen spears us?' Donna wailed.

'Yeah, her demons are gonna chase us and bite off our heads!' Pearl cried.

If Mizuki felt alarmed she didn't show it. Bronwyn halted. The music stopped.

Mizuki opened her arms. 'Welcome to our peace party,' she smiled with her mouth but not with her eyes, then commanded, 'Nadia, Evie, the butterflies!' The little ones scurried to open their mosquito-net-tent to release two dozen butterflies. Large and small, glorious and plain, fluttered free in all directions.

While the butterflies distracted the crowd, Katey watched how Mizuki dithered in the rocky space between Bronwyn and the fire as Bronwyn raised both hands to mirror Mizuki.

'From this moment, my friends are your friends,' Bronwyn announced, ' My home is your home.' The two girls embraced. Although Mizuki was physically taller, Bronwyn's hair and feathers, or possibly her arrogance, made her appear higher.

Without turning, Bronwyn beckoned behind her. 'Gifts,' she said. Sparrow passed something to Roxy. Roxy stepped forward and handed it to Bronwyn. A pulley-light, still in its box, brand new, never opened.

'There's instructions inside,' Bronwyn said as

Mizuki received it.

Katey shouted, 'We know what to do with them lights. We don't need your stuff. We already got what we need.'

'But we could use another,' urged Mizuki, waving a hand to shut Katey up. 'Lights won't last forever, even these. We accept.'

Bronwyn clicked her fingers. Claire approached carrying a screwdriver, a wrench, and a rusty tin full of bolts. Bronwyn said, 'We found a ton of this stuff. It's pretty useless, but you . . .'

Katey spat, 'We don't need no tools.' *Accept a gift, lose a child.* Who would Mizuki sacrifice for this junk? Stephie? Joy? What if Mizuki handed her, Katey, into the hands of the enemy? Her stomach knotted and gurgled like she'd eaten bad berries.

'We accept,' countered Mizuki.

Katey glared at Melissa, *Back me up!* but Melissa remained mute among the Home Rock crowd.

Another flick of the wrist from Bronwyn brought Lydia near. Lydia handed her a grubby plastic bag containing something flat and floppy. Bronwyn offered it to Mizuki who said, 'I know what this is. You didn't disappoint.'

The Home Rock girls were eager to see, but Mizuki set the bag upon a rock. 'No one touches this. If you do . . .' she started, but she couldn't think of a consequence, '. . . just don't touch. Claire, Lydia, Roxy, fetch the fish. Let's party!'

Katey could hardly believe her ears - Mizuki giving orders to Helizone girls as if she knew them. What's more, they obeyed her. Katey observed Bronwyn Bowen select the most comfortable rock for herself and lie back on it as Claire, Lydia and Roxy kicked off their trainers and waded into the lake.

The fish-trap had been constructed in the shallows, where the water was thigh height. It was a mishmash of sticks and stones forming a scruffy sort of nest with a rush-mat lid weighted down with stones. The three girls removed the mat then, with great difficulty, hauled out a net, dragging the trapped fish over the wall and through the water. The fish fought and flapped, battering against the girls' legs in their bid for freedom. Lydia squealed, but Roxy hissed, 'Shut up,' as she glanced back to check for Bronwyn's reaction, relieved to see her sunbathing with her eyes shut. They clung on until they reached the shore, dragged the hapless fish up the beach and dumped them, gasping, close to the fire. They then returned to collect a second net.

Mizuki squatted, opened the net and thrust in her hand. 'Katey, come, choose your favourite.'

'Don't boss me. I'm not your slave,' hissed Katey.

'For crying out loud, don't be such a baby and do as you're told for once,' Mizuki snapped. She grasped a large fish in both hands, stood up, lifted it high above her head and smashed it down hard onto the shingle. The stunned fish stopped flapping 'though it was not yet dead.

With one eye, the fish accused Mizuki. *You took me from my home. Dumped me where I don't belong.* Mizuki cocked her head. *Did I hear that fish speak?*

She felt herself swaying and steadied herself by setting her feet apart, but she could not steady her mind. Shadowy beings loomed over Mizuki. She could see right up their flaring nostrils. They mocked her, '*Don't be a such baby! Look everybody, look at our big, old cry baby.*' The mouths of the beings opened and closed. Mizuki peered in, loathing their furry tongues and strident voices, hating the black gaps in their rotten teeth. She stood totally still. *Bullies get bored if they get no reaction. Bullies like a fight. Dear God, help me be still. I won't play their mean game.* Mizuki did not flap nor flinch like a stupid fish. She knew not to accuse grown-ups. 'Don't look at me with your mean eye or . . .' The dying fish lifted its head.

'Kill!' shouted one of the Helizone girls. Mizuki blinked. I'm by a fire, with a fish at my feet. She dropped to her knees. Her hand found a rock that perfectly fit her palm. She raised the rock and looked the fish in the eye.

'Kill!' they screamed.

Mizuki smashed down and the fish never flinched. Smash, mash, mash! Light, shade, light, shade, as her arm rose and fell between Mizuki and the sinking sun.

'Stop, it's dead, stop! What're you doing? There's blood all over. Stop, it's dead!' Katey cried.

Mizuki stared at the bloodied rock in her hand and sunk back into Katey's arms.

Melissa and Freya rushed to help but Mizuki blindly pushed them away. With one hand on Katey's shoulder, Mizuki struggled to her feet. She looked at one Home Rock girl then another; the Blaze House girls at Heathrow, immaculate in their brand-new custard-yellow tracksuits, shiny hair brushed in neat bobs or plaits or ponytails, faces shining in anticipation of a hopeful tomorrow. Someone cried out, 'Stop, it's dead!' but it was only that kid Katey, Katey with a yer, that angry, filthy, ragged kid from Castle Care.

Leaning on Katey, Mizuki hobbled to the water's edge to wash away the stink of blood and scales and glare of the one accusing eye.

*

Ash glowed between the hot stones. Mizuki placed the fifth fish onto the moss-pan on the saturated bamboo platform. She covered the fish with a layer of moss, green side down. Smoke oozed through until the fish flaked apart. Freya and Melissa shared out the steaming flesh until both teams had eaten their fill. Everyone, bar the Silent One, sat around chattering, remembering, sharing, exaggerating, spilling over with memories about life in the *Before*.

The stunning sun-disc balanced precariously on the zig-zag horizon, carving a rippling path of orange-gold up to shore. Myriad birds swooped low over the water, catching flies. To one side of the lake, deer emerged from the trees to drink. Nearby, an echidna snuffled for worms and ants. The Helizone girls scratched their bites and chewed their nails, waiting for Bronwyn's next command, but she was fast asleep on her rock beneath a halo of tatty feathers.

*

Very early the next morning while the half moon was high, Katey felt Mizuki tapping her arm, 'Hey, wake up. We have to go, shush, come on.'

Katey rubbed her eyes. One by one the Home Rock girls were woken. They yawned as they reached for a hand, any hand, anyone to walk home with.

'Where's Bronwyn?' Katey whispered. The moonlight shimmered over the abandoned rock where Bronwyn had lain.

Mizuki explained, 'She left hours ago. They've all gone. I let you lot sleep.' She turned her back and, with the filthy plastic bag flopping over one arm, she set off towards the Flower Palace and on to Home Rock, knowing that her girls would follow.

15

Replay! Replay!

Atracker from the Kasua tribe called urgently from the darkness of the forest. First to respond were Kristofer Helgen, curator of mammals at the Smithsonian's National Museum of Natural History in Washington DC, Muse Opiang, a biologist with the Papua New Guinea Institute of Biological Research, and Gordon Buchanan, a Scottish wildlife filmmaker.

'My heart's in my throat,' gasped Kris, hardly able to breathe for the thrill of the discovery.

'Oh, my word, have a look at this,' laughed Gordon directly into the camera. 'This is the biggest rat I have ever seen. It is one of the largest rats in the world and here we are, holding it. It looks so different from any rat you have ever seen. It's the size of a cat. Bigger! Almost a metre long. It's a spectacular new species. Back in Scotland, rats give me the heebie-jeebies, but here he is, docile as a puppy.' Gordon reached out to stroke the creature's back. It snuffled and twitched its whiskers without so much as a flicker of fear.

The expedition HQ had been set up on a small area of level ground. The team had constructed an open-sided wooden 'room' covered by a rain-proof tarpaulin to protect tables of laptops and iPads, microscopes and microphones, nets and containers for catching insects.

Back at HQ, Gordon related the news to the other scientists; 'It's a giant woolly rat, about the size of a large cat and with a long, naked tail. We found it inside the crater just wandering around, happily munching on tubers, feeding very well. Totally unafraid of people - obviously never encountered people before. Never before seen by science.' He shook his head in disbelief.

'As a biologist, I've spent so many cold, muddy nights in the rain, but never expected to be rewarded like this!' added Muse, with a grin.

'He was tractable and fairly tame, not afraid of us at all,' explained Kris, 'and quite a handsome beast with all that silvery, shaggy fur!' Another British scientist, naturalist George McGavin, inserted the memory stick from the remote camera trap into a laptop. Everyone crowded in for a look, gasping as the rat came into view. Several other creatures had triggered the camera's infrared light; a striped possum, similar to a small badger, but with a long finger to winkle grubs out of holes and curled claws, sharp teeth and a long foxy tail; the bizarre silky cuscus, for all the world like a child's teddy-bear with the addition of a strong, prehensile tail; a giant bird, the cassowary, its footprints the size of a man's hand; as well as deer, beetles, spiders and small rodents.

'Hey, what's that?'

'What's what?'

'Replay! Replay!'

'Stop! There, it's just behind the . . .'

'There, in those trees!'

'Won't you look at those enormous eyes!'

The team fell silent. They craned their necks at the screen, puzzled by the grainy image glowing in the background, mesmerised by two bright, unblinking eyes and a crown of hair that stuck out stiff and wild as brambles. The delicate shadow-creature slipped softly into the foliage and vanished.

Gordon gasped, 'But what was it? It's tiny, to be sure. Bipedal. I'd say . . . not ape - too upright. Anyway, not in these parts. Nocturnal - sees in the dark. Displays no fear. Small, even for a local tribesman, and tribesmen rarely enter Mount Bosavi – most regard this place as sacred. Doesn't appear to be hunting. Three seconds isn't enough. Play again. And . . . stop right there. Take some measurements. If it is humanoid it's a miniature race. It almost looks . . . no, that's impossible. My heart is racing - this is epic. Can we head down there right now, reset the camera, take another look?'

Led by the Kasuan, the naturalist and the cameraman retraced their steps tentatively covering the short distance to where the woolly rat had first been sighted. It would be all too easy to slip in the dark, or step on a venomous snake, or get lost deep within the long-extinct volcano, in this fragile yet vast jungle. The excitement was palpable as the three men negotiated their way through the micro-ecosystem, cocooned from the world by a mighty wall of fierce mountains, the near-vertical sides covered in dense foliage, a barrier that prevented interbreeding with creatures outside the crater, and offering protection from ancient hunters and modern-day tourists.

'Here we are. I reckon this is the right place.' The men reset the camera trap. They directed the beams from their head-torches to scan the foliage high and low, but they saw nothing of interest, and attracted only moths. Reluctantly they agreed to return to base to catch some sleep, if sleep was at all possible in the heat and noise of Mt Bosavi.

16

Bronwyn, Jody, Elle-Marie, Claire, Lydia, Sparrow, Roxy

Claire and Jody were being sick, chucking up all over the place. Sparrow and Roxy ignored their groans, happy to play in the cage, absorbed in a game of 'waterlogged-teddy meets smoke-damaged Elsa-doll'. What with all the comings and the goings the entrance had expanded and the underlings no longer bothered to block it at night because the slaves were content to stay inside the driest, least contaminated place in the Helizone. They never tried to run away.

Sparrow and Roxy had learnt from Melissa how to weave mats and overlap rubbery leaves to water-proof their roof. Since returning to the Helizone, they lost themselves in home-making, hair-dressing and singing, or foraging for fruit and what they called 'baby sticks.' These were tiny, new bamboo shoots that had to be harvested early each morning while they were still sweet because, later, those same plants shot up and became tough and bitter-tasting. Best of all, Bronwyn had become bored of her slaves so pretty much ignored them.

Elle-Marie tossed stones at paint cans. When she hit one, her listless audience Lydia cheered a half-hearted 'Yay!' from her chosen spot, leaning on the precarious propeller. Lydia rubbed a small section of the helicopter round and round with her forefinger, until that one spot glowed bright as a full moon.

Lethargy was the enemy of the underlings who slept longer each morning. When they woke they picked at their bites and scratches, some of which were painfully infected. Bronwyn no longer dangled her legs out of the helicopter, but wandered between the trees, paying no attention to the snakes and arachnids that lay in wait for smaller prey than she. Her matted hair hung almost to her waist, impossibly tangled with feathers, grime, beads and bones. She licked her dry lips until they cracked and bled.

A bird of paradise dipped down then up across her line of vision. Bronwyn thought, 'A hot, crusty flying pie, steam trailing behind.' She reached out and swiped the air to grasp its streamer-like tail, but the bird was long gone and, blankly, she stared after it and then at her empty fist, wondering how on earth she'd missed. The sun burned unbearably bright. Bronwyn sidled into the warm shadows, where her thumb found her mouth; a crumb of comfort.

Distant thunder rumbled between the mountains and rolled over the treetops.

A drop of water fell.

A cloud burst.

A skyful of dark clouds opened the hatches.

A shower. A waterfall. A torrent.

Bronwyn threw back her head and opened her mouth, relishing the liquid that ran down her throat, or through her hair and over her shoulders.

Roxy and Sparrow crawled out from their dry cage. The rain hammered against the Super Puma and, where the ground was already marshy, it formed a deeper pool. The little ones stamped through it, splashing, holding hands, laughing, looking up, lapping with their tongues at the generosity of the heavens.

Claire and Jody clutched their stomachs but, despite their agony, they too lifted their faces to receive their gift. Pure water. Life. Strength, just enough for today.

And what is a day but a room in which to live, a stage between dawn and dusk, a carpet of sunlight between two ebony curtains?

The sun is born. It is destroyed by night, but the darkness cannot overcome it.

So again light is born. Again it dies beneath the night.

There it is then, life, after-life.

And hope. There is always hope.

The rain stopped. Bronwyn's blood sugar had fallen dangerously low. She forced herself to think. *What's wrong with me?* Why can't I see straight? She blinked repeatedly, scrabbling through her mind for a shot of clarity. The fuzzy treetops came into sharp focus.

'I'm tumbling out of the sky, crashing through the trees, thump, thump, thump. An almighty jolt, falling, smoke, screams, dust, blood, fear. Both pilots dead, the guardian staggering like ghouls. That blonde kid, Katey, grabs my hand, squeezes tight. Go away! Can't breathe. The massive door is mangled, hanging half-hinged. I lean out but I can't see the ground for smoke. It must be far below. Need air. Must jump. I land in a swamp. I think I see Mizuki leaving the scene of the accident. She swings on a rope and is gone. Katey is pulling my arm. "Are we dead?" she asks. I shake my head. Dead? I'm still standing, so no, not dead.'

'Dying,' Bronwyn spoke into the Helizone. Is that my voice? She heard someone speak in the space above her head, clear as the plink of a final raindrop on glass. She felt herself enveloped in warmth, not the usual stuffy, sweaty heat, but a peaceful sense of other. A gentle, comforting presence. A still, small voice.

'Go.'

Bronwyn heard herself calling, 'Follow me!' and she set off along the track. One by one the others followed as she had trained them, but this was no triumphal procession. Merely seven starving children trailing wearily through the tall wildness.

Bronwyn recognised the plateau as the place where she'd pushed Joy, where she'd thrown delirious parties, body and mind adrift, high above the roof of the jungle. Without looking back, the abdicating queen trekked beyond her known world; her underlings could follow or not, but she would rather die than return to the Helizone. Beyond the plateau, Bronwyn stumbled onto an animal track, one that Mizuki had investigated during one of her night-time ventures. The underlings had strung out, exhausted, hardly able to raise their eyes to check where Bronwyn led.

The virgin mountainside rose ever more steeply, forcing the girls to pick their way over rocks, between giant roots and around skinny tree trunks. Jody's feet hurt in her tight trainers. She kicked them off. Her feet felt free and light. She marvelled the way her bare feet moved, one baby-step after another.

Claire came upon Jody's trainers, abandoned, splayed open like two huge, woodlice with frayed antennae-laces. 'What are you?' she asked. Claire rocked forwards and backwards. The creatures loomed up at her, then shrank back. Claire fell. Her cheek smacked the black ground. A man called Jim was in her head, saying, 'You're an innovator. People like you can change the world.'

The grass tickled Claire's eyelashes so she opened her eyes. 'I'm an inner-vator,' she said. A massive millipede with spines along its back, rippled around her forehead almost touching her skin, but not quite. It appeared gigantic, but Claire didn't flinch. She smiled as it moved away. It was just one of those jungle things.

Elle-Marie tripped over Claire. *Before*, she'd have sworn and kicked Claire for being an ignoramus, a dork, for being in the way, but she had no fight in her. Fight or flight? Were there really only two options? Try flop. She sunk down beside Claire and reached for Claire's hand. The tips of their fingers touched, interlocked. They looked, blinking, into each other's eyes.

They heard the voices of men.

Elle-Marie shut her eyes. 'That's social services coming round without an appointment. Dad's gonna totally smash their heads in.'

*

Bronwyn's legs stopped obeying her brain. She imagined she was walking briskly, but her hand was above her head, clutching an overhanging branch. The branch swayed and the earth rocked. Beneath her armpit, Bronwyn saw the hazy image of a petite girl staring up at her. Bronwyn smiled with a strangely beatific expression. 'Do I know you?' Bronwyn rasped.

The girl's head moved from side to side like a cockatoo, inquisitive, trusting, quiet.

'Joy?' Bronwyn mouthed. With superhuman strength, she threw back her head, rolled her tongue and trilled as gloriously as any bird of paradise. The incredible sound carried up the mountainside, terrifying many jungle creatures, then stopped abruptly.

Bronwyn said, 'I taught you to do that.' The child shook her head – *not me, no* – but Bronwyn continued,

'Remember we tricked them? They believed I brought you back to life! They believed my powers, adored Queen Bronwyn. What a scam! What a buzz!' The child came into focus. Not Joy. A different slave with a long-forgotten name. Possibly no name.

Footsteps. Bronwyn glanced up - someone's coming! In a single step, the infant melted backwards beneath a fountain of huge, pinnate leaves.

'Is there anyone else with you?' A man spoke. He touched Bronwyn's shoulder, 'How many of you are there?' Bronwyn felt herself carried through the air. She felt light as a feather. The quadrant of sky swung hypnotically above her, left, right, left. A leaf shook off a drop of water which fell slowly, slowly, timed precisely to land on Bronwyn's face, roll down her cheek and into her ear.

'Anyone seen the tiny one? The one we captured on camera?'

Are they talking to me?

'Here.' A flask touched Bronwyn's lips. Water trickled from the side of her mouth, over her jaw, down her neck.

'We found five survivors. Best send the tracker down to search for more.'

They're talking to each other. I'm rocking like a baby. They're looking for the Home Rock girls. They can look all they like, it's not my problem.

Bronwyn grinned at the pile of junk littering the front garden of number 47. A comforting sight. The bin-men had refused to empty the recycling because her mum refused to sort the vodka bottles from the cornflakes' boxes, then the overflowing wheelie bin had been kicked over by idiots and the wind had blown a gale. Blame the wind for the real damage. The paint cans rolled in that wind. Their lids fell off. White paint spilled, drying over the dandelions and doggy-doos. *Mum never bought paint in her life; she swiped every penny for her next drink.* Julie Slingerland's dog was barking like a nutter. Her partner swore at it. He kicked it and the dog yelped.

A cool, blue cloth moved over Bronwyn's face, dabbing gently, the way a real mother washes a real child, taking care not to cause distress. Bronwyn recognised her mam's trademark fag-burn bullet holes in the blue flower curtains. She peered through one of the holes and spied a beautiful woman with soft, brown eyes. The woman gently tugged at Bronwyn's hair, removing beads and feathers one by one.

17

Silver Dolphins

'Can you hear them, 'cos I can't.' Melissa had been sitting cross-legged on Hog Rock, but now she was standing up, and had pinned back her ears to catch the silence beyond the drill of cicadas and cackling of the kookaburras. And the silence unnerved her.

The Home Rock girls busied themselves braiding hair, chopping fruit, and sweeping bugs. Narrow pathways ran between the shops, the huts and the toilet, which Stephie regularly swept free of stones, twigs, bugs - anything that threatened vulnerable feet. Melissa and Freya had constructed a 'cupboard,' a wood-frame tied at each intersection with sturdy grasses, with parallel bars from which an assortment of clothes and rags were draped on makeshift hangers. Lower down were shelves, rudimentary racks of bamboo for storing footwear, trainers mostly, of various sizes and condition. Most shoes no longer fit the original owner. The unspoken rule said anyone could use anything from the cupboard. Most shoes and clothes had been customised with berry-dyes, threads, or beads knotted onto laces. The colours faded because of the daily rain-drench then merciless drying under the baking sun.

At the 'Thinking to Help' shop, Mizuki reacted to Melissa's alarm. She stopped pretending to listen to Pearl's latest whacky scheme and strode over to Hog Rock. Melissa scrambled down to meet her, 'Something's wrong. I can't hear them. Actually, I don't think I've heard them for at least two days.'

'Can't hear who? The Helizone girls?' Mizuki and Melissa stood stock still, sifting out the sounds of wildlife in search of human silence.

'No voices. No banging,' said Melissa, 'Something's changed.'

'And I haven't seen Bronwyn for days. We kind of lost touch since . . .'

'But what if,' Melissa imagined the unthinkable, 'what if they've died?'

Mizuki pulled forward her plait and wrapped it around her wrist to admire the freshly added red and blue seed-beads, 'No way's anyone died.'

'Or if they got an illness? Or them mushrooms were poison. Or . . .'

'Shall we go see?'

'Now?'

'Yes now, if it helps you stop stressing. I don't get why you're so bothered about them anyway.'

'Because of Sparrow. Roxy's tough enough, but little Sparrow, she's just . . .'

'They'll be fine,' said Mizuki, shifting her feet, embarrassed because she'd long since forgotten about those kids. She forced a cheerful tone, 'Come on then, let's do it now, but don't tell the others. We'll be quicker on our own.'

'Do what? What's you up to?' Pearl had followed Mizuki from the Thinking to Help shop. She grabbed Mizuki's arm and stuck on like a leech, 'I knew you wasn't listening to me. You're supposed to listen. That's your 'ticular job, don't you know? You two's not doing nuffin without me. You going swimming? You got secrets? I bet you just wanna have all the fun without us lot.'

'None of your beeswax,' snorted Melissa, unpicking Pearl's hand from Mizuki's arm and flicking her away, 'Go get something for supper. And tell Nadia there's a ginormous bug on that leaf – yeah, that thing there with the antennae and white spots. Now get lost.' She made a 'thick' sign by pressing her tongue against her inside bottom lip, while wiggling her fingers on her forehead to imitate antennae.

'But what arrrre you gonna do?' whined Pearl.

'We're gonna check out the Helizone, see what them others are up to,' said Melissa. Mizuki glared at Melissa, '*What d'ya go and tell her the truth for?*'

Pearl snorted, 'You can stick that yucky place, an' don't aspect me to come with you . . . and do you know?'

'Know what?' smiled Melissa, pulling her mouth into her sassy better-than-you know-all way.

'Do you know, them Helizone girls keep sweet little baby kittens in cages and starve them to absolute death. Katey told me. Jus' think. Poor baby kitties without no food!'

'You mean chickens.'

'I said kittens and I meant kittens. It's mega disgusting what some people do.' Pearl spat on the ground to nail her side of the argument. She huffed back to the others where she took an exaggerated breath to attract everyone's attention and announced, 'You know what? Melissa and Mizuki are gonna check out the Helizone if anyone's int'rested, which you aint - obviously.'

'But we're doing choir, aren't we?' Donna pleaded, 'I wanna do choir. Can we do them megglies again, please, please, please Freya?'

'Yeah, that's what we planned,' smiled Freya, pleased to be in demand. 'Oy, Katey, what's that medley you taught us the other day? The one about God's mountains protecting all around? Yes. And we'll do Five Green Speckled Frogs for Nadia and Evie 'cos it learns them proper words.'

Katey noticed Mizuki and Melissa laughing at Pearl behind her back. Her eyes narrowed. No one had disappeared in a while, but something shifty was going on with those big girls.

Mizuki saw Katey watching. She called out, 'Stop fretting little sister. Melissa's coming with me to check out the Helizone. Just to make sure Bronwyn's lot are okay.' Mizuki approached Katey, arms wide. She smiled down at her, 'Trust me for once. Stick around and help Freya with the little ones. Want a hug?'

Katey shook her head with a definite no, then for no apparent reason, she crumpled into uncontrollable sobs. Mizuki wrapped her arms around the little girl, 'Hey, don't get so upset. Chill down and cheer up. We'll be back, both of us. And maybe we'll find something nice, just for you.'

'I told you already, I don't want nuffin nice.' Katey pulled back, her dusty face streaked with her own tears, and sweat from Mizuki's t-shirt.

Melissa tugged Mizuki's arm, 'Let's go or we'll be too late. You might like creeping around in the dark, but I hate it. I want to be back before this lot are asleep.'

Melissa looked at Freya to check she was happy to be left to get on with things.

Freya nodded. *Go, it's okay, I've got this.*

With Melissa and Mizuki away, Freya felt responsible, a special thrill of being in charge. Being number one was a big deal, if only for an evening.

*

The songs of the choir mingled with the vibration of the jungle. Mizuki and Melissa made their way to the lake, then strode on past the arrow tree, along the trampled, littered trail. Mizuki stopped, pulled a face, and retched.

'Puke, pong!' Melissa held her nose. They covered their faces with their hands until their stomachs could handle their revulsion then set off again. As they approached the Helizone, their feet squelched over the polluted marshy ground.

'Let's go back,' Melissa whispered, but Mizuki

shook her head. She side-stepped a fly-ridden carcass of a tree kangaroo. Something brushed her face and she jerked back in alarm, but it was only a cord attached to a broken pulley-light, swinging from a branch.

Carnage. The rusting helicopter had sunk lower and lower until Bronwyn's upturned 'throne' was almost at ground level. One of the gigantic broken blades had slipped and crashed to the ground. All around were mud-streaked clothes, tatty trainers, plastic bottles, battered paint cans, feathers, bones of small beasts, and wrecked cages.

'But where are they?' Melissa started.

With a finger to her lips Mizuki tugged Melissa's arm and dragged her to the base of "Katey's tree." They shinned up the trunk and stretched out along the broad branch, their lithe bodies melting naturally between the hairy vines, shiny ferns and orchids that sprouted from every nook and cranny.

'Men!' Melissa gasped, eyes wide, covering her face with her hands to stop herself crying out. Both girls held their breath. A squirrel kamikazed down from the canopy, bounced off Mizuki's back and into the undergrowth. Birds squawked warnings and fluttered up and away. The girls heard the swish of sticks from "Bronwyn's track" as they beat it wider, left, right, left, right.

The men spoke a strange kind of English, 'Eureka, we found it. That Welsh gal's directions were spot on.' An Australian. Shorts, tee-shirt, walking boots, binoculars, rucksack.

'Crikey, what a stink!' said another, thick set,

bearded, sunglasses on his head.

'Where d'ya start with this little lot then?' This from a third man in a grey cap, who reported their findings into a voice recorder, mumbling this and that, mostly about the condition of the Super Puma, 'Won't you take a gander at this beauty!' He patted the Super Puma, then wiped the rust from his hands on his cargo pants, 'Never seen anything like this monster bird up close - 'course it's hardly worth a zack in this smashed state.' The first man agreed. He fiddled with the cord of a GravityLight, raised the counter-balance two metres, then let go. He puffed out his cheeks, 'Well, blow me down if this isn't some kind of dim light without 'lecky!'

Using iPads, the men took photos in all directions including skywards towards Mizuki and Melissa, capturing only the underside of the branch. The girls did not move a muscle, not even when a magnificent butterfly settled on Mizuki's arm. She was positive she could hear its tiny heart thrumming and brumming through her skin.

'It's goin' to be tough getting a permit to bring in what's needed to deal with this little lot. I hear it took the Brits the best part of thirteen months to secure a deal to cross the boundary into Mount Bosavi for their TV show. There'll be restrictions but we'll have to bring in team to locate the black box, scout the area, see what gives.'

'Can't see any sign of bodies. Poor kids must've been so excited for a new beginning, only to lose their lives in this hell hole. Strewth, the stench is enough to knock a grown man from here to kingdom come! I say we mosey on back before we lose the light.'

Mizuki eased herself forward. The butterfly took flight, briefly alighting on the bearded man's sunglasses before moving on. Mizuki pushed her face through a tree-fern and peered over the edge of the branch. The man in the grey cap placed his fingers on a curiously shiny spot on the helicopter, then he slapped the Puma farewell. All three headed back up the track towards the plateau.

When the coast was clear, Mizuki and Melissa descended the tree, their senses alert in case the intruders returned. Shoulder to shoulder they stood with their hands over their noses and mouths like gasmasks, because of the smell. All around, Bronwyn's magazines lay scattered, torn, and drenched. A GravityLight strewn and broken like some discarded toy. Nothing of value to take back to Home Rock, except . . .

Mizuki spotted something shiny; a small, silver object, partially submerged in rainwater, trapped within a trumpet-shaped leaf at the base of the tree. She bent the leaf and shook the water droplets onto the palm of her hand. Out fell a pendant. Two silver dolphins arched in opposite directions with a loop for threading a necklace.

'Freya,' Mizuki mouthed. She tucked Freya's forbidden memory deep into her pocket, then beckoned Melissa with her chin. 'Promise me something,' she said, 'Don't tell anyone at about those three guys.'

18

The Sky Shook

Mizuki's lanky legs hung over the lip of Hog Rock as she sat in her favourite place. She crossed her ankles and called everyone to order. Melissa hauled herself up alongside Mizuki. The rest found their own space here and there, sitting back to back, or lounging against rocks, or simply standing, quietly chatting.

'There's things we've been forgetting,' began Mizuki, without having planned her speech. 'One's days. Freya has been forgetting to mark the days. I totally trusted you, Freya.'

'But you said, "Who cares about days?" I tried to show you but you . . .'

'Don't blame me for your failings,' Mizuki said, suddenly remembering the way she'd squashed Freya's enthusiasm, 'You shouldn't have taken any notice of my opinion. You shouldn't give up on a job just because no one praises you.'

'But the varnish dried up,' protested Freya.

'Because you never twisted the lid on proper,' Pearl

accused.

'So that's it then. No more birthdays,' Katey sighed. She twiddled with the bead necklace around her neck, then she grinned, 'Hey, no days means I'm never gonna have to be a teenager. Phew! Teenagers always get done for doing bad stuff.'

'But *I* want birthdays. I want to be seven and eight and nine *and* ten,' wailed Joy standing up to make herself heard, aware of being little, and remembering how big people took more notice if a person stood up.

'You can't have everything just 'cos you want it,' Pearl said, thinking of the white dress she'd ordered that never arrived.

'I know, Pearl. I want birthdays, not for presents, but so I can be grown-up.'

'Huh, grown-ups! Just be yourself, Joy,' Mizuki said, but the blood rushed to her ears, so she could hardly hear herself think. Nevertheless, she stammered on, 'Joy's right in a way. We'll sort out the birthday problem. Give me time and we'll think how to do it. We had a birthday not so long ago, so don't get your knickers in a twist about the next one. The next thing we forgot . . .'

'Toilets,' Melissa prompted.

Mizuki nodded, 'Yup. The toilets need sorting and fixing. I've had this idea for improving the pipes so when it rains the water runs faster. We need bigger pipes, open lengthwise, and more of them, coming in a bit steeper, like this,' she demonstrated the angle with her arm. 'Freya, Pearl, Melissa and the Silent One are the Diggers, so you can work on this with me.'

'What about *her* working for a change? That fat slob, she never does nuffin to help no one,' declared Pearl, 'You can't call her a Digger.'

'Don't be nasty, Pearl. Anyway, you can't talk. She made us necklaces. And she did carry some earth. She's a bit slow but when she's feeling okay she can lift more than me,' said Freya, 'Calling her fat is being mean. She can't help how she looks. It's her disease. You'd better say sorry, Pearl.' Freya sat down cross-legged, rocking her head so the ends of her eight beaded plaits swooshed and bashed against her knees.

Pearl tugged at her own hair until her scalp hurt. Some came out in her hand. She selected a single strand, winding it tight around her finger until the skin beneath her fingernail turned white. The hair snapped and the blood rushed back again. 'I'm not mean,' Pearl insisted, but the conversation had already moved on.

Katey lay back, thinking. Since being in the jungle she'd worked out how to line up words inside her skull to make whole sentences. She couldn't see the words with her outside eyes, but inside her mind the letters hung one by one through her brain like socks on a line. She discovered she could, simply by thinking, unpeg them and hang new words in their place. A sentence formed in her mind; '*Mizuki's talking funny. She's up to sumpfink.*'

Katey sat up and called out, 'Why're we fixing up Home Rock, Mizuki? Why are you talking about toilets and days and stuff?'

'Because,' Mizuki sighed, 'if we're gonna live here

forever, we gotta work together an' be happy.'

'Forever?' echoed Freya. By itself, "forever" felt like a punch in the head. A punishment. Katey spelt out *forever* in the speckled darkness behind her eyes but the letters loomed large and took up too much space.

Freya waved a hand and asked, 'But what about Ethan Cook? What about the THP? I was getting my own room with windows that open and white curtains blowing and a duck-egg duvet and a place to hide my tin . . .'

'You aren't supposed to bring your memory tin,' Pearl said, 'Staff said . . .'

'Shut up about staff. Who cares what your lot said about rules. Mine told me Ethan Cook's rule of leaving memories behind was ridiclious,' Freya said, close to tears.

Pearl mocked, 'Freya, Freya, disobeyer, if you hadn't brung your tin on the aeroplane, you wouldn't never have gone and lost it.'

Freya leapt up. Like a wild cat she flew at Pearl, fingernails flashing, lashing, scratching, biting, tearing Pearl's hair. Pearl screamed. She lurched at Freya, sinking her teeth into her shoulder. Donna was quick to leap to the side-lines, punching the air, yelling, 'Kill, kill, kill!'

Melissa grabbed Donna's arm. She screamed, 'Stop doing that!' but Donna's eyes burned with the thrill of a fight and no one could pull her away. Nadia and Evie clung to each other as Freya thumped Pearl with every ounce of her being.

'Kill!' screamed Donna's-a-Goner-Moore, raising

her fist and bringing down an imaginary knife.

A tremendous noise. An immense thrumming. A huge engine roaring, shaking the sky, so close the vibrations shook a million leaves off the trees and stopped the fight.

'Hide!' commanded Mizuki, leaping from Hog Rock and landing like a gazelle beside Pearl. The children, apart from the Silent One who languished in her hut, scattered into the undergrowth as two helicopters churned overhead. Mizuki grabbed the not-so-yellow shirts from the cupboard and scanned Home Rock for other tell-tale signs of family life. She stuffed as much as possible under a huge-leafed bush, then hid.

Standing perfectly still, Mizuki blended in with the jungle. She noticed how far the jungle had encroached on their carefully constructed huts, so that some branches overshadowed them, and bamboo had sprouted where it didn't used to be. Home Rock was so overgrown no one would ever find them.

The others squatted in the undergrowth. Freya, her face scratched and bleeding, sobbed, 'What if that is my mum? She said she'd never stop looking for me. She said, "*Never believe what they say about me, you'll always be mummy's princess.*" I want to go back to England, even if I do hate flying, and you can't stop me.'

'Think of a happy ending,' whispered Joy, more to herself than Freya who couldn't have possibly heard.

'Shh!' warned the others, afraid of being heard over the racket of the engines. From the sound if it, the helicopters were hovering over the Helizone or nearer, maybe this side of the lake.

Freya lost it. She leapt up, waving at the sky, sobbing and screaming, 'Help! Help! We're here. Please find us. I don't want to be here no more. Help!' Melissa held on to her but could not console her.

Mizuki had a brainwave. She delved into her pocket, shoving her hand right down into the corner, feeling with her fingernails for a tiny object. She thrust it under Freya's nose. 'Remember when we said you were a ghost, the time you came out of the bushes and you said about a necklace?'

Freya stared at the thing in Mizuki's palm, trying to fathom how something so small and precious could appear just like that, a breath-taking sign of hope in such terrible chaos. She mouthed, 'My dolphins!'

Hesitantly, Freya reached for the silver pendant in case Mizuki was playing a mean trick. What if she suddenly snatched it back, or worse, chucked it into the bushes. Then it was in her hand. She held it to neck and said, 'It had a chain, but the Helizone girls broke it.' Freya closed her eyes, remembering.

*

Because of the shouting, Freya had come downstairs in her dressing gown. The bread on the side was mouldy, but she took a crust and sucked on it. Bacon fat congealed in the grill-pan on the counter. There were pawprints and grooves in the fat where the blind kitten had been. The kitten smooched against Freya's leg, mewing as it wound a figure of eight around her ankles. Across the hallway, in the sitting room her mum and dad were fighting. A vase smashed against the wall. The front door slammed. Windows rattled. Freya jumped, and the kitten hissed.

Freya blinked at the bloody footprints along the hall carpet. In the blood lay her mum's cheap dolphin necklace. Freya felt in her dressing-gown pocket for her phone and, not for the first time, dialled 999. Someone asked, 'What's the emergency?' Freya picked up the necklace . . .

Someone tapped her arm. Freya opened her eyes, annoyed by the interruption.

Joy.

Joy said, 'What you got? Can I see?'

Freya sighed and opened her hand, 'It's mine. Don't touch.'

Joy looked up, 'I got something else for you, something what I found all by myself. Look, here, can you get it off me? I've kept it 'cos I didn't know it was yours.'

Freya's eyes widened, 'My chain! Where did you . . ?' But this was no time to chat because the trees were shaking. Men were closing in, shouting and hollering.

'They're saving us,' explained Joy.

'They're still miles away,' Melissa said, in a stage whisper.

'No, not miles,' Mizuki said, 'This side of the Helizone. We've gotta decide what to do. And quick.'

'I'm not going in no helicopter,' Katey said, 'We already crashed once.'

'I wanna stay here with you lot for ever and ever,' Pearl said, rubbing her bruised arms from Freya's beating, while glaring daggers at Donna for cheering Freya on.

Donna couldn't make her mind up. To go or not to go.

'Zoo here,' Nadia said, clear as a bell.

Evie waved her newest notebook. 'Zoo stay,' she agreed. The bushes rustled. Something or someone was pushing through the foliage.

'Hide!' commanded Mizuki and once again the girls dissolved into the greenery, their grubby faces camouflaged. They could no longer hear helicopters. Had they given up and gone? Or had they landed?

Someone, not a Home Rock girl, was standing very close, very still.

Without warning, Donna ran towards the person shouting, 'I wanna go home with you. Take me back. I want to go with you!' The others froze, *No, Donna, no!* Mizuki considered running in the opposite direction but she stayed rooted to the spot. *Nothing, no man, no woman, no one, can make me go with them.*

'Shut up, Donna Moore,' said a familiar voice, 'We ain't taking you nowhere.'

'Sparrow!' The little ones rushed to greet her. 'Sparrow's here! Look everybody, look who it is!' Joy, Evie and Nadia fell on Sparrow, hugging her and dancing like crazy. Sparrow's eyes seemed larger than ever in her bony face. She flashed them an urchin grin, the broad smile of a ragged child who knew no better than to be content. To exist forever in the dirt.

'Roxy's with me,' Sparrow said. Roxy emerged timidly, clutching a teddy-bear with dried-stiff fur. It had been a while so she didn't want anyone too close. It was clear Roxy didn't want to be hugged.

Sparrow gabbled, 'We was walking with Bronwyn. Bronwyn said, "We're gonna die if we stay in the Helizone," so we followed her but she went too far. It got too steep. Them lot didn't wait for us, so me and Roxy went back to the Helizone to play for a bit. We was in our room playing dolls waiting and waiting, but Bronwyn never comed back. Then Vix came running and said, "*Quick, hide!*" She showed us which way to Home Rock. She gave us bananas to eat and . . .'

'Vix?' Mizuki said it first.

'*My* Vix? My nearly-sister?' Joy shook her head in disbelief.

'Vix what runned away?' Donna gasped.

Sparrow and Roxy nodded. *Yes, that same Vix what legged it from Bronwyn Bowen.* They stepped back and there she was; tiny, fierce, barefoot Vix, tight-mouthed, fists clenched, still wearing her Blaze House aertex and jogging bottoms.

19

Spy Survivor

Joy's eyes narrowed. *Why's Vix talking to Mizuki, and not me? I'm her pretend sister. We played at the Flower Palace and by the lake. She looks different. Older. Sharper. Scarier. Like she doesn't need me no more.*

Everyone hushed. Mizuki lifted one hand to signal everyone to sit. They checked the ground for insects, brushing some away before taking their places. Mizuki spoke quietly, 'Vix, you'd best tell us all where you've been.'

Vix grinned, 'I went up the mountain and made my own house in a tree, very high up, and I got lots of new friends.'

'Friends?' someone piped up.

'Rat. Bird. Hedgehog what's not a hedgehog. Bear.'

'There's no bears here,' Pearl said.

'Ssh. She means them funny kangaroo things, what look like bears but they're not bears,' Freya explained, 'Carry on, Vix. What happened? What did you see?'

'Bronwyn Bowen came walking up my mountain,

and them others - you know Jodie and Claire what fell over? Also, Elle-Marie and Lydia. I hid in the bushes but she saw me.'

'Bronwyn saw you?' Pearl again.

'Ssh, don't interrupt,' Freya hissed.

'Some men talked to Bronwyn. The men what's growing vegibles in a special garden with a net to stop the birds. I nicked some food and hid when the men came. They said, "It's rats what made them holes," but it were me all along. In their big massive tent, they cook hot soup and vegibles. And they creep out in the night with lights stuck to their heads. They catched a big rat, same as our rat, but they didn't catch it in a cage like Bronwyn did. They just stroked it.'

'Did you say vegetables?'

Vix nodded, 'Green ones and red ones, for feeding the TV people. They've got the massivest tent ever. And computers. They catched bugs and did photos of them on computers. And there's a mummy.'

'A mummy? Who's mummy is it?' Freya's eyes widened with hope, 'You better not be lying.'

'Yeah, I bet she's telling porkies.' Pearl stuck up her nose. Vix got all the attention round here. 'The one about a mummy is a stinking fat lie.'

'A mummy with brown eyes and long black hair. She's got a camera with a big round bit sticking out. The mummy pulled feathers out of Bronwyn's hair.' Vix rolled her eyes to help her remember all the confusing pictures; 'Them men talked to Bronwyn 'bout lots of things. Glasses Man said, "These must be *our* girls, the ones from the accident! Them's the Transfer Hope girls what was on the news," and Beard Man said, "Are there people out there alive?" and Bronwyn said, "No."

'Bronwyn said "no?"' Freya gasped.

'"No."'

'Stinky liar, pants on fire!' Pearl hissed.

'Shut up, Pearl. Vix is saying true stuff,' said Donna.

'I didn't say she's a liar, I said *Bronwyn's* a liar because what about us? We are alive.' Pearl's face crumpled. Her eyes filled with tears so she could hardly speak, 'Bronwyn said we aint alive, but we are, aren't we?'

Vix did her best to remember, 'Glasses Man asked Bronwyn Bowen, "What about the pilots?" then Bronwyn said, "One's a skellington and one's stinking. Sunk in the marsh." Claire and Jody chucked their guts up - I saw the mummy give them medicine. Then Jody said, "Where are our slaves?" Then Bronwyn went "Ha, ha, ha," like that. Then she said, "Shut up, Jody, what you going on about? There's no slaves in no jungle." Then Bronwyn gave Jody the evils . . .' Vix slit her eyes as Bronwyn had done, '. . . and the grown-ups said, "This is going to affect our expe . . . exped . . . expedition." And the mummy said to Glasses Man, "Did you get through to the police?" He said, "We's sending a search party soon as." So that's when I snicked off quick, and I ran here to tell you to hide 'cos them men's coming to get you. I ran through the Helizone and there was Roxy and Sparrow just playing. I said, "Do you want to get saved by them men or don't you want to get saved?" and Sparrow said, "No," didn't you Sparrow? Roxy said, "Quick, tell the Home Rock girls," so we runned here, but helicopters came - not the same helicopter as ours what crashed . . .' Vix gasped for air, '. . . and them men's coming here right now. We took a short cut, the one what them Helizone girls used to spy on you.'

'Enough,' said Mizuki, raising her palms to calm Vix down, 'If the men are really coming we've gotta decide quick who wants to go with them to Transfer Hope and who wants to stay at Home Rock. Everyone who wants to stay can go to the waterfall.'

'The one where we had our birthday party?' Katey asked.

'Yes. Everyone who wants to go to THP best walk to the Helizone, because that's where they'll find you. But – and I mean this - whoever goes has to promise on your life to say exactly the same as Bronwyn, that no one else is alive. Otherwise they'll never stop looking for us.'

'I told you already, I'm staying at Home Rock.' Katey jumped up, quickly followed by Nadia and Evie.

'Stay.'

'Stay zoo.'

Donna stood up. 'I've changed my mind. I don't wanna go with them men. I'll stay if Mizuki stays.'

Mizuki stood. 'Staying,' she said.

Stephie stood.

Sparrow.

Roxy.

Melissa.

Freya's eyes filled with tears. She caressed the dolphins at her neck. 'This is the best transfer hope place in the whole wide world,' Freya stood up, 'and

I hate flying, so I'm staying here for ever.' She rubbed the ridged scars on her wrist where her teeth had drawn blood on the long flight from Heathrow.

'I dunno,' shrugged Joy, 'because what about TV?'

'Staff said TV is rubbish at Transfer Hope,' Melissa warned, 'They said it's gonna be a whole different life, new country, new house, new school, new . . .'

Joy's eyes widened, 'What about Paw Patrol? And Mr Tumble?'

'Yeah, and what about my white dress?' Pearl pouted, 'I totally love dresses, don't you know, so I'm going with them to get a dress from an actual shop. Fact: when I go to Transfer Hope I'm getting me twenty hundred dresses.'

'What are you going on about? You'd swap Home Rock for a stupid white dress?' Melissa spat on the ground.

Joy asked, 'What I want to know is, Vix, are *you* staying or going?' Vix shrugged like she didn't care either way. Joy frowned. Vix wasn't the same best friend who'd left her that day by the lake. It was as if Vix didn't need her any more, like she didn't need anyone at all.

'I think it's good here,' Stephie said, 'with no school.'

'When they go away, we'll make our own school with our own teachers,' Mizuki nodded, '. . . so it's agreed. No one wants to go the Helizone, except for Pearl. The rest of us are going to the waterfall.'

'I changed my mind - I'm coming with you, 'Zuki,' giggled Pearl, 'You aint getting rid of me that easy.'

Suddenly she swung round whacking Donna's arm in the process, 'Hey, what's that weird noise?'

No one dared say what they could hear, for fear of being right, yet each one knew. Guilt flickered between them fast as lightning. *The Silent One! We forgot to ask her to vote.* But this was not about voting. The terrible noise increased.

The impossible had happened.

20

White Dress

The intense cry wailed like a siren. From fever pitch it fell to a sigh, then a shudder, then high again; *Me, me, me, me, me!*

'No!' Mizuki cried as she rushed to hut of the Silent One. 'Wait, stay back!' she warned the others, then ducked inside. Her breath caught in her throat for there was the Silent One in her baggy sweatshirt, curled around a squirming baby, still with its pulsating umbilical cord attached, its furious face streaked with creamy vernix.

Faces crowded the doorway; shiny, grubby children, wide eyed and mouths gaping. Mizuki was acutely aware of the dirt under her own fingernails, that she was neither clean enough nor, for that matter, worthy enough to approach the infant.

Melissa said matter-of-fact, 'You have to cut that rope thingy.'

Donna pushed Melissa aside, 'Let *me* see. Is it real?'

Katey shoved her back, 'No, Donna's-a-Goner

Moore, it's a doll. And that's why you aint no nurse!'

'We can't cut it,' Mizuki said, 'because nothing's clean. We've got no microwave and no scissors.' The baby stopped crying and nuzzled its sticky face into the sweatshirt.

Mizuki backed out of the hut. 'Let me out, I need fresh air!' She burst into the open and looked up, 'God help me!' she called instinctively, and instantly had an idea, 'Pearl's dress . . . I almost forgot!' Mizuki rushed to her hut where she rummaged for the soiled plastic bag she'd kept since the beach party with Bronwyn.

Pearl was close on Mizuki's heels, 'I heard that. My dress? You got it? Why didn't you tell me before?' She barged into Mizuki's hut as Mizuki opened the filthy carrier bag and pulled out a large piece of folded white cloth, two white towels and a man-sized brown leather belt.

'That's not a dress,' Pearl whined, 'Where's my real dress what you promised? Big fat liar, pants on fire. You're a big fat liar, Mizuki.'

'Perfect!' Mizuki pushed Pearl aside and, clutching the materials, ran back to where the others were near hysterical with excitement, all talking at once,

How did that happen?'

'A baby came out of her tummy!'

'My sister had one . . .'

'I know how to make babies . . .'

'Who said she was dying?'

Mizuki raised a hand, 'Okay, be quiet and listen. First, we've got to wash our hands, faces, the lot. And I mean properly wash. Nobody's to kiss that baby

259

because . . . because, well, look at us, we've got bugs all over. Just 'cos we can't see germs doesn't mean they're not there.'

Pearl peered around Mizuki's shoulder, wanting to shower accusations on her, searching for proper grown-up words to drive her point home about the dress, but nothing came.

Mizuki continued, 'I got these sheets from Bronwyn, for making Pearl a dress. I thought Melissa and Freya could pretty it up with some dyes, find a way to wrap one round Pearl, hold it on with this belt, but I forgot . . .'

'You can stop going on about it, Mizuki. I get it,' Pearl snorted, 'that dress what you got special just for me, you wanna give to someone else, just 'cos she's gone and got herself a baby. Filthy sponger! Moan, moan, moan, that's all she ever does, makes a few necklaces, has a baby. Do what you like – give it to her, see if I care! Anyway, that's not my sort of dress. I was thinking of more like a silk prom dress with lace and . . .'

'Hands!' reminded Melissa, and everyone rushed to where the mountain rose away behind Home Rock, and the purest water tumbled over the rocks.

The Silent One groaned as her body expelled the placenta, then heaved herself away from the squishy, rufous lump that flopped like a slimy upturned lily-pad, its pale stalk still connected to the new-born. The Silent One closed her eyes. She bent her chin towards her child, pressing her nose to its downy head, inhaling the sweet scent, so intoxicating, so beautiful, more delicious than anything she'd ever known in all her thirteen years.

The Home Rock girls raced back from their cursory wash, drying their hands over their grubby clothes. Pearl was first to the door. Seeing the Silent One so still, she threw up her hands, 'Too late, that one's a goner!' She slapped her palms hard on top of her own head the way her mother did in a crisis.

'Let me . . .' Mizuki pushed past Pearl, knelt down and pressed the back of her hand against the cheek of the mother, 'No, not dead – just sleeping.' Mizuki beckoned Freya, who was hovering ashen-faced at the entrance to the hut. *Pass me a towel*. Mizuki lifted the baby and swaddled it, take care to avoid the cord and the placenta. Freya passed Mizuki a sheet. Mizuki placed it beside the Silent One, so when she woke, she could lie the baby on it.

The Silent One opened her eyes and whispered, 'What is it?'

'What is what?' Mizuki repeated.

'Boy or girl?'

'Oh, right, it's a boy.'

'He's all right? Fingers? Toes?'

'Yes, I think so - legs, arms, the lot,' Mizuki grinned, unnerved by the serene voice and controlled demeanour of the mother. It dawned on Mizuki that during the whole time, the girl had never complained, never demanded, merely retreated and coped alone.

'What do I do?' Mizuki choked back her tears.

'String,' came the whisper.

'Tell me, I mean, *can* you tell me what is your

name?'

'I am Geraldine.' The young mother shut her eyes and allowed herself a long, deep sigh.

Mizuki bowed her head and removed the precious necklace created by Geraldine. She bit off the end, and the beads scattered over the rush matting.

'Tie the string round the cord, near to his tummy button, tight as you can.'

Mizuki squeezed shut her eyes and opened them again. The throbbing umbilical cord was as repulsive to her as the fat white grubs they'd found when collecting wood. 'I can't do it,' she began, 'my fingers won't work. I want to . . . I want to help, but . . .'

'Let me.' Katey had crept in. Taking the string from Mizuki, she too knelt on the mat. Katey winced as she opened the blood-soaked towel, lifted the cord and somehow tied the string and dared to pull it tight, close to the baby's belly. As she did so, she pressed the back of her hand against the soft skin of the new-born.

'When it drops off, chuck it,' Geraldine said softly, 'and then will you get me a banana, oh, and some coconut milk, if that's okay.'

Tears trickled down Mizuki's cheeks. *Let me do that. Yes, I can find you a banana. Milk too.* Gasping for air, she stumbled into the sunshine where the Home Rock girls with their mostly clean hands were anxiously dithering. She pushed past them and ran, sweeping her hand along the Daystone as she headed out of Home Rock, onto the trail that led to the Flower Palace.

With Mizuki out of the way, the girls squeezed into Geraldine's hut to gawp at this wonderful thing that had happened to them all.

21

Transfer Hope

'Hello?'
'Hello!'
'Anyone there?'

Alone in the Flower Palace, surrounded by butterflies and crickets and beetles and birds, Mizuki caught her breath. She lay back in the long grass and allowed the intoxicating combination of scent and colour and life to calm her spirit.

'Hello!' Those outsiders again. Intruders, strangers, all searching for her, just as she had once searched for Vix. And just as she had given up hope of ever finding Vix, she knew they'd eventually have to give up on her. Those men could stand a metre away but would not see her. She inhaled deeply, enjoying the tightening of her skin as the sun dried her tears on her cheeks. The men sounded excited, shouting about the signs of human activity they'd discovered: the blackened stones by the lake, the singed moss and the fishbones, the paint cans and plastic bottles strewn far and wide, an arrow fixed to a tree.

Mizuki froze. Cutting through the cacophony of the forest, she heard the unmistakable tread of footsteps, the snap of a twig, the shiver of foliage.

'O:sulu tepela! O:sulu tepela! Ahem!' cried the bird as it swooped by, its impossible white tail slicing east from west, the *Before* from the *Tomorrow*.

'It's a warning! Got to hide my girls . . .' Mizuki sat up, '. . . get everyone to the waterfall!' Mizuki sprinted back the way she'd come, calmer now, more confident of what she had to do.

At Home Rock Mizuki stopped short, shocked yet pleasantly surprised to see her girls congregating near the Daystone, with its spattering of chipped and faded varnish, waiting to go with her wherever she might lead. The Blaze House crew had pulled on the remains of their yellow sweatshirts, some had personal rucksacks on their backs. Donna Moore clung to her shiny, shoulder bag with the diamante pattern, holding tight to the straps with both hands. Evie held her pink jewellery box to her chest, its lid hanging like a milk-tooth by a single rusty hinge. Nadia's little rucksack was cram-packed with notebooks and blunt, chewed pencils. She clutched a lunch-box containing two praying mantises, the larger munching on the smaller one.

'Big one eat wive,' Nadia informed Stephie, who told Freya, 'Nadia says its eating its wife.' One day, Nadia would understand that, in reality, the bigger one was the 'wive' who was devouring the smaller male after mating.

'Impressive!' exclaimed Mizuki, puffing out her cheeks, 'Well done for being so quick to get ready. The white-tailed bird warned me to tell you to hide. They're coming! We must escape to the waterfall, and fast. One of you help Geraldine carry the baby.'

No one moved.

'Hurry! They'll catch us if we don't get a move on.'

The girls shuffled their feet, exchanging wide-eyed glances with one another. Mizuki hesitated, her eyes narrowed. The way they were acting was all wrong. They were being deliberately obtuse. Mizuki stamped her foot. She shouted, 'You heard me - I'm trying to save us. Don't just stand there gawping like a bunch of stupid sheep. We've got to leg it now! *Men* are coming to get you. Did you hear what I said? *Actual men!*'

*

Geraldine emerged barefoot from her hut. Melissa had brushed her hair and pulled it back into a smooth ponytail, lifting her face so her cheekbones shone beneath her flushed cheeks. Katey had cradled the baby while Freya wrapped Geraldine from head to knee in a white sheet, cinched twice round the waist by the thin leather belt. The corner of the sheet had been machine-stitched using scarlet thread with the letters *THP*. The second sheet formed a sling around Geraldine's chest and over her shoulders, then knotted at the back. The sleeping baby, swaddled within it, was soothed by his mother's beating heart.

Geraldine's eyes met Mizuki's.

Mizuki frowned.

Neither moved.

The coup hit Mizuki in the gut. 'No, no, no!' she cried, grabbing at the sudden pain in her stomach, 'You're giving up on us. Home Rock is home. At the Transfer Hope Project they've got adults in charge, bossy ones who'll make you do stuff you hate. You don't want that, do you? You *weren't* with us when they voted to stay. They said, "Stay," and I said, "Stay." We agreed. Hey, what about the zoo? Nadia, Evie, you can't leave those poor little creatures all alone with no one to feed them or clean them and no one to care. And what about our shops? Freya, you're a brilliant weaver - and Geraldine, you make beautiful necklaces. Sparrow, Roxy, you came back here when you could have followed Bronwyn. You *chose* Home Rock. Think straight for once! Bronwyn's gone. Without Bronwyn guarding the Helizone, we can take all the stuff we like whenever we like, with no trade.' Mizuki looked desperately from one child to the next but was met with mute stubbornness. Her shoulders sagged and she whimpered, 'You promised me you'd stay.'

Geraldine cleared her throat. Speaking with gentle authority, she said, 'While you were having your *moment*, we had a bit of a chat. We agreed it was better for all of us to go to Transfer Hope. Back at Blaze House, when they first told us about THP I hated the idea, but I was only pretending to hate it because hate is what I did. Hate was who I was before. *Before*, I hated everyone and everything. Hated my birth name even. No one knew it, but I visited the Transfer Hope website so many times I fell in love with the place, and from the moment we left Blaze House, the taxi to the airport, the long flight from England, the helicopter, ever since the crash, I've never stopped dreaming about the THP. It's so beautiful. We get our own rooms with pretty shutters, and gardens with flowers and benches and a fish pond. And when we're ready, they'll match us to forever families who sign a form to say they'll support each other for a lifetime. Which means my new mum will be an aunty to *all* of you, and your new dad, Mizuki, will be my uncle and that's how the whole thing's going to work. And we'll be given what they call an 'overseer' for our whole lives, a counsellor to help us cope with money and work and grown-up stuff. We'll get one-on-one training to learn trades like Diggers and Searchers, but better. Donna Moore can learn to be a nurse.'

'Me? I can be a real nurse with no more pretend?' gasped Donna.

Mizuki patted the scar on her forehead, 'We don't need a real nurse,' she tried to say, but the words stuck in her throat because the Home Rock girls were listening, not to her, but to the outcast who had found her voice.

*

From behind Mizuki, a stranger spoke, 'You're right, sweetie, with our support, Donna can train to become a real nurse.' Mizuki swung round to see a middle-aged woman, tall and tanned, with kind eyes and wavy hair, wearing blue jeans and a yellow cotton over-shirt rolled up at the sleeves. Her accent was familiar from the TV.

Donna's eyes opened wide, 'That woman said my name! She knows me already. She saw me first before you lot!' Donna imagined running into the woman's arms, being accepted and loved and chosen, but terror rooted her to the spot.

'Hush, Donna Moore, we know all of your names. And mine is Lilian Cook. My husband, Ethan, heads up the Transfer Hope Project. Pretty soon you'll meet him because he's right behind me somewhere.' She lowered her voice, aware her next words would always be meaningful, 'He's right behind me – and he's looking for you.' Lilian threw open her arms, "Yes, looking for you, you gorgeous gals!'

They didn't know how to react. The woman wasn't shouting at them for being filthy dirty. She wasn't yelling or swearing. Not even the resi staff from Before had called them gorgeous, so they didn't understand that they could run to Lilian and throw their arms around her, that with Lilian it was safe to hug and be hugged.

Steph, Roxy, Pearl and Donna jostled forward, to be closer, but Mizuki whispered to Vix, 'She's pretending to be nice. Trying to trap us.'

'Come with me,' whispered Vix.

'Tell me where you went after you escaped Bronwyn?' Mizuki nudged Vix, her face questioning.

269

Vix grinned, 'Come and I'll show you.' Looking up, Vix saw how Mizuki's dark hair shone blue in the sunlight.

Mizuki shrugged, 'I can't, Vix. I'm not strong like you.'

'Don't be scared. There's no baddies in the dark,' Vix whispered, reaching out and squeezing Mizuki's hand.

Lilian mumbled something into a walkie-talkie, then did her best to comfort the girls with her words, 'Ethan and I and the whole THP family know your names and faces inside out. Goodness, I feel I know you better than my own children. Ever since we first read your files over a year ago, we've loved every one of you. And then - the accident,' she paused remembering, '. . . devastated. I thought, we thought . . . we cried. Cried a monsoon. And prayed, boy, did we pray! Day in, day out. Prayer gave us hope. An itsy-bitsy shred of . . . hope.' Lilian blinked, sniffed, rubbed her nose, cleared her throat, 'Then something wonderful. Gerald's travel bag arrived in the post - it is Gerald, isn't it?' Lilian looked about, trying to identify the right child. She recognised the tallest girl, standing behind the others, 'They told me you prefer being called "Gerald." Apparently, you left your bag in a taxi in London. How dreadful for you! They posted it to us immediately, even before the accident happened. Having your precious things gave us a teeny bit of hope. It was tough to keep believing when the whole world is saying, "Give 'em up, Lilian. It's hopeless.

You're not doing your mental health any good. They can't possibly survive in a jungle. Accept reality. Move on. There're plenty more kids in care for you to love." But I couldn't forget you. Even though I couldn't see you, I kept imagining you lost, starving, crying out to me. Then came the miracle. Your five beautiful, brave friends were found by a film crew from your very own nation. The story made international headlines! Sadly, we haven't yet met those precious young ladies because they're still in hospital and . . . I'm gabbling, forgive me, but I can't believe you're here, right in front of me. I'd hug you, I would, but I don't want to scare you. It's going to be all right, I promise. Your rooms are waiting; lovely clean sheets, your very own shower . . .'

Mizuki's eardrums were beating hard, as if she were underwater. She'd hardly heard a word. She felt powerless to fight, too weak to run, unable to do what she really wanted to, to throw herself kicking and wailing onto the ground. But maybe there was another option, one that didn't involve taking flight, nor getting into a fight, nor flopping down and giving up. She could have faith. Dare to trust Lilian. One stranger. Mizuki examined Lilian's face. The woman seemed genuine enough with her auburn hair, dimpled cheeks, soft wrinkles around her lips and kind eyes with crow's feet. Mizuki self-consciously touched the lumpy scar on her forehead. She felt ugly and ashamed. The rest of the Home Rock girls were not thinking of themselves but staring open-mouthed in the presence of an angel.

'Being inside Mount Bosavi is unheard of. Ordinary

mortals are rarely allowed here. Locals call this sacred ground so the tribes rightly protect it. Your helicopter was supposed to fly west of here but a storm was brewing. Usually the pilots turn back, but for some reason . . . oh, you don't want to know all this grown-up stuff. The authorities are investigating. Oh dear, I'm at it again, gabbling on but it's so amazing! Can't get over seeing our girls. All this chitter-chatter's just me being in shock. Ethan won't be a mo. He'll catch up and he's not going to believe . . . I wish he'd get a move on, but there's no rushing that guy. He's got a far better sense of direction than me so he should be . . . and blow me down, look who it isn't? Hey, Ethan, over here, we've found them!'

Two men strode in, tall, with long legs and giant feet. One had binoculars, the other an iPad, plus a camera slung round his neck. The girls huddled together. Geraldine held back, suspicious, protective of her sleeping infant. She recognised Ethan's broad smile and grey eyes from the photos, DVD and website, now he was right here, in real life, with another guy. They looked okay.

'Hi,' said Ethan, raising his hand like a scout leader promising to do his best, as if, for him, it was perfectly normal to take a stroll through an uninhabited jungle and chat to a bunch of filthy, stinking, skinny, foreign kids.

'This must be where you hang out,' he noted, raising an eyebrow towards the shanty town of disintegrating wigwams, rain-battered sheds, and wonky channels with a mishmash of mud walls and haphazard bamboo constructions, 'D'you young ladies mind if Mike here takes a pic or three on his thingamajig?'

'This is our place what's called 'Home Rock' and yes, photos would be very nice,' ventured Pearl, quivering with a sense of her own bravery because she was the only one speaking, breathlessly hoping against hope that the new people would like her the most. She couldn't help herself adding, 'D'you know what? You know how memories are not allowed at your Transfer Hope place, well, Freya's got her silver dolphins on a necklace from her birth mum. She smuggled them in her tin, 'cos staff at her resi said it was a ridiclious rule leaving our memories, but I think it's a good rule because . . .'

Pearl was interrupted, not unkindly, by Ethan, 'I'm sure Freya is totally fine to keep her dolphins. Who told you memories are not allowed? Memories, like manners, maketh man – and child. I've no doubt you lot'll have a ton of fascinating memories after almost seven months in this paradise. Crikey, how ya survived without our famous chiko rolls I, for one, can't imagine!' He scratched his head, 'Righty-ho, who's up for giving us oldies the grand tour, then?'

Pearl and Melissa broke ranks, rushing to show off their toilet system, pointing out the direction of the 'swimming pool' and proudly announcing their row of shops.

'What's this?' Mike asked, photographing the fading sign: 手伝

Katey stepped forward, 'That's my big sister's "Thinking to Help" shop. She's half Japanese and she's

273

called Mizuki.' Katey shot a look at Mizuki and caught the briefest of smiles. Encouraged, Katey added, 'Actually, she's nearly my adopted mum, but she's only twelve so I'm much too much 'sponsability for her.'

'I see,' grinned Mike, screwing up his face and wiggling his cheek bones comically, one side then the other, then scrunching his nose like a rabbit. Nadia, Evie and Joy giggled, but they held hands in case this was a trick, in case he suddenly yelled, or swore or raised a hand and battered them. Mike clicked his tongue to indicate that he'd made a grown-up decision, 'I'm done with the stills. If you lot are good and ready we oughta get going before the rain.'

Pearl rushed to Lilian, grabbed her hand and with boundless enthusiasm led the way to the Flower Palace, pointing out this bug and that butterfly, this tree and that rock. Donna stared longingly at Lilian's other hand. Her own fingers flexed and clenched, flexed and clenched, but it was no good, Donna had no idea how to reach out to Lilian the way Pearl had done. Instead, she satisfied herself by trotting alongside, trying to outdo Pearl by chattering nineteen to the dozen, not understanding that Lilian could hardly comprehend her British accent. Behind them, Nadia and Evie hopped and skipped, while the praying mantises rattled in the box. Mizuki, Vix and Katey, kept their distance from the adults so they could whisper conspiratorially. Melissa and Freya watched Geraldine gliding, gracious as any goddess among the throng.

Joy attached herself to Steph, Roxy and Sparrow but she didn't feel much like talking. Vix had rejected her, but that was fine. She looked up to where the tree tops bumped heads with the blue sky, happy to be a child and skip towards the Helizone with grown-ups in charge.

Mike hung back to film what he would later tag: 'The British THP Girls Depart Home Rock.' He adjusted the settings on his iPad, then hastened to catch up with Ethan and the rest. Beyond the Helizone, before the V, he brushed past a child standing perfectly still in the undergrowth.

*

Two helicopters were on the plateau, parked between the V, where the Searcher's had spied on Bronwyn, and 'The Stage' where she had danced. Some men were loading objects from the Helizone onto one of them.

At the sight of the huge beasts, Freya turned to run, but her legs gave way and she fainted. Lilian dropped Pearl's hand and rushed over to Freya. Freya opened her eyes immediately, but Lilian knelt beside her, 'Don't get up, not just yet. It's best to lie still.' Then, 'You can sit up now, slowly. Rest your head on your knees.' Lilian wrapped her arms around Freya, softly saying, 'Breathe, you're okay, breathe Freya, breathe.'

Pearl watched. Her eyes narrowed, 'Freya's snitched my new mum.' She muttered, 'I'm gonna make Lilian hate Freya so Lilian will stop hugging her.' Pearl inhaled noisily, hoping her voice would come out extra loud and command attention, 'Um, everybuddy listen. Do you know what?'

Lilian smiled generously up at Pearl, 'What now, I wonder?' fully expecting yet another exaggerated story. She helped Freya to her feet, keeping her arm around her waist to steady her.

Mean words were stumbling up Pearl's throat, tripping over each other to be first out, when Pearl slammed her hand over her own mouth to stop herself because, well, because Freya was no longer Freya. Hadn't that ghost-girl been virtually an adult? Wasn't she one of the big people in Home Rock? The best hut builder and best Digger ever? Yet, next to Lilian, Freya was a skinny weakling with streaks of snot and dirt-stained cheeks. Not a big girl, not a ghost, not a Digger nor a Weaver, but a little girl. And because Freya was only a child and not a threat, Pearl forced herself to swallow her mean words, and covered her confusion by taking a second noisy breath to tell a different story, 'Did you know? Well, um, today when Geraldine got her baby, I very kindly gave her my dress what was s'posed to be for me, what Mizuki forgot to give me after the party for them horrid guests and . . .'

Lilian nodded. Another tall tale, yet somehow something rang true. Lilian considered Pearl's eyes, read her body language, heard her natural chatter, her desperate, self-serving story. Lilian frowned. 'You're not talking make-believe, are you? Did you say Gerald had a baby?'

All the girls nodded in unison. Even Freya was nodding. Lilian gasped, thinking the baby must surely be dead and buried deep in the jungle, because during the trek from Home Rock to the plateau, in the excitement of being rescued, not one child had so much as mentioned any baby, and Geraldine had walked the whole distance without a word.

Every child faced Geraldine. Up until now, Lilian had assumed that Geraldine's arms were wrapped around her body as self-protection, but now it was obvious that the white sheet concealed the outline of a little one, with mucky stains leaking through, and that Geraldine's arms were in fact, supporting a minute baby. A miniscule pink foot poked through the folds in the sheet.

'Goodness me child, I had no idea . . . you should have said something. You must be exhausted. Here, let me help you, poor mite.' Compassion overwhelmed Lilian. She reached out too quickly.

Geraldine stepped back, curled her shoulders over the baby, and commanded, 'Don't touch my son!' *Papa who? Kangaroo. Who am I? If only you knew.* Geraldine stood up tall, almost eye to eye with Lilian, and spoke with absolute authority, shocking even herself with the strength of her words,

'Don't call me Gerald. I am Geraldine.'

*

Two helicopters rose above the plateau. Cocooned within one of them, the children ascended, white-knuckled. Freya bit her own arm. Nadia and Evie giggled over the bugs they'd smuggled on board. Katey snuggled up to Mizuki. When no adult was looking they exchanged knowing glances. Katey dared to mouth, 'Vix.' Mizuki put a finger to her lips. *Hush little sister, we agreed to be silent forever and ever. It is what Vix wanted.*

*

Alone by the lake, where the heron stalked fish, and terrapin stretched their ancient necks, an infant warrior raised her face to the sky. As the helicopters throbbed away from the approaching downpour, Vix lifted her hands the way Mizuki had taught her.

'Thanks,' she said for her friends, for their salvation, for their hope.

A stunning, black and white bird flew low over the water, its impossibly long tail separating the sky above from the water below.

'O:sulu tepela! O:sulu tepela!' was its plaintive cry.

O:sulu tepela.

Peace be still.

The End

Footnotes

p49[1]   Chelonia Depressa – Terrapins
p115[2] Hello – Adele
p115[3] Like a Child – Backstreet boys
p163[4] A pear-shaped fruit called a noni
p158[5] All tree kangaroo species in New Guinea are threatened by human hunting, logging and land-clearing for oil palms. As no humans live in Mt Bosavi, tree kangaroos exist freely there.

p18   O:sulu tepela - 'Be peaceful' from the Kasua New Testament:
1 Thessalonians 4:11 "Live peaceful and quiet lives."

With reference to weaving, digging, hut-building, jewellery-making, hair-dressing, and other creative activities described in this book, I like these words of Sir Terence Conran: (March 31st 2015 – Campaign)
"We have the most amazing craftsmen in this country and, added to the fact that the UK's creative industries are the finest in the world, it saddens me that, as a nation, we are losing that pride in the simple pleasure of making things."

ACKNOWLEDGEMENTS

For generously reading earlier versions of this book and advising, encouraging, and enthusing me to keep going, I'm indebted to Kirsty-Jane Lamin, Charis Smith, and Wendy Rowe. Thanks to the Creative Network writers' group in Preston, some for reading my work, others for turning up month after month to explore this 'creative thing' called story.

Thank you, Catherine Cousins for your help, and all at 2QT for your ongoing support and friendship. Thank you, Tom. Love this cover! Your wizardry for inventing 2D and 3D games and toys and your artistic scribblings never fail to inspire and impress www.tang-mu.co.uk   And to my rare and beautiful friend, Meg. We go back a long way. Thank you for your art.

I know, I'm obsessive. Always writing. Or editing. Or proofing. Thank you, Andrew, for supporting my efforts, emptying the dishwasher, and not complaining (to my face).

Note: Chapter 15: Replay! Replay! I based this chapter on a factual account from the documentary, 'Lost Land of the Volcano' has been included with the kind permission of the BBC Natural History Unit, Bristol. May I add particular thanks to Gordon Buchanan who graciously read and agreed the relevant pages, and to his agent for putting me in touch with the right people. The discovery of a child by his team is, of course, total fiction.

Note: The product GravityLight has been referred to with permission from members of the GL02 foundation. May 12th 2018 @GravityLight tweeted that they'd taken the extremely difficult decision to close The Foundation. For more information on this innovative group please refer to @Deciwatt or @GravityLight or see gravitylight.org/blog.

About the Author

Katharine was born somewhere in Kent, quite a long time ago. She's lived in Europe and Asia, but mostly "up north" in Lancashire. Her favourite thing is swimming in big waves. She also likes digging holes then filling them with water for fish, frogs and flowers. If she'd had proper careers advice, she'd have studied natural history, but she became a teacher which was fun while it lasted. She's fostered teenagers and taught excluded youngsters in the community. Many of those children are hidden within the characters in this book.

Other books by Katharine Ann Angel

Being Forgotten: 8 short stories about teenagers, fiction based on fact, with discussion aid
The Froggitt Chain: a novel
The Burglar's Baby: a novel
Stegalegs at Spinning River: for 8-10 year olds
We Were Nobbut Grocers: a memoir

An Insight from my Childhood

My brother and I were pre-schoolers when Dad, an army anaesthetist, took us into the jungle. 'Hush!' he said, 'Tread softly!' Then, 'Stop! Listen to the bird-song,' 'See that butterfly,' 'Let's swing over on this liana.' Chris, aged two, stood on a twig which disturbed a swarm of bees which attacked us, stinging Dad many times as he tried to protect his son with his own body.

Another time, I spotted a massive conker-coloured millipede rippling towards me from beneath the garage door. Then there were the home-invaders - the minor bird that flew through our lounge squawking semi-comprehensible messages and the soldier ants that devoured every crumb from the kitchen floor before marching out in triumph, single-file. Locals brought creatures to our door, knowing Dad would care for them; a fish-owl, a tiny monkey, snakes, spiders, tortoises, a puppy or two. One winter, the army whisked us back to an icy, snow-covered London. I'm certain my mother would rather have been attacked by jungle bees than move her children halfway around the world to stay with her in-laws in chilly Shooters Hill.